THE UNION T

BOOK I

Blinded by the Light

Joe Kipling

Cillian Press |

First published in Great Britain in 2013
by Cillian Press Limited. 83 Ducie Street, Manchester M1 2JQ
www.cillianpress.co.uk

British Library Cataloguing in Publication Data.
A catalogue record for this book is available from the British Library.

Paperback ISBN: 978-1-909776-00-5
eBook ISBN: 978-1-909776-01-2

Cover Design: Billie Jade McNeill

Published by
Cillian Press – Manchester - 2013
www.cillianpress.co.uk

For my dad who introduced me to Sci-Fi and my mum who would have told everyone in park.

Acknowledgments

I'd like to thank the following people for their help with this book: To the many friends and family who listened to my ideas and commented on the various drafts, including: Helen Coen, Richard Power and Nikki Harris. Thank you for your time and patience. Special thanks to Annwyl Port and Bekka Kipling who's insight and thoughtful comments helped to shape this book. Michele Lemon as always your encouragement and enthusiasm was gratefully received. Thanks to the Olive Tree Bistro in Holmfirth for keeping me well supplied with Cappuchino's and home made scones. To Mark Brady and Sonia Devons at Cillian Press thank you for your expert guidance and support. Finally, thank you to Will, Jake and Max for letting me use your names.

CHAPTER 1

Stranded

The sun shimmered like a blood red orange, its bright rays reflecting vibrantly across the darkening city skyline. The deep orange hue backlit the clouds and glinted off the glass and steel buildings below giving the Neighbourhood an otherworldly, almost magical feel.

'It's beautiful,' I gasped, as Reese and I sprawled out across the grass.

Reese took a noisy gulp from his can of beer. ''S because of the pollution,' he slurred.

'I don't understand?' I frowned.

'The pollution makes the sky that colour. All the crap in the air filters the light and turns it orange.'

'Oh,' I responded.

'Not so beautiful now is it MaryAnn?' he laughed. 'Now that you know that it's the pollution.'

I tried to ignore the sneer in his voice. Reese was the coolest boy in school. I'd spent six months trying to get him to ask me out on a date and I wasn't going to waste time arguing with him about a stupid sunset. I'd already spent most of our first date squeezed into the front seat of his convertible. His best friends Danny and Charlie had sprawled out across the back seat, drinking beer and shouting insults at any girl who was unfortunate enough to be passing by.

By the time we'd arrived at the park I was desperate to escape the confines of the car and breathe the clean fresh air outside. Thankfully Danny and Charlie had grabbed a six pack and, after making a couple of lewd gestures at Reese and me, they'd disappeared off in the direction of the kids' playground. The last time I'd seen them they were drunkenly trying to push each other off the swings.

Reese had grabbed the remaining beers off the back seat and had led me over to the edge of the park where we had a magnificent view across to the Neighbourhood. I thought it was very romantic.

I rolled off my stomach and sat up straight, turning my back to the setting sun so that I faced Reese. I crossed my legs and leant towards him trying to make myself look as alluring as possible. If Reese didn't ask me to be his girlfriend then I'd be the laughing stock of the school on Monday.

Georgina and Natalie, my two best friends, were waiting for me to get back from my date so that I could fill them in on all the gossip. The anticipation had been building all week until we were almost giddy with the excitement of it all. We'd discussed my hair, makeup, wardrobe, how I should behave, topics to talk about. We'd planned everything. In fact with all the planning that had gone into the event you would have thought that I'd never been asked out by a boy before. It wasn't my first date, but we all understood the importance of this particular 'date'. If everything went well and Reese asked me to be his girlfriend then by Monday I'd be hanging out with the coolest group of Alphas in school. Alphas were the social elite, not just at school but across the whole Neighbourhood. Even though I was Alpha too, Daddy was a politician not a celebrity. So I was pretty popular at school, but not popular enough to be invited to all the best parties; the really glamorous ones that all the celeb kids went to.

Reese was in a whole different league, his mother was the model, Diana Temple. She wrote her own fashion blog on the Portal and

EVERYONE followed it. Daddy once said that if she told the Neighbourhood that wearing a teapot on their head was fashionable then everyone would be rattling around in one.

Georgina, Natalie and I met up every Thursday after school and waited impatiently for her blog to be uploaded onto the Portal so we could find out what to spend our weekly credit allowance on. Reese's father was a famous singer too, so it meant that his social status was pure gold and I was hoping that some of that gold would rub off on me and make me sparkle.

With this thought uppermost in our minds Georgina and Natalie had arrived at my house early this morning to help me get ready. Georgina said I needed to go for *the girl next door look - with a touch of sexy* . . . . She said *that was what boys liked*. As Reese had spent most of the afternoon drinking and belching with his friends rather than paying any attention to me, I was beginning to wonder whether Georgina really knew what she was talking about. Although, now we were alone, Reese finally seemed to be giving me his undivided attention; even if he was peering down my top.

I pulled self-consciously at my vest but Reese leered at me. 'Leave it. I was enjoying the view.' I flushed red with embarrassment. Reese snorted and took another loud gulp of beer.

'You want?' He opened a can and thrust it under my nose. I hesitated. I didn't want any more beer. I'd never been able to handle my drink very well and I'd already had two cans in the car. My head was feeling a bit woozy and I didn't want to risk getting drunk, but I didn't want to look like a total fool in front of Reese either.

After a moment's hesitation I grabbed the beer from his outstretched hand and took a reluctant sip. I hated the taste and I tried not to grimace as I swallowed it down as quickly as possible.

Reese was laughing at me, 'You don't like it?'

Crap! He really did think I was a loser. 'No,' I protested, 'it's good.'

'Not a problem.' He snatched the can out of my hand and poured the contents out on the grass. 'There's more where that came from.' He drained the remnants of his own can of beer, crumpled it up and threw it on the grass in front of him.

'Don't you think you'd better pick it up? We'll get into trouble for dropping litter.'

'I'm just keeping Delta in a job.' He gave me a crooked smile. '*One Neighbourhood working in harmony,*' he repeated a Light slogan. 'I'm a real humanitarian.' He laughed loudly and kicked clumsily at the empty can with the toe of his shoe so that it bounced away from us across the wet grass.

I nodded in agreement. The city employed Delta to do all the menial jobs; like sweeping the streets and cleaning houses. Daddy said that it showed just how benevolent the Light had been in giving them a safe place to live, so they could still contribute to society. Still, there were strict rules about dropping litter in the Neighbourhood. Daddy said that with so many people living in the Neighbourhood, if we all dropped just one piece of litter a day we'd soon be drowning in waste and that would lead to disease and infection. I gave a shudder of revulsion at the thought.

'It's not the Delta I'm worried about,' I said. 'If we get caught dropping litter and Daddy finds out he'll kill me.'

'You've got to be kidding. You're the Legislator's daughter; I thought he'd protect you.'

I shrugged. It was true, Daddy was very influential in the Light and he would do anything for me. I had him wrapped around my little finger, but I didn't want Reese to think I was spoilt.

'He might decide to make an example of me,' I said. 'He could get into lots of trouble if I break the law and he ignores it.'

'Yeah right! Wasn't it your father who helped when you and your friends got drunk at the school party last year?

I squirmed in embarrassment at the memory; Georgina had sneaked a bottle of vodka into the end of term party and Natalie and I had got incredibly drunk (did I mention that I don't handle my drink very well?). All three of us had ended up dancing in the school fountain in our underwear. Daddy had been incredibly embarrassed, but he'd spoken to the headmaster and dealt with the situation. Someone at school had obviously been gossiping to Reese. I wasn't sure whether I was upset that someone had told him such an embarrassing story, or happy that he'd been talking about me. If he'd been listening to gossip then that must mean he liked me.

'What about the time you were caught shoplifting in the Hub,' he continued. Crap, he knew about that too! I wondered who he'd been talking too, probably Melissa Carter; she had such a boring life she was always gossiping about something.

'It was a joke,' I stammered. 'To see if we could get away with it.'

'And obviously you didn't!' he replied.

I was embarrassed. 'No, no we didn't.' It had been a stupid bet anyway and mostly Georgina's idea. It was Daddy who had had to sort out the mess, and he'd been so angry with me.

'So if we get caught then your father will just bail us out.'

'Hmmmmm, maybe.'

'Of course he'll bail you out; your father would do anything for you.'

'That's where you're wrong,' I protested. 'He didn't help my brother when he got into trouble.' I clasped my hand across my mouth, but it was too late. I hadn't meant to mention my brother.

Reese looked interested. 'Brother! I didn't know you had a brother.'

Of course he didn't know about my brother, he was the best kept secret in the Neighbourhood. He'd left home when he was fifteen and had disappeared without a trace. I was only eleven at the time and still didn't understand what had happened to him. Mummy and Daddy refused to talk about it. I'd heard rumours that he'd gone across the

Boundary, but I didn't believe them. I couldn't understand why he would run away from the Neighbourhood to live Outside when it was a death sentence? At school we'd been shown broadcasts of the Outside and they terrified me. The Ferals who'd survived the virus had been driven mad by the disease and they fought each other for food. The reporter had said that some of them were even cannibals. It was too horrible to think about.

I couldn't imagine why my brother would cross the Boundary, but there hadn't been a sighting of him since he left home four years ago. I sometimes fantasised that he'd sneaked onto a bus and gone to one of the other Neighbourhoods; he could have travelled up north to Edinburgh or gone south to London. He'd always wanted an adventure. Our Neighbourhood had never been big enough for him.

Reese had only moved to our Neighbourhood six months ago so he'd never met my brother. He'd travelled to Manchester from London, which was another reason why I was so desperate to date him. People rarely travelled between the three Neighbourhoods as the buses were used for transporting supplies. It took months for the Light to authorise travel permits because we had to conserve resources.

Daddy said that before the virus people would catch buses and travel across the country any time they wanted. I couldn't imagine what that must have been like. Some people still travelled across the Outside, mainly traders moving between the Neighbourhoods, but it was incredibly dangerous because there was no protection from the Feral Echo. There was also the risk of disease. People travelling between the Neighbourhoods had to undergo weeks of quarantine in case they brought any infection with them. Daddy said that we couldn't risk another outbreak of the Sandman Virus. The next outbreak could be the end of us all.

I'd never met anyone else who'd travelled from another Neighbourhood before so just sitting and talking to Reese made me feel excited and slightly dangerous. When he'd first arrived at the school that's all anyone could talk about; the boy from London. We'd listened enthralled as he told us his story over and over again. How he'd travelled across the Outside for a full day on the bus. We'd all cringed in disgust when he mentioned the Feral Echo, starving and deformed by disease, living in hovels by the side of the road. I shuddered at the horrors that he must have seen.

'MaryAnn, I said I didn't know you had a brother,' Reese interrupted my chain of thought and brought me back to reality. He was staring at me, obviously waiting for a response.

I picked at the sleeve of my gloves and avoided looking at him. 'He went away,' I said uncomfortably. I was aware that I was flushing self-consciously and I desperately wanted to change the subject. I didn't want Reese to find out about my brother, to hear the rumours that he was living Outside with the Ferals. I didn't want to see the look of disgust on his face and I definitely didn't want to ruin our date.

'Went where?' he probed. I realised I must be behaving strangely because he had a curious look on his face.

I didn't know how to respond. I desperately wanted to change the subject but my brain was like treacle and I couldn't think of anything else to say.

'Went where?' he persisted. He obviously wasn't going to give up.

'Can we just drop it?' I was so anxious my voice came out louder than I expected.

Reese's brow crinkled in annoyance and he jumped to his feet, scowling down at me. 'Don't shout at me . . . stupid bitch.' He stormed away across the grass.

Immediately I regretted raising my voice. Panicked, I jumped up and ran after him, angrily berating myself for upsetting him. Why did I always get so defensive about my brother? He'd run away from home and I should just accept it. Now my stupid temper could ruin my date with Reese.

I found Reese standing under the shade of a broad oak tree with his back to me. I moved beside him. 'I'm sorry,' I said. Reese didn't respond. Instead he bent over and made a strange choking noise . . . then he threw up all over my brand new tiger print pumps.

I stared in horror as the slimy vomit soaked through the thin material of my shoes. Reese bent over again, but this time I managed to jump out of the way. He groaned loudly as vomit splattered across the grass.

'Too much beer,' he moaned. 'Need to go home.' He staggered away from the tree in the direction of his car.

'What about Danny and Charlie?' I called after him.

'Don't care,' he said. 'Got to go home now.' He dug into his pocket and threw a metal object at me. It was the key card for his car.

'You have to drive,' he said.

'What?' I shouted in alarm. 'I don't have my licence yet.'

'Can't drive,' he answered. 'Too drunk, and daddy won't let you go to jail. I get caught driving drunk and I'll be in serious trouble.'

I tried to think of a response but before I had chance to come up with a reason why I couldn't drive the car Reese had opened the passenger door and climbed inside.

I hesitated, not sure what to do next. If I was caught driving illegally I'd be in big trouble, but what other choice did I have? I briefly toyed with the idea of calling Daddy and asking for his help, but I dismissed it right away. Daddy would help me out, but he'd have that disappointed look on his face when he arrived to collect me. Besides, Georgina was having a party at her house at the end of the month and there was a chance that Daddy might ground me for drinking beer. I couldn't risk it. I had to drive Reese home.

Reese was sprawled out across the passenger seat. His face had a green tinge to it and he smelled strongly of vomit. It made me think of disease and sick people and my sensitive stomach heaved slightly. I opened the driver window to let in some air and took a couple of deep breaths to calm my nerves. I'd only ever driven a car once before in the car park behind our apartment after I'd persuaded Daddy to give me a driving lesson. I tried to remember what he'd taught me, but all his instructions were jumbled up in my head.

I took another deep breath and inserted the key card into the ignition. The engine roared into life. I checked the rear view mirror, remembering vaguely that Daddy had said it was important to make sure there was no-one behind the car. I think it had something to do with people on bikes. Sometimes when Daddy started talking at me I just switched off and made sure I nodded in all the right places to make him think I was listening.

Gripping the steering wheel tightly and hunching forward a little so I could get a better view of the road I slowly released the handbrake and cautiously pulled away from the kerb. I was grateful that the car was an automatic so I didn't have to worry about the clutch and gears.

I drove slowly out of the park. The road to the exit was unsealed and bumpy and Reese groaned as we lurched uncomfortably along the path. 'Take it easy,' he snapped before making a gagging noise. I yelled at him to hang his head out of the window and thankfully he made it just in time.

When we arrived at the main road I was relieved to find that it was quiet and there was very little traffic. Reese lived on the other side of the Neighbourhood to me and even though I'd travelled the road as a passenger in Daddy's car I still had to concentrate hard to remember the way.

By the time we pulled up outside his house Reese had fallen asleep and was snoring loudly. I prodded his arm gently and he woke with a start. With his grey face, mussed up hair and smelling sourly of vomit he looked dreadful and nothing like the cute boy that I'd been so desperate to go on a date with.

I waited expectantly for the concierge to open the car door. When nobody arrived, Reese opened the door on his own and staggered drunkenly out of the car. Annoyed, I switched off the engine and climbed out too. If our concierge had behaved so irresponsibly then Daddy would have been furious. It was incredibly bad manners.

Reese was unsteady on his feet and swayed alarmingly for a moment. I thought he was going to fall over, but somehow he managed to regain his balance. I escorted him up the porch steps and once we were at the top he grabbed at the heavy wooden door frame to steady himself.

'Are you going to be okay?'

He didn't respond, just grasped for the handle and opened the door.

'Key card,' he mumbled.

'What?'

'I want the key card for my car.' He held out his hand impatiently. 'Give me my card.' His voice was slurred and almost incoherent.

I handed the card back to him. 'How am I going to get home?'

'I dunno,' he said as he stepped into the HealthScan. It flashed green and he entered the house, closing the door behind him without giving me a backward glance.

I remained on the step staring at the closed door thinking that he wouldn't really abandon me with no way of getting home, that he would at least let me inside so that I could call a taxi. Eventually I realised that he definitely wasn't coming back and I sank down onto the cold stone steps unsure what to do next.

I shivered. It was getting cold and I was only wearing a thin vest. It was a cute hot pink vest that Georgina had chosen especially for the date. She said the colour really suited me and that I looked great in it. At that moment I would have gladly swapped it for a less sexy jumper. I opened my handbag and pulled out my phone. The battery was low; too low to make a call but it allowed me to check my credit. Great! I had no credit left. I'd meant to ask Daddy to top it up before I'd left the house this morning but in the excitement of getting ready for the date I'd completely forgotten. I couldn't call anyone or connect to the Portal to top up my credit so that I could at least order a taxi. 'Really!' I muttered to myself, could this day get any worse?

With no phone and no credit it seemed that the only option was to walk home. It was at least four miles to my house which meant I had a long trek ahead of me and I hated walking. It seemed such a stupid way to travel. I gave Reese's closed door a final, hopeful glance before climbing down off the porch and heading in the direction of home.

I was about half way home when I heard the first crack of thunder. Moments later the heavens opened and it started to pour with rain. Within minutes I was soaking wet, freezing cold and angry at myself for leaving my jacket at home. I muttered a string of obscenities that would have gotten me grounded if my parents had been around to hear them. At least the puddles of water that filled the street were able to wash away the vomit from my new shoes. It seems there was a silver lining after all!

CHAPTER 2

Welfare

It took forever to walk home and it was already dark when I arrived at my apartment block. The concierge greeted me with a nod as I entered the Atrium.

The apartment was in darkness, which meant that Daddy and Mummy must be out; probably at a charity event or a dinner party. I was relieved that I didn't have to explain to them why I'd arrived home so late, soaked to the skin and shivering with cold.

I was exhausted, the day had been a complete failure and all I wanted to do was crawl into my bed and go to sleep. I switched on the hall light and then clambered wearily up the stairs, squelching wetly along the corridor until I reached the door to my room.

As I entered my room I almost jumped out of my skin as two people leapt off the bed. 'MaryAnn,' they chorused in unison. 'Where have you been? We've been waiting here for ages.'

With my heart hammering wildly in my chest I realised it was Georgina and Natalie, who it appeared had spent the evening camped out in my bedroom.

'We fell asleep,' said Natalie.

'You're soaked,' Georgina said, her dark brown eyes quickly taking in my bedraggled appearance and sodden clothing. 'What happened to you?'

I was too miserable even to speak and threw myself dramatically across the bed. I felt the mattress depress as they took a seat on either side of me. Natalie pulled the hair back from my face and I screwed my eyes shut so I didn't have to look at her. 'Tell us what happened.'

I shook my head. I deliberately kept my eyes closed, refusing to look at either of them. The day was too awful to talk about and I just wanted to be left alone.

'Sit up and tell us what happened,' Georgina spoke in the tone she used when she expected to be obeyed. I'd learnt from experience that it wasn't wise to ignore Georgina when she was in one of her moods, so I reluctantly sat up. My hair hung limp and wet against my skin, sending rivulets of cold water running uncomfortably down my spine.

Georgina was examining me, waiting for me to speak.

I tried to hold her gaze but my face crumpled – I felt so humiliated. 'It was awful,' I sobbed. 'Just awful.'

'Oh it can't have been that bad,' Natalie said kindly.

'It was horrible, the worst date of my life. We drove around in Reese's car for ages -'

'The convertible,' Natalie interrupted.

'Yes the convertible,' I murmured.

'Sweet.'

'Natalie, shut your big fat mouth and let MaryAnn talk,' Georgina hissed. Natalie fell silent.

'It would have been sweet if Danny and Charlie hadn't been with us. We drove round and round for hours while they all drank beer. It was horrible, the car smelt like feet and it made me feel sick.' I could hear the high pitched whine in my voice, but I was so miserable that I didn't care.

Georgina scowled. 'What happened next?'

'We drove to the park and Reese and I went up to The Point. You know at the edge of the park where you get those great views over the Neighbourhood?'

'Very romantic,' Natalie murmured.

This comment elicited another scowl from Georgina.

'I was just saying that it's very romantic,' she protested feebly.

'No-one wants to hear what you think so just shut your big mouth.'

'It was really romantic until Reese drank too much beer and threw up all over my new shoes.'

They both stared at my feet. Natalie pulled a face, but didn't comment.

'So after he threw up on your shoes what happened?' Georgina asked in a measured tone.

'He was too drunk to drive so I had to take him home -'

'You drove his car?' Natalie squealed excitedly. 'You actually drove his convertible. Now that really is sweet.' She whistled softly through her teeth.

'But he took the key card off me when I got back to his house and I didn't have enough credit for a taxi so I had to walk all the way home, in the rain. It took me hours.' I hid my face in my hands, too ashamed to look at either of them.

'What an idiot. I can't believe he left you to walk home on your own,' Natalie patted my damp shoulder sympathetically.

'I told you it was the worst date ever,' I said, basking in the sympathy I'd been craving. At least my friends cared about me and understood how awful my night had been.

'It wasn't that bad,' Natalie sounded unconvincing. 'It could have been worse.

'How?' I howled in despair. 'How could it have been any worse? He threw up on my shoes.' I indicated my feet and she wrinkled her nose in disgust.

'You idiot,' Georgina hissed so vehemently that both Natalie and I jumped in surprise. I stared at her, my mouth hanging open. Georgina wasn't renowned for her compassionate nature, but surely even she understood how horrible my night had been.

'Do you realise what you've done? There's no way that Reese is going to ask you to be his girlfriend now. This was our big chance. We invested time in you and you blew it. You've ruined this for all of us, and all you're concerned about is a pair of stupid shoes. You're pathetic MaryAnn. Absolutely pathetic.'

I continued to stare at her open mouthed. I wasn't sure how to respond. I'd expected sympathy from my friends, not an attack.

'I don't think I can ever forgive you for this,' she continued.

'What could I have done? He was drunk. He threw up on me. I couldn't stop -'

'Of course you could have stopped him,' she interrupted. The venom in her voice was unmistakable. 'You could have stopped him drinking at any time. You could have refused to get in the car with Danny and Charlie. You let things get totally out of control.'

Natalie raised her eyebrows at me, but didn't say a word. I didn't blame her. It was wise to keep your mouth shut when Georgina was annoyed. She could often be relied on to follow a tirade with a hard slap across the face.

Georgina sprang up from the bed. 'Come on Natalie. We're going home.'

'But what about MaryAnn. Shouldn't we stay with her? She looks so miserable.'

'She deserves to be miserable,' Georgina hissed.

'But . . .' I started.

She rounded on me. 'You don't see boys messing me around do you? Getting drunk and throwing up on me.'

It was true. I don't think there was any boy in the Neighbour-hood brave enough to mess around with Georgina, and if they did I suspected they wouldn't live long enough to tell the tale.

'You're so selfish MaryAnn, this wasn't just about you. We spent ages getting ready for this date and now you've ruined it for all of us. There's no way Reese or his friends will ever invite us to any of their parties now. You've totally killed our social life and probably made us a laughing stock. I don't think I can ever forgive you for this. In fact I don't know whether I even want to be friends with you anymore.' With that parting shot she stalked out of the room pulling her coat from the back of the chair as she went. Natalie hurried after her, throwing me a sympathetic smile as she closed the door quietly behind her.

Alone in my room I lay down miserably on my bed. My clothes were still damp and I pulled a blanket around me so that I was cocooned in its safe warm interior. I closed my eyes. This was not how my evening was supposed to end. I should have arrived back from my date jubilant and excited, Georgina and Natalie should be hanging on my every word as I told them all about my date, the romantic conversations in the park, the moment he asked me to be his girlfriend. Instead I'd been humiliated by the coolest boy in school and my friends had disowned me. Life was so unfair.

If anyone tells you that things look better in the cold light of day, then they're lying. I know this because when I woke up the next morning things were worse. I'd slept in my clothes and woke up feeling cold and damp and achy. My insides were tied in knots at the thought of facing Reese at school and I couldn't even bear to think about my tattered friendship with Georgina and Natalie.

There was a knock at the door and Mummy called for me to get up. Mummy was not a morning person and usually woke up in a bad mood so I'd learnt not to antagonise her by being late for breakfast. I lay in bed for a few moments before I gave myself a mental shake, *MaryAnn Hunter stop wallowing in self-pity and get out of bed.*

Throwing off the bedclothes I reluctantly dragged myself into the bathroom. I peeled off my clothes and stepped into the shower. 'Hot, Massage,' I commanded and a hot stream of razor sharp droplets immediately hit my head. The water felt good and soon I began to feel a little better. The chem rinse that followed the shower stung my eyes and as always I gagged at the smell. After my date from hell the previous evening I felt that I deserved the misery. For once I wasn't tempted to cut the rinse short and risk my parents' wrath when they found out. Instead I stayed under the rinse for the prescribed five minutes.

As I stepped out of the shower I heard the tinkle of a bell that signalled that breakfast was about to be served. Everything was run with military precision in the Hunter household. Daddy liked to keep things in order. I used to sometimes wonder if he behaved the same way in the office and whether he used a bell to signal lunch or break times to his staff.

I towelled myself dry before pulling out my green dress from the wardrobe. Once I was dressed I opened the bathroom cabinet and took out a series of bottles. I didn't have to count the bottles: I knew that there were ten in total, each containing a health supplement. I swallowed each supplement in turn. They were all artificially flavoured to make them more palatable. My favourite was the orange tasting one; a high dose of vitamin C combined with an anti-viral that the Light had manufactured to prevent colds and flu.

I swallowed the final supplement and then pulled a clean pair of gloves out of the cupboard. As I pulled them on I marvelled at how they so easily formed a second skin. Only a few years ago we'd been forced to wear thick material gloves as a protection against the spread of disease. Then the engineers developed a new synthetic fibre that was so cheap to produce that even Delta used them. It meant that once the gloves were fitted they were barely noticeable and everything you touched felt so real.

I headed downstairs, carefully avoiding my vomit stained shoes that were still lying on the bedroom floor, and arrived in the dining room just as breakfast was being served.

Daddy and Mummy were already seated at the table. As I approached the table Daddy dropped his newspaper and offered me a nod and I returned it before slipping into the seat next to him.

'Your hair's wet,' Mummy commented.

'I didn't have time to dry it.'

'Well don't go out with it like that. I don't want the neighbours to see you with wet hair . . . and you could catch a cold.'

Mummy was very keen on keeping up appearances and she thought that she could scare me with the threat of a cold. It wouldn't do for the Legislator's daughter to leave the house with wet hair. Being a member of my family sometimes felt like I was part of an elaborate theatre production; perfectly groomed, perfectly dressed and perfectly behaved. There was no room for mistakes, especially not if those mistakes affected Daddy's job with the Light.

Thankfully Mummy was distracted by the arrival of breakfast and she turned her attentions to Anita our maid who carefully set out a series of sterile tubs containing scrambled eggs and sausages. As always there was far too much food for the three of us, but Mummy said that extravagance was a sign of our status. It was important that our wealth and prosperity be demonstrated at every opportunity. Mummy usually ate like a bird, picking at the crumbs on her plate, while Daddy often ate at the office. So there was always a lot of food left after each meal. Mummy personally supervised the disposal of the food into tightly locked waste bins to make sure that the servants didn't pick through any leftovers. Not only did sharing food and leftovers spread disease but Mummy also believed that giving Delta free food destroyed their work ethic and made them lazy.

Daddy took a gulp of his coffee and smiled at me over the rim of his newspaper. 'Poppet, you remember that we have tickets to the charity ball next week don't you?'

I nodded in response, my mouth too full of scrambled eggs to answer him.

'Do you need a new dress?' he asked.

I quickly swallowed the last of my food. 'I have an old dress I could wear. The red one that I wore to the Christmas gala,' I added.

'That old thing,' he said. 'That won't do at all. We can't have everyone in the Light thinking that my daughter has to recycle her old dresses. I'll add some credits to your phone. Would a thousand be enough?'

I smiled at him. There was no way I'd ever wear an old dress to a party. It made Daddy feel good if he thought he was spoiling me and a thousand credits would buy a very nice dress and shoes too.

Appearances were very important to Daddy too. He always expected us to look our best. He never left the house without being perfectly groomed. He had a manicure and facial every week and all his suits were handmade. I'd never seen Daddy casually dressed, he was always formal in a suit, accompanied by a waistcoat, tie and an ornate gold pocket watch, that he said had belonged to his father.

The sound of a car horn beeped in the distance. Daddy folded up his newspaper. 'Back to the daily grind,' he said before draining the last remnants of coffee from his cup. I knew he didn't mean it, Daddy loved his job. Mummy always referred to his job as his second wife. She sometimes complained that he paid more attention to his job than he did her. I knew that wasn't true, Daddy absolutely adored her. He was always buying her nice things and planning extravagant surprises.

'I'll walk you out,' Mummy said as Daddy prepared to leave.

Once they'd left the room I finished the rest of my breakfast, trying not to think about the day ahead and how awful it was going to be. Instead I focussed on the prospect of buying a new dress, which helped to cheer me up a little.

Mummy didn't return to the table, so once I'd finished breakfast I went back to my room to dry my hair, put on my makeup and get ready for school. I also checked the Portal, but there were no messages from Georgina or Natalie, just a big empty space of nothingness on my Contact page.

I usually met up with Georgina and Natalie outside the Olive Tree Café so we could walk to school together. Today I wasn't surprised to find that there was no-one waiting for me. I lingered outside for ten minutes hoping that at least Natalie would turn up, but she didn't. After the events of last night I hadn't expected that either of them would be there, Georgina would be determined to make me suffer and Natalie would be too scared to go against her wishes. Finally I lost all hope and walked to school on my own.

I tried to convince myself that I didn't care, but I was used to being popular and having my best friends around me and I cared a lot more than I liked to admit. I was feeling really miserable by the time I arrived at the school gates.

I made my way to the entrance and stepped into the HealthScan. It held me for two or three minutes and I was just getting concerned when it flashed green and released me into the interior of the school.

On a positive note, school wasn't as bad as I'd expected. Reese obviously hadn't told anyone about our date and when I bumped into him in the corridor he stared right through me as if I didn't exist. While I hated being invisible to him, it was better than everyone knowing the excruciatingly embarrassing details of our date. Georgina also seemed determined to ignore me. She barely glanced at me during any of our classes. Natalie cast a few sympathetic looks my way, but kept her distance too.

Break time was miserable. I didn't want to hang around the common room as I didn't want Georgina to see me on my own. I thought I would hide out in the girls' toilets, but I found a SanTech outside who told me they were out of order. He wouldn't even let me use the toilets for five minutes to reapply my makeup. I lost my temper a little and told him it was a stupid idea to work on the toilets during break time, but he ignored me. When I tried to insist that he let me inside he muttered something rude under his breath and rifled through his tool bag refusing to speak to me again.

After resisting the urge to punch him in his stupid blonde head I stalked away in disgust. Once I'd left I regretted not taking note of the name on his ID badge so I could report him to security. He was designation Delta and should show more respect to an Alpha. I was in such a bad mood that I would have enjoyed getting him in trouble. It would teach him to mind his manners. The altercation had made my head throb, so I went in search of an empty classroom and hid out there for the remainder of the break.

By early afternoon I was sure that something was wrong. When I'd woken up I'd put the achy body feeling down to sleeping in my clothes, but by lunchtime my head started to throb and my throat was scratchy and sore. I informed my teacher and he called Welfare who immediately escorted me to Isolation.

The School Isolation Unit was white and clinical and simply furnished with a metal bed and chair. I lowered myself onto the bed and waited for Welfare to take me home. This was only the second time I'd been in Isolation but I knew the procedure, everyone did. We'd been drilled on it so many times.

My head was starting to throb painfully. I curled up on the bed and leant my cheek against the white pillow, enjoying the cooling sensation against my hot skin. I expected that Georgina would totally hate me now. She and the rest of the class would have been escorted to quarantine and given painful anti-virals. If they didn't present symptoms in the next eight hours then they would be released and allowed to go home.

The door to Isolation opened and two people in orange suits and helmets entered the room. The uniform worn by Welfare made it difficult to tell if they were men or women, but by the size of the two people who entered the room I thought they might be men. In voices muffled by their helmets and oxygen masks they told me that Transport had arrived to take me home. They both escorted me out of the back of the Isolation Unit into a white tiled corridor. The tiles of the corridor gleamed brightly in the harsh strip lighting and the glare hurt my eyes. I mused to myself why all Isolation Units looked the same; white floors, white walls, white ceilings, even white handrails for people who were infirm and unable to walk unaided. Who decided that Isolation had to be white? I wondered, why wasn't it red or blue or even green? It would be much more welcoming. White was so horribly clinical and cold.

The long white corridor ended in a plastic tunnel and it crackled and popped as I clambered through it into the back of the Transport. Once inside the Transport we travelled back home to my apartment. During the short journey I was treated by the doctor, who took my temperature, blood and urine samples. It was so embarrassing giving the urine sample and I hoped that the doctor looked away, but I couldn't tell as it was impossible to see his eyes through the dark visor of his Isolation Suit.

Transport pulled into the car park at the back of my apartment block and I clambered out to find Mummy waiting for me. At least I recognised the familiar shape of Mummy as she was wearing her Isolation Suit too. Mummy's suit fit much better than the Transport doctors and you could tell that it was expensive and designer made.

The Atrium had been cleared so the Welfare Officers were able to escort me up the stairs and into our own Isolation Unit.

As I entered the Isolation Unit I gave Mummy a tight smile and she dipped her head in response. The door closed automatically behind me and I heard the click of the lock as it activated. I'd entered Locker One so I quickly took off all my clothes and stuffed them into the orange contamination bags. I shivered in the slight chill that pervaded the room. All Isolation Units were purposely kept cold so that germs couldn't incubate.

I quickly moved into the shower room. If I hated my daily chem shower, then the infection showers were a million times worse. I'd only been sick a few times before but could vividly recollect how horrible the showers were. I remembered fifteen minutes of hell, as high grade antiseptic chemicals were sprayed over my body. No matter how tightly I shut my eyes they still stung horribly. My eyes had been red and sore for a week afterwards.

The intercom clicked loudly and the sound echoed eerily around the room. 'Ready?' a grainy voice asked.

'Yes,' I replied and then braced myself for the onslaught. There was a loud hiss followed by the clattering of pipes as the liquid spurted out overhead and hit my body with such force that it squeezed a hiss from between my clenched lips.

The smell of the antiseptic filled the room like a thick fog around me. It was almost suffocating. I tried not to gag. Gagging would involve me opening my mouth and then I might swallow some of the liquid. I shuddered at the thought. The last time I had an infection shower I'd held my breath for so long trying not to breathe in the horrible smell that I'd felt light headed. I'd opened my mouth to take a much needed gasp of air and instead had gotten a mouthful of antiseptic liquid. I spat it out immediately but some of it had trickled down my throat, where it seemed to burn a trail all the way to my stomach.

This time I mashed my lips into a tight thin line as the liquid poured over me. I started to count out the seconds in my head, one, two, three, four . . . fifty eight, fifty nine, sixty, another minute had gone by. I only had to endure another fourteen more minutes. I concentrated on each number, forming it in my head, focusing on its shape until thirteen minutes had gone by, then fourteen and finally the fifteen minutes were over and the shower stopped. Even without the liquid spraying over me the air was still heavy with the sharp sting of the antiseptic so I continued to hold my breath as best I could. My eyes were watering furiously and my vision was blurry.

'Move out please,' the intercom crackled into life.

I stepped out of the shower and groped my way into the drying room where warm drafts of air buffeted my body and dried away the last remnants of the shower.

When I was completely dry I stepped into Locker Two. This time, instead of the orange bags, there was a sterile white nightgown, gloves and socks waiting for me. I pulled the nightgown over my head, slipped the socks on and then pulled on the gloves. I moved over to the door at the end of the room and pressed the bright red buzzer. The door opened for me and I exited Locker Two and entered the Isolation Unit. This would be my home for the next week. Thankfully this room wasn't as stark and white as the Isolation Unit at school. Mummy had added some home comforts and the white walls were covered in tasteful prints. There was also a PortPad so I wouldn't be bored. I could see Mummy waiting on the other side of the large glass window that connected the room to the rest of the house. Now that she was out of danger she had taken off her Isolation Suit.

'Are you alright, darling?' she asked using the intercom on the other side of the glass. She was frowning slightly and there was a look of concern on her face. She was alone so I assumed that Welfare must have already left the house.

I nodded and gave her the thumbs up for added reassurance.

'The doctor says you have a cold,' she said. 'So you need to stay in isolation for the next seven days.'

I gave her another nod in response.

'You need to get into bed and rest,' she said. 'Daddy will come and see you when he gets home from work.'

She waited until I'd climbed into bed and then gave me a small wave before heading back into the main part of the house. I was glad that we were rich enough to have our own Isolation Unit. If we hadn't been able to afford one then I would have had to go to Community Isolation. In Community Isolation I would have been facing a week of boredom staring at four white painted walls with no PortPad to keep me amused. Gillian Davies, a girl in my class who was designation Bravo, so of course didn't have her own Isolation Unit, had to spend two whole weeks in Community Isolation last year with a throat infection. She said it was the most boring time of her life. She said that it had been so boring that she had even been looking forward to going back to school!

CHAPTER 3

Party

When Daddy arrived home he came to visit me straight away. He promised that he would arrange for my favourite designers to come to the house and model dresses for me so that I could choose something for the charity ball.

It was actually a lot of fun to sit in bed and watch the designers and models parade outside my window in an array of fabulous dresses. I made them turn one way and then the other, showing me the back and front of each dress. In the end I selected a beautiful royal blue strapless silk dress. It was floor length and Mummy said that it would fit me like a glove.

By the evening of the party I was declared fit and well. All sign of infection was gone and I was able to leave Isolation. Mummy collected me and accompanied me back to my bedroom.

'Daddy and I are heading to the party early,' she said. 'He's meeting VIPs and doesn't want to be late. We've asked the chauffeur to pick you up at seven thirty. Is that okay with you darling?'

I smiled in response, grateful she didn't expect me to spend time with Daddy's stuffy VIPs. I wanted to have fun at the party. I didn't want to be bored by lots of old people.

When we arrived at my bedroom Mummy fingered the blue dress

hanging up on the rail. 'You'll look beautiful in this darling,' she said. 'I told Daddy all about it and he can't wait to see you in it.'

The dress certainly was beautiful and I couldn't wait to put it on.

'I'll see you later,' Mummy said as she left the room. 'Please don't be late. You know how much it upsets Daddy.'

As I didn't have to leave until seven thirty I had enough time for a long relaxing soak in the bath. I scrubbed and exfoliated my whole body to wash away the last remnants of the nasty antiseptic smell of the Isolation Unit. Then I moisturised and carefully sniffed myself all over to make sure that I smelt normal again.

Once I was satisfied that no trace of antiseptic remained I slipped into my dress and twirled around in front of the mirror admiring my reflection. The dress really did look good and it brought out the blue of my eyes. My dark brown curly hair bounced playfully on my shoulders. Originally I'd planned to wear my hair up, thinking that it would make me look sophisticated, but since I'd run out of time I left it hanging loose, gripping the fringe with a diamanté clip.

At seven thirty I skipped down the stairs in my new sliver sandals and found Daddy's limo waiting for me in the drive. Normally Daddy used the limo to travel to work or for official engagements but on special occasions it was made available for all the family to use. It was important that the Legislator's family arrived in style.

The inside of the limo smelled like old worn leather and the woody scent of Daddy's aftershave. I settled comfortably into the soft leather seat and my stomach was full of butterflies as I thought about the party. I was hoping there might be some cute boys there, maybe that would make up for my epic failure with Reese.

We drove to the Hub, which was the name we gave to the centre of the Neighbourhood. As we rounded the corner the Building of Light came into view. This building served as the headquarters for the Light. It was located at the northern edge of the Square of Light.

The square was filled to bursting with people. My attention was drawn to the centre of the square where 'Our Hero' stood. The stone sculpture showed a doctor wearing an Isolation Suit standing tall and proud above the afflicted. What caught my attention was the stream of light which illuminated the statue, changing it from red to white and then blue; the colours of our national flag. The Light must have arranged this show especially for the gathered crowd. Daddy always said that the Director had a flair for the dramatic.

The statue commemorated all of the brave doctors who gave their life during the worst days of the Sandman Virus. Each year on Boundary Day, everyone from the Neighbourhood gathered in the square so that each citizen could lay a single white rose at the statue. The rose, a sign of purity and cleanliness, was our Neighbourhood emblem. Of course it was difficult to find real roses nowadays so most of them were synthetic.

The car crawled around the square until we reached the Building of Light. Above the entrance, proudly displayed in a haze of red, white and blue, I read the familiar words 'The Light is Right. The Light is Might' etched into the moulded stone.

This was the slogan that the Light had used when they took control of the Neighbourhood twenty years ago. The Sandman Virus was still raging across the country and hundreds of people were dying every day. The government had lost control, they couldn't cure the disease and they couldn't stop the food riots that followed. It was the Light who had discovered the Cure and it was the Light who had funded the building of the Boundary so it was right that they took responsibility for the people inside.

Daddy had been a legal assistant with the Light during the worst days of the virus. By the time my brother was born he'd worked his way up the ranks and had been named as the Legislator, the head of the Legislate. His position meant that I got to enjoy the perks of his job, like being invited to some of the really good parties. It wasn't the same as being part of the celeb crowd and being invited to all of the celeb parties, but it was still fun. Georgina and Natalie's parents worked for the Light but they were only minor partners which meant they didn't always get invited to the same parties as Daddy. Usually I was able to arrange an invite for them both and we'd have a great time mingling with anyone that was famous and trying to get our pictures posted on the Portal.

Tonight I was going to the party alone, and it felt strange. I wondered what Georgina and Natalie would be doing this evening. I expected that they would be watching the party on the Portal. Maybe this was the opportunity I was looking for to show my friends what a great time I was having without them. Normally I attended parties with Daddy and Mummy and they quickly ushered me past the photographers. Neither of them were interested in being celebrities and they definitely didn't want my picture all over the Portal. Daddy told me that once a picture was online it could never be removed. We had to be careful that nothing got onto the Portal that could hurt his position in the Light.

Tonight without my parents protecting me I had an opportunity to make my mark. If I could get my picture on the right blogs looking fabulous in my new dress then big things could happen. I could be voted 'best dressed' and reinvent myself as a style icon. Maybe I'd get a dedicated blog or, even better, a guest appearance on a reality show. That was how lots of people in the Neighbourhood became famous. Maybe I could become a celebrity in my own right. Georgina and Natalie would have to come crawling back to me, begging to be my friend – that could possibly be the sweetest revenge of all.

I fumbled in my purse and pulled out the little jewelled mirror that Daddy had given me for my birthday. I flipped it open and reapplied my lipstick. If I was going to make the right impression then I needed to look perfect.

There were crowds of people outside the Building of Light clamouring for a view of the party guests.

'Here we go,' I muttered as I popped the mirror back into my handbag. The chauffeur opened the car door and I took a deep breath as I exited into a blaze of lights. Normally at this point Daddy would pull me away, sometimes throwing his coat over me to shield me from the photographers and insisting on 'no pictures'. This time I was alone and could behave how I wanted. There were journalists and photographers everywhere and I stopped to pose for the cameras at every opportunity. Some of the photographers even knew my name and I blushed with pride as they called out to me. This was definitely going to be my night.

Eventually another car drew up and the photographers' attention turned to its occupant. I walked towards the entrance of the building blinking madly in an attempt to get rid of the yellow spots that danced across my vision.

Halfway up the stairs I came to an abrupt halt as I thought I spotted a familiar face in the crowd. I lurched forward as someone bumped into me from behind. It was Dr Butters, the Head of Environmental Affairs. His blonde head bobbed up and down manically as he accepted my apology for stopping so suddenly, his face beetroot red and shining brightly. I remembered that Daddy didn't like him and referred to him as 'that blithering idiot'. I let him pass me on the stairs, his massive girth pressing me uncomfortably into the brick of the building. As soon as he was gone I quickly turned back to the crowd, but the familiar face had disappeared.

I proceeded up the stairs towards the entrance to the building, sure that I couldn't have seen my brother in the crowd. I must have imagined it. Once inside the building I handed my invite to the Watch and then pushed through the throng of guests as I tried to locate my parents. I noticed Daddy and Mummy entertaining a group of octogenarians in the corner of the great hall. Not wanting to waste my time talking to old people I gave them both a brief wave and made my way to the bar. Mummy frowned at me but I pretended not the notice. I knew they would expect me to introduce myself to the VIPs and play the loving, attentive daughter. But if I was going to make the most of the party I needed some time to myself, just for a little while.

I hadn't seen any eligible boys so far, but I thought I might find some in the bar area. I ordered a fruit mocktail from the cute barman. For a moment I even considered flirting with him to pass the time, but I checked myself almost immediately. It would be totally inappropriate given that he was Delta.

I took my drink and scanned the bar and was delighted to see two or three cute boys. I noticed an attractive dark haired boy talking to a group of men. He was dressed in a flamboyant purple velvet dinner jacket which stood out vibrantly against the stuffy black suits worn by the older men in his group. I caught his eye and he gave me a brief smile. I watched him for a few moments while I finished my drink and handed the empty glass to a passing waitress. I ordered another drink, keeping one eye on the cute boy who was still talking animatedly to the group of older men. He'd glanced over in my direction a few times so I knew that he was interested. I decided to leave the room to see if he would follow me.

I took my drink and headed to the door. I could feel the boy's eyes on me as I walked across the room. Before I exited the bar I turned and threw him an encouraging smile.

Once I was out in the hall I slowly headed towards the ballroom. I turned a few times but was disappointed to find that the boy wasn't following me. I'd been so sure that I'd made a good impression.

In the ballroom the orchestra was taking a break and guests milled around the room chatting in small groups. I scanned the room. Everyone appeared to be in couples and I couldn't find any unattached men.

'Miss Hunter,' a waiter appeared beside me, an empty tray in his hands. I nodded, surprised that he'd addressed me directly and that he appeared to know my name.

'I have this for you,' he said uncertainly. He offered me a folded piece of paper. I took it from him, and he hovered nervously as I opened it. *'Meet me outside in 15 minutes.'* I turned the paper over but there was nothing else written on it. Nothing to identify the author.

'Who gave this to you?' I asked the waiter.

'A young man,' he said. 'He was waiting outside in the rear gardens.'

Curious, I asked him to describe the man.

'Dark hair, dark eyes,' he said.

'Attractive?'

The waiter shrugged. 'I suppose so,' he said.

I smiled to myself. So the dark haired boy was interested and now he wanted to meet me out in the gardens. How exciting and romantic.

'You can go,' I said as I dismissed the waiter.

He seemed relieved to get away from me.

I immediately headed out of the ballroom and down the rear stairs into the gardens. The gardens were deserted, everyone else was inside at the party. It had been raining earlier in the day and I had to lift up the hem of my dress so it didn't get wet. As I fussed with my dress I realised that someone had stepped out onto the path.

I looked up excitedly, expecting to see the dark haired boy. I let out a gasp. It was a dark haired boy, but not the one I was expecting. Standing on the path in front of me was my brother. He was older and a little bit taller, but I would recognise him anywhere. His messy hair still stuck out at right angles, his clothes slightly too big for his slender frame. He didn't say a word, he just stared at me while the hint of a smile played on his lips. I opened and closed my mouth like a goldfish.

My brother found his voice first. 'Hello MaryAnn,' he said. It seemed too casual a greeting from someone I hadn't seen for four long years.

'Daryl,' I responded a little unsteadily. 'What are you doing here?'

'I came to see you,' he said. 'I missed my little sister.' He gave me an appraising look.

There were a million things I wanted to ask him but most importantly I wanted to find out where he had been for the last four years. When I asked him this he simply shrugged in response. 'Here and there,' he said evasively.

'Here and there?' I queried. 'That's not a proper answer.'

'It doesn't matter where I've been.'

'What do you mean it doesn't matter? We've all been so worried about you.'

He cocked an eyebrow. It was an expression I remembered well. 'Really, you were ALL worried about me?'

'You just disappeared and no-one knew where you'd gone. Daddy and Mummy were distraught.'

'Oh I bet they were.' There was no mistaking the sarcasm in his voice, but I wasn't sure what it meant.

'Of course they were,' I said. Then I paused uncertainly. In reality, Daddy and Mummy had barely spoken about Daryl after he'd left, usually changing the subject or telling me to hush if I asked about him. I'd found it extremely frustrating but had come to the conclusion that his disappearance was too painful and that they couldn't bear to talk about him.

'I expect our parents were more concerned about whether I'd damaged our father's esteemed position in the Light,' he said bitterly.

'Stop it,' I said. 'You make them sound so callous. It was horrible after you left. Everyone was miserable.' I was ashamed to hear my voice crack with emotion.

My brother's face lost its scornful look and it was replaced by something akin to shame. 'I'm sorry. It must have been horrible for you. If it makes you feel any better I missed you too. I came back because I wanted to see you again.'

There was a part of me that desperately wanted to believe him, but, as happy as I was to see him again, something wasn't quite right. There was a tension in his face that made me feel uneasy. I recalled the rumours I'd heard about him going Outside and the memory made me step away from him in horror. Frantically I fumbled in my bag for my antiseptic spray and wipes. I needed to sanitise myself immediately.

'What's the matter?' Daryl asked. He frowned when he saw the spray and wipes in my gloved hand.

'MaryAnn,' he said, through gritted teeth. 'I'm not sick. I'm fine.'

I ignored him and instead wiped frantically at the bare skin on my arms.

'MaryAnn,' he repeated. 'I am NOT sick.'

I continued to scrub at my arms. 'I heard that you went Outside. What if you've brought the infection back with you?' I said.

He shook his head, 'MaryAnn, Outside isn't what you think it is,' he said.

I stared at him, confused. Outside was a horrible place filled with disease.

'MaryAnn, I'm fine, honestly, but if it makes you feel better I'll keep away from you.' He took a few steps away from me as if to prove his point.

I hesitated, torn between revulsion at the threat he posed and curiosity about where he'd been for the last four years. He didn't look sick. Maybe a little bit thin, but he definitely didn't have the pallor of someone who had the Virus. I'd seen broadcasts in Wellbeing at school about the infection and these had shown people bleeding from the eyes and ears. A fact that made me want to gag a little.

I was still a little unsure but then he smiled and I immediately softened. I'd forgotten about his smile, how it didn't just stay on his lips but played across the muscles of his face until it finally reached his eyes. That's why he'd been so popular at school. People always fell for his easy charm and ready humour. Despite myself I smiled back.

'You look good,' he said. 'And all grown up.'

'Well it has been four years. That's what happens to eleven year olds, they grow up you know.'

'So you're, what, fifteen now?' he asked.

'Yes, sixteen in ten months.'

'You look like our mother,' he said. 'That's how I recognised you.'

Damn! Daddy and Mummy. I'd forgotten about them. They were still inside at the party and would probably be looking for me, expecting me to entertain their VIPs.

'Daryl, I'm supposed to be inside at the party with Mummy and Daddy's guests,' I exclaimed. 'You know how Daddy gets if we make him look bad in front of his friends. He'll be furious.'

I was going to ask if we could meet again when my brother surprised me by grabbing hold of my arm. 'Don't leave,' he said. 'We have so much to talk about.'

I pulled away in horror. 'Daryl, you promised, let go of me.' I tried to twist my arm free and was startled at how strong his grip was.

'Daryl, I'm going to be in so much trouble if I don't go back to the party. Let go of my arm.'

Rather than release my arm my brother's grip became even tighter and he was actually starting to hurt me. Daryl's eyes were darting around nervously and his smile no longer looked soft and welcoming. It was stretched taut and thin across his face.

'Daryl,' I hissed a warning. 'I want you to let go of my arm right this minute.'

He ignored me and instead pulled me onto the lawn, physically dragging me away from the building. My heels sank into the grass and I stumbled.

'You can't go to the party,' he said in a very quiet voice. 'You have to come with me.'

Alarm bells began to sound in my head. There was definitely something wrong. After Daryl had left home my parents had told me he'd *got in with the wrong crowd*, but they'd never explained what that meant.

He continued to drag me across the grass. 'We have to make them listen,' he said unexpectedly. 'Stay with me and you'll be safe.'

At his words I mustered all of my strength and, taking him by surprise, I wrenched my arm roughly out of his grasp. As soon as I was free I sped back across the lawn. In my haste to get to the building I left my shoes behind in the grass and was running barefoot, but I didn't care. If I was safe out here with Daryl then there was something dangerous in the building . . . and Daddy and Mummy were inside.

Daryl bellowed loudly behind me. I was so desperate to reach my parents that I ignored the stones that ripped at my naked feet and ran for the door. As I pulled it open I could hear my brother yelling; his voice high pitched and screaming.

There was a deafening roar; loud like a thunderbolt, followed closely by a blinding light. I was flying backwards through the air, my arms flailing helplessly. I felt something rip into my face, my head slammed against something hard and blackness engulfed me.

Chapter 4

Aftermath

My head hurt and my throat was dry. My cold was back worse than ever. A loud beeping noise was making my head pound sickeningly. It must be time for school I thought as I reached out to turn off my alarm clock.

My arm didn't respond. I couldn't move. I was paralysed. My eyes flew open and I squinted myopically against a harsh bright light. Pain tore through my head and I choked back a wave of nausea. My body felt like it was on fire and I cried out, my breathing a heavy rasp.

I lay very still and slowly the pounding in my head began to subside until I was left with only a dull ache. With the pain under control I was able to take in my surroundings. It was obvious that I wasn't at home. The walls of the room were white; stark white and clinical like a . . . like a . . . 'Oh no, I think I'm in Isolation again,' I muttered to myself. My voice sounded ragged and hoarse.

My vision was obscured by a large white machine and I realised I'd located the source of the annoying beeping noise. The noise made my head hurt and I wanted more than anything for it to stop. There was a long tube leading from the machine and it was connected to my arm.

I concentrated on moving my other arm and with a herculean effort I grabbed at the tube. White hot daggers of pain hit me and I heard myself groan loudly. Despite the pain I managed to grasp the tube tightly and with all the effort I could muster I tore it out of my arm. Rather than resolve the problem, the beeping noise became a wailing siren. A siren that hammered shards of pain into my delicate, shattered head.

The door flew open and I heard raised voices as people ran to my bedside. I could make out two people; a man and a woman dressed in white. Neither of them were wearing Isolation Suits and for a moment I was confused. I obviously wasn't in quarantine so I couldn't be sick. I must be in hospital, that meant I wasn't infectious . . . was I injured?

The man bent over the machine and reinserted the tube into my arm. Mercifully the wailing stopped immediately and the beeping noise started again.

'She's awake,' said the female, addressing the man next to her. I thought she was stating the obvious and wanted to make a sarcastic comment, but my throat was dry and I could only make a guttural groan.

'Get her some water.'

The man left the room and returned moments later with a glass of water and a straw. He lifted my head slightly and brought the water to my mouth. Ignoring the shards of pain that hammered into my skull I sucked hard on the straw. Once the water was in my mouth I found that I couldn't swallow it and I gagged. I was embarrassed as water poured down my chin and onto the bedcovers.

'Slowly,' the man cautioned.

The nod I gave him caused such an intense explosion of pain in my head that for a moment I thought my skull was going to split in two. When the pain subsided a little I pulled on the straw again. This time I found I was able to take small sips without choking.

Once I'd finished drinking my voice came back a little.

'Where am I?' I croaked.

The man and woman exchanged glances. Maybe I was mistaken but I thought I saw the female shake her head slightly.

I felt angry. Why wouldn't they tell me what had happened. I tried to remember what my last memory had been. An image of myself in a midnight blue gown flashed through my mind. I was going to a party, but what party? I struggled to remember. There was something important about the memory. A wave of fatigue washed over me and my eyes flickered wearily. I tried to force myself to keep them open, but there was only darkness.

When I woke again the room was pitch black and the hospital was quiet. There was a chair opposite my bed, but it was empty. Lying alone in the darkness I thought about my parents. They should be by my bedside. I felt a stab of annoyance at their absence. Maybe they'd decided that the party and the VIPs were more important than me. It really wasn't fair that they'd left me alone in the hospital. I tried to move to a more comfortable position and a wave of white hot pain drove daggers into my skull. When the darkness descended again I welcomed it like an old friend.

The next time I woke the room was flooded with light. I could hear movement outside my room, the clip clop of heavy footsteps and the deep metallic clang of a trolley being wheeled across a stone floor. I moved my head cautiously, mentally grimacing against the expected pain, but to my delight there was nothing.

The door opened and a blonde female nurse entered pushing a trolley. She was heavily made up and she smiled at me. Cherry Red. That was the colour of her lipstick. It was the colour that Georgina always wore. I noticed that some of it had stuck to her front teeth.

'I have to give you an injection. Part of your treatment.' I was too tired to argue so I lay stiffly as she jabbed a needle into my arm. The pain made me wince slightly and she patted me on the shoulder. 'All done,' she said kindly.

As she was about to leave the room I called out to her. My voice was hoarse through lack of use. 'Where are my parents?' I asked.

Her smile seemed to waver a little. 'Erm, I'll get someone to come and speak to you, sweetie,' she said as she left the room.

I didn't want someone to come and speak to me. I just wanted my parents. I knew they were very busy and I was being selfish, but I couldn't help feeling a little bit sorry for myself. Why weren't they sitting here by my bedside waiting for me to wake up? Where could they be? Maybe they were in the hospital restaurant having a coffee or something to eat, I reasoned. It felt like I'd been in the hospital for a long time and they would need to eat. I decided that this was probably what had happened and that someone had already gone to fetch them. I waited expectantly, glancing eagerly at the door every time I heard footsteps in the hall. Each time I was disappointed as they passed right by my door.

Eventually the door to my room opened. I looked up expectantly but to my disappointment it was the male nurse and not my parents who entered.

'You awake?' he asked.

'Yes,' I mumbled.

'I'll get the doctor.'

'What happened to me?' I asked before he had chance to leave the room.

'I'll get the doctor,' he repeated, and then exited the room closing the door behind him.

I was starting to feel angry. Why was no-one answering any of my questions? When the doctor arrived I resolved that I was going to get some answers.

The nurse returned and was followed into the room by a stout bearded man. I presumed that he must be the doctor.

The doctor smiled at me, but I refused to smile back. 'So you're awake Miss Hunter?' he said.

'Obviously,' I answered in my most disdainful tone.

He looked a bit taken aback. 'Well let's take a look at you,' he said. 'Make sure everything's where it should be.' He used what he obviously thought was a kindly tone, but I wasn't interested in his bedside manner, I wanted some answers.

'What happened?' I asked.

'Let's have a look at you first before we start asking questions,' he gave me a patient smile.

I shook my head and if my arms hadn't been numb and too heavy to lift I would have crossed them combatively across my chest. 'Tell me what's going on first and then I'll let you examine me.' It was an empty threat, my body was numb and there was no way I could physically prevent him from examining me. Even so I saw a flicker of annoyance cross his face.

'I need to examine you,' he insisted.

'Absolutely not,' I shook my head. 'I want some answers first.'

The doctor's patient smile was replaced by a stern and very imposing frown. My resolve wavered a little in the face of his determined gaze, but somehow I managed to maintain my composure.

'I'll make you a deal,' he said. I need to examine you first. Then I'll answer all your questions. No examination, no questions,' he said firmly. 'If you don't submit to the examination then I'll have you forcibly restrained.'

I got the impression that this wasn't an empty threat so I reluctantly complied.

A light breeze whispered through the trees that bordered the small rose garden. I sat on a hard wooden bench and waited for the Director to arrive. The Director had volunteered to be my guardian and today he was taking me home to live with his family. The doctor told me how lucky I was, to be taken in by the leader of the Light when the only other alternative was foster care.

I certainly didn't feel lucky. My parents had both died in the explosion that ripped through the Building of Light on the evening of the charity ball. They told me Mummy was killed instantly and Daddy had died a couple of hours later in the hospital. The doctor said that they had tried very hard to save his life and I had no reason to question this, after all Daddy was a very important man, he was the Legislator. I suspected that they did everything they could to save him. It didn't make me feel any better. In the end it didn't matter, they had failed and he had died anyway.

Whenever I thought about it I felt numb. It wasn't just my body that was numb; there was numbness in my brain as well. Like there was too much information to process so it had just stopped working. I liked it that way. Being numb made it easier to function; to get up in the morning, get dressed, go to physical therapy, engage in stupid inane conversations with the therapists. It was all pointless, but my numb brain seemed able to tolerate it. Sometimes when I needed a break from reality, my brain would just switch off altogether. When I returned to reality I'd find that I'd been staring into vacant space for an hour or more.

I was lucky, the doctors said. I'd survived because I was so far away from the blast. The emergency exit door had been blown off its hinges and slammed into me. The force of the impact had broken my ribs and punctured a lung. I'd stopped breathing in the Transport a number of times but the doctors had been able to resuscitate me.

I fingered the dressing across my cheek; the hinge from the door had ripped into my face causing a deep gash. The doctors didn't think that it would heal properly and told me I would have a permanent scar. Yesterday while I was alone in my room I'd carefully lifted up the dressing so I could study my reflection in the mirror. What I saw made me quickly replace it in a cold sweat. My cheek was ripped wide open. A jagged red gash ran across its full length from below my eye to the tip of my mouth. Not only did I look like a monster but it also served as a permanent reminder of the night my parents died. Now every time I looked in a mirror I would be reminded that they were gone.

It was funny that it was the scar that brought tears to my eyes whenever I thought about it, while my parents' death just made me feel empty.

My life since the explosion had a surreal edge to it. My days had been filled with examinations and physical therapy, which was so far removed from my normal life that it didn't seem real anymore. A part of my brain hung on to the fantasy that this was a horrible dream and that soon I would wake up at home in my bedroom. The bell would be ringing for breakfast and I'd go downstairs to find Daddy and Mummy sitting at the table. As long as I held onto the vain hope that I was stuck in a nightmare then life somehow seemed more bearable. It gave me the energy I needed to get up out of bed every morning and face the day.

There was the crunch of gravel and the Director's silver car slid gracefully up the drive. His chauffeur climbed out and opened one of the rear passenger doors. I was astonished to see the Director get out of the car himself. I'd expected him to send one of his aides to collect me from the hospital. The Director was a tall, broad shouldered man; his face rugged and worn, but attractive in a way that screamed of good health and fitness. Daddy said that he was very charismatic and that this was why he made such a great leader. Men wanted to be like him and women fell in love with him, or at least older women did, he wasn't my type. I preferred to stick to the boys at school.

I surveyed him as he climbed out of the car. His suit fit expensively across his broad shoulders, giving him a toned athletic look. His blond hair was cut short and perfectly groomed. He was the embodiment of the Light: tall, strong and healthy. No wonder he'd risen so quickly through the ranks of the Light. He looked like he'd been born to be its leader.

The Director gave a smile as he came towards me and covered the ground in only a few strides. His face was sympathetic as he approached me - an expression I'd seen many times since I'd arrived at the hospital.

He gave me a small bow while offering the standard party greeting. 'Good health and prosperity.'

I returned the greeting, 'In the Light we trust.'

'I'm so sorry about your parents.' He bent down and startled me by suddenly grasping my hands in his as he stared intently into my eyes. Momentarily I was astonished at how forward he was. It was unusual for anyone but exceptionally close friends and family to engage in such intimate contact. Once I'd got over the initial shock I was repulsed to find that even through the material of our gloves his hands felt cold and slimy. I cringed away from him slightly. It took me a few seconds to compose myself, but he didn't seem to notice my discomfort and flashed me a sympathetic smile before straightening up and patting my shoulder softly.

'It'll take some time to recover from the shock,' he said reassuringly. 'We'll take you home so that Maud can look after you.'

He held out his hand to help me up from the bench. I grabbed it reluctantly, cringing a little at the wet cold texture. *Stop it,* I scolded myself mentally. This was the Director, the leader of the Light and my new guardian. There was no reason to cringe away from him . . . *but he has horrible slimy fish hands* an inner voice whined at me. I told the voice to shut up and followed the Director to the car. 'Let's get out of this awful place,' he said.

I couldn't have agreed more.

As befitted the leader of the Light, the Director lived in a large house on the edge of the Neighbourhood. Daddy told me that the building used to be a castle. It was situated in a secure location with picturesque views of the surrounding hills. It was only fifteen miles from the Boundary. In the early days when Boundary incursions had been common, a fortified perimeter wall was erected around the building for security.

When the Boundary had first been erected and the Neighbourhoods created there had been protests from the Echo left Outside. They banded together and formed the Union; a partisan group that had caused some real problems for the Light. They'd planted bombs, disrupted official events and shot people in cold blood. It had been a difficult time, but ultimately the Unionists didn't stand a real chance. They'd been poorly trained and were no match for the highly skilled officers of The Watch, who had hunted them down and killed them all. Those that weren't killed by the Watch quickly succumbed to the Sandman Virus until in the end they were no threat at all. All that remained Outside were bands of starving Ferals scavenging around for enough food to eat.

Nowadays the walls around the Director's house were no longer guarded as there hadn't been a Boundary incursion for years. No-one inside the Neighbourhood posed a threat to the Light or its Director.

The Director's car manoeuvred through a set of iron gates that opened automatically as we approached. Once inside we travelled along a wide gravel drive until the car came to a halt outside the house. The Director's daughter Maud was waiting for us at the entrance. Her face was partially hidden behind a thick curtain of jet black hair. She was a sickly looking girl, her eyes deep set and rimmed by dark circles. Mummy once told me that because she was so sickly looking it made people feel uncomfortable around her so the Director kept her at home. She was home schooled and rarely left the house except to escort her father to official functions. She was incredibly timid and barely said a word.

After I'd climbed out of the car she stepped forward and gave the Director and me a stiff bow. 'MaryAnn, I'm so sorry,' she said, her voice so quiet it was barely audible.

I followed the Director and Maud through the HealthScan and into the house. I'd visited the Director's home before but the pure extravagance of the entrance hall, with its ornate flooring, gold decorative mouldings and diamond chandeliers always caused a sharp intake of breath. It really was quite beautiful and wonderfully ostentatious.

The Director addressed me, 'MaryAnn, I hope you don't mind but I have work to do. I'll leave you in Maud's expert care.'

He gave each of us a quick bow before striding away down the hall.

Maud peered at me timidly through her thick fringe. 'I'll take you to your room.'

I followed as she led me through the massive entrance hall and up a large carpeted staircase. At the top of the stairs we travelled down a long corridor which was luxuriously decorated with vivid green and gold wallpaper. About halfway down the corridor we stopped outside a wooden door. 'This is your room,' Maud indicated. There was a sign on the door: 'MaryAnn's Room'. The sign was decorated with pink and yellow flowers.

'I painted the sign myself,' Maud said proudly. 'My room is further down the hall, so we're practically neighbours.'

She gave me a wide smile and her pale face lit up for a moment. She opened the door to my room and stepped inside. As she gestured for me to enter there was an air of expectation.

Once inside the room I couldn't help but gasp with shock.

Maud seemed nervous. 'Do you like it?'

I couldn't speak, I just stared around me. The room was the exact replica of my bedroom at home. The wallpaper, the curtains, the carpet; everything was the same.

'We took pictures of your bedroom and then tried to recreate it.' Maud said. 'So you'd feel at home right away.'

I was too busy fighting the urge to be sick to answer her.

As the silence lengthened Maud's already pale face began to turn a startling shade of white and she looked close to tears.

'Did we do the wrong thing?' She asked.

I detected a quaver in her voice. I couldn't bear the thought of her bursting into tears and didn't have the energy to comfort her. I knew that she had meant to do the right thing, to make me feel at home, so I managed to give her a thin reassuring smile.

'It's perfect,' I stammered. 'Just like home.'

Her face relaxed and she clapped her hands in delight. 'Great,' she almost squealed. 'It was my idea. I told the Director that we should try and make you feel at home. He left all the arrangements to me.' She gestured for me to follow her and I silently trailed after her as she chatted about the complexities of recreating the room. I was barely listening, I was still trying to get over the shock of seeing my bedroom, the room I never expected to see again, recreated here in a stranger's house. It felt ghoulish and I shivered.

'You poor thing. You're cold.' Maud reached behind the bedroom door and pulled out my fluffy pink bathrobe. I was repulsed at the idea of putting it on, but Maud was already pulling it over my shoulders. I tensed slightly but let her finish. Once the bathrobe was on she nipped the front together and tied it firmly with the silk belt. 'There you go. That's much better isn't it?'

I nodded stiffly.

'You must be exhausted. Maybe you'd like to lie down for a while.'

She pulled back the cream bedspread covered in silk flowers that I used to love and indicated that I get inside. I wanted to cry, but instead I dutifully crawled between the sheets and lay down.

'Try and get some sleep,' she said. 'I'll come back and get you for dinner.' I closed my eyes obediently, but when I opened them a few moments later she was still standing there by the side of my bed. There was a look of such intense pity on her face that I quickly squeezed my eyes shut again without saying a word. A few seconds later I heard the bedroom door click shut as she left the room.

I lay very still with my eyes tightly shut, wishing that I could just fall into a deep sleep and forget about everything; Maud, my bedroom and especially my parents, but I'd spent so much time resting at the hospital that I just couldn't sleep. I sat up and took some time to study my 'new' bedroom. It really was an exact replica of my room at home; there was nothing out of place. I couldn't detect even the smallest of differences. I knew that Maud meant well, but I didn't like it. It was downright creepy. If I was going to sleep in my bedroom then I wanted to do it in my own home and not here in the Director's house.

I climbed out of bed and padded around the room picking up various objects and then putting them down again. I was careful not to make any noise as I didn't want Maud to know that I was awake. I expected she would waste no time coming back to my room to take care of me. I opened my underwear drawer and shuddered. Even my underwear had been arranged perfectly. I wasn't sure I liked the idea of someone going through my things and recreating my underwear drawer. That was just plain nasty. Despite my uneasiness I had to admire the attention to detail. The amount of time and research that had gone into recreating the room was staggering.

I found a copy of the book I was reading just before the accident. It was lying open on my dressing table. Most people read books on their PortPad as paper books were so difficult to get hold of. But I liked the feel of holding real paper in my hand so Daddy often let me read books from his own personal collection. The book hadn't been a particularly riveting read, but welcoming the diversion I picked it up and climbed back into bed. I was just finishing the third chapter when I heard a gentle knock on my door and Maud entered.

'Time to get up,' she said. 'The Director likes us to dress for dinner.'

'Okay, thanks. I'll be right down.'

'You need any help?'

I shook my head. Did she think I was incapable of dressing myself! She'd be offering to take me to the toilet next.

'Well I'm just down the hall if you need me.' She hesitated for a moment and then stepped over to the bed and extended her hand shyly. 'I have this for you,' she pressed a silver bell into my hand. 'Just in case you need any help,' she said. 'You can ring it, and I'll be able to hear you in my room.'

I took the bell and placed it on the dressing table. I tried to give her what I hoped was a grateful smile.

'Fifteen minutes,' she said before she left. 'The Director likes us to be punctual.'

After she'd left the room I climbed out of bed and picked up the bell. I turned it over in my hand and it tinkled lightly. I didn't know very much about Maud, we'd only met very briefly when she attended official functions with the Director. She didn't seem to have a mother. I think Daddy had mentioned that she had died when Maud was very young. It was almost as if she had taken over her mother's duties and at functions she spent most of her time attentively listening to guests and handing out drinks and canapés. She always referred to her father by his title 'the Director' and never daddy or dad or father as my friends did. I decided she was a little bit odd and I certainly wouldn't be ringing the bell to get her attention.

Dinner was served in the dining hall. It was a large room with a table that was large enough to seat at least thirty people. The Director was already seated at the head of the table with Maud at his right. To his left was another place setting which I assumed was mine. The Director gave a tight bow as I entered and took my seat.

'You look lovely,' Maud said. 'Purple suits you.' I wasn't sure what dressing for dinner meant. At home we'd just worn our everyday clothes unless we had guests. So I'd chosen to wear the purple silk dress that Daddy had brought me for Christmas last year. I noticed that both the Director and Maud were dressed very formally. The Director in a dinner jacket and Maud in baby pink chiffon dress that drained the colour from her face and did absolutely nothing for her already pale complexion.

Dinner was a formal affair. The room was very quiet and all I could hear was the clinking of cutlery against the china plates. Servants hovered in the background ready to leap forward as soon as a napkin, spoon or another serving was required. The atmosphere in the room felt stifling and I tried to break the uneasy silence.

'So Maud, I hear that you're home schooled?' As soon as I spoke a tense look swept across her face and her eyes darted anxiously across to her father.

The Director pursed his lips slightly but continued to eat without making a sound.

'There's no talking at meal times,' Maud whispered across the table. 'The Director likes to enjoy his meals in peace and quiet.' Then Maud startled me by giving a high pitched laugh. 'But you're new to the family so you wouldn't know that, would you? I'm sure the Director won't mind you talking this one time.' Her eyes darted nervously across to her father.

I thought I saw the Director's head bob slightly, but apart from that small movement he made no other response.

We finished the rest of the meal in silence.

When the plates had been cleared away and coffee served, the Director stood up. 'I'll leave you two girls to chat over coffee,' he said. Maud jumped to her feet and bobbed her head in a bow. Following her lead I scrambled to my feet as well. The Director gave us both a perfunctory bow and then left the room with his coffee cup in his hand.

'Does he always behave like that at home?' I asked curiously after we'd sat back down.

'Like what?'

'You know, so stiff and formal.'

Maud frowned, 'I don't think I understand what you mean.'

'I've seen him at functions before and thought that he always seemed so relaxed. I hadn't expected him to behave so formally at home.'

For a moment I thought I saw a flicker of annoyance cross her face and I was afraid I'd offended her. Then she smiled.

'The Director is a very busy man,' she said. 'When he's at home he likes to let go of his public face and enjoy the peace and quiet.'

'Don't you think it's a bit weird that we can't talk at the dinner table though?'

'The Director is a very busy man,' she repeated firmly. 'He should be able to enjoy a little bit of peace and quiet in his own home?'

I gave up and changed the subject; she obviously wasn't going to listen to any criticism about the Director.

'So you must have spent a lot of time organising my bedroom,' I said. The thought of the room still made me feel slightly nauseous but I didn't know what else to talk to Maud about. We didn't exactly have a lot in common.

Her face brightened immediately and she spent the next hour telling me about the complexities involved in recreating my room. How she had taken over five hundred photos and then employed an interior designer to work on the details. It was an easy conversation and I barely had to respond apart from the odd yes and no.

When we'd finished our coffee she asked me if I wanted a tour of the house and I eagerly jumped at the opportunity. After weeks of being cooped up in the hospital I was keen to get some exercise.

The house and grounds were extensive and so too was the Director's security system. The threat of Boundary incursions may have ended long ago, but the Director still had a state of the art security system. Panic buttons were located all over the house and Maud informed me that pressing just one of the buttons resulted in a total lockdown. It also alerted the Watch who would respond in a matter of minutes.

'I even have my own personal alarm,' Maud confided. She delved into her neckline and pulled out a pendant on a long gold chain. 'I press this here,' she indicated the middle of the pendant, 'and the house goes into immediate lockdown. It also activates a GPS signal so that I can be located if I'm kidnapped.' It seemed excessive to me, but I didn't want to risk offending her again so I kept my thoughts to myself.

CHAPTER 5

Alone

The weeks dragged by. I didn't go back to school, instead the Director had decided that I would be home schooled with Maud. I suppose that it was logical that I join Maud in her lessons as the Director already employed a number of tutors who came to the house on a daily basis. Unfortunately it meant that I was becoming a recluse. Maud had no friends and no social life to speak of, so we rarely left the house or its grounds. It wasn't long before I began to feel isolated.

At first I'd logged onto my Contact page every day to keep up with my friends. I read their status updates and looked at their photos, but that just made me feel even lonelier. My friends' lives were carrying on as normal. They posted Contacts about how much they hated school, who had a new boyfriend, details of the latest scandal, pictures of all the coolest parties – but I wasn't part of that scene anymore. None of my friends had come to visit me in the hospital. I reasoned that they must have been embarrassed about what had happened and didn't know what to say. I expected I would probably have felt the same way if it had happened to one of them. I'd had a few stilted conversations on the Portal when I'd first arrived at the Director's house, but it was obvious that they felt uncomfortable around me so after a while I'd stopped posting altogether.

My social life was non-existent. We were expected to escort the Director to political functions, but these were often boring, dreary events and none of my friends ever attended. It seems that Maud didn't accompany her father to many of the fun events that Daddy used to invite me to.

Finally, when I couldn't bear the social isolation any longer, and I'd become so desperate to escape the confines of the house, I'd managed to persuade the Director to let me meet up with my old friends Georgina and Natalie. I'd thought that talking to them face to face might be easier than posting Contacts on the Portal.

The Director had agreed to the trip but on the condition that I take Maud along with me. The whole experience had been excruciating. We'd met Georgina and Natalie at one of our old haunts; the Olive Tree Café. The café was located in the Hub; in the very heart of the Neighbourhood. Maud had never been into the Hub without a chaperone and was incredibly nervous about the trip. She'd also chosen to wear a skirt and top that wouldn't have been out of place on a sixty year old grandma.

When we entered the café I noticed that both Georgina and Natalie scrutinised her, their eyes taking in all the details of her clothes, hair and makeup (non-existent). As we approached their table they both glanced at each other and openly sneered. Maud must have seen the look that passed between then because she shrunk behind me and stared at the floor as I introduced her. As Georgina and Natalie cast an appraising eye over my outfit they both visibly winced as their attention was drawn to my face. I noticed that Natalie's hand flew subconsciously to her cheek and I had to restrain myself from touching my scar in response. I'd only recently had my bandage removed and was still getting used to the reaction it provoked.

I took a seat on the opposite side of the table and sat down as calmly as I could. Maud timidly slid into the chair next to me. Maybe it was just nerves, but Maud's need to please went into overload and she fussed around like an old lady, ordering from the menu and paying for coffee and cakes. This made Georgina smirk even more. I'd forgotten how mean she could be.

Georgina was dating Reese and she told me this with an almost gleeful look on her face and a challenge in her eyes. In the old days I would have been upset, but now I realised I didn't care. Reese had been part of my old life, and anyway he was an idiot, he'd thrown up on my shoes. After everything that had happened, my infatuation with him seemed foolish. In my opinion Georgina was welcome to him. I resisted the urge to tell her that she could probably do better as I knew she'd take this as jealousy on my part.

Natalie was dating someone from the football team and she giggled about spending time with him in the park. Georgina made a crude comment. I forget what it was, but it made Maud shuffle uncomfortably in her seat. Aware of her discomfort Georgina seized on the opportunity to make a series of even cruder comments that caused Maud's eyes to nearly pop out of her head. Her naivety annoyed me almost as much as Georgina's obvious pleasure in making her squirm.

They invited us both to a party; all my old school friends would be there. I politely refused. I couldn't endure the torment of taking Maud to a school party. It would be full of impeccably dressed teenagers who would poke fun at her all night. Eventually, after one of the most uncomfortable hours of my life, I made our excuses and Maud and I left the café.

'So those were your best friends,' she murmured as we climbed into the car the Director had arranged for us.

I shrugged my shoulders in response.

She stared out of the window and didn't utter another word all the way home.

After that social disaster I'd given up on my old life altogether.

I'd even stopped using the Portal so I lost touch with all my friends and the outside world altogether. As the numbness of my parents' death began to fade it was replaced by a feeling of loneliness and isolation. I wanted to embrace my new life, but I felt trapped and claustrophobic in that large mausoleum of a house with only Maud and the Director for company.

There were days when I'd wake up in the early hours of the morning gasping for breath, feeling like I was going to choke to death. The whole weight of the house seemed to press down on top of me, squeezing the air out of my lungs and threatening to smother me. I'd fly to the window and throw it open, gulping down lungfuls of fresh air until I felt better. Sometimes I'd have to sit at the window for over an hour before I was able to return to bed and go back to sleep.

The problem was that despite my isolation and seclusion from the outside world I was never truly alone; Maud, the Director or a servant was always hovering close by and I hated it. I wanted to get away, to escape the feeling of claustrophobia that constantly enveloped me. I felt like someone was slowly suffocating the life out of me.

It was December and I'd been living at the Director's house for almost five months. Christmas was fast approaching and I thought this might give me a much needed opportunity to escape the Director's house and be on my own for just a little while.

I set my plan in motion one afternoon after the Director had returned home from the office. I knocked on his study door and when he told me to enter I crossed the room to his desk. He continued to scribble on his PortPad for a few moments while I squirmed awkwardly in front of him, determined not to lose my nerve. When he looked up and indicated that I should speak I asked if I could go into the Hub on my own to buy Maud a Christmas present. At first he simply refused, but I told him that Maud had become such a good friend that I wanted to buy her something special and that I couldn't do that if she came with me on the shopping trip. After some consideration he agreed but on the condition that I used one of his cars.

I was so excited I could barely wait for the weekend. Maud's eyes had filled with tears when I confessed that I would be going alone. I told her that I wanted to buy her an extra special present for Christmas and in the end she said that she understood, although her eyes still glistened with tears as I left the house. I didn't care whether she understood or not. We spent every day together and I just wanted to experience some much needed freedom.

The chauffeur introduced himself as Mr Murray. He had dark skin with close cropped curly hair peeking out from under his chauffeur's cap. I could see his grey jacket straining across his broad shoulders as he held the car door open for me.

We drove through the Hub and he dropped me off outside the mall. I practically skipped with happiness as I made my way to the busy entrance. I stepped into the HealthScan and received a green light. I didn't have a temperature and there was no sign of infection so I was free to enter the mall.

As I stepped out of the scanner I was buffeted by the noise. Christmas tunes blared out loudly, teenagers were shouting, babies were crying and there was the general feeling of excitement that always pervaded the mall at Christmas time. For a moment I was stunned by the sheer volume of the noise and it almost overwhelmed me. It had been such a long time since I'd been surrounded by so many people. It was bliss. I was giddy with excitement and could feel the tension of the last few months fade away.

I spent the morning in a fabulous haze of excitement as I bought some new clothes for myself and some Christmas gifts for Maud and the Director. I'd obviously spent too much time closeted in the

Director's house as a number of times I had the uneasy feeling that I was being followed. After I'd glanced over my shoulder for the third time that morning, finding nothing but a bunch of overexcited girls window shopping, I had to laugh at my paranoia and decided it was time for lunch.

I had a fabulous meal at the pizzeria in the mall. The Director disliked fast food, and insisted that his chef only prepare healthy meals so it had been ages since I'd eaten pizza. When it arrived at my table I took a moment to breathe in an aroma of freshly baked bread that mingled sweetly with tomatoes and cheese. Pure heaven.

I gorged myself on margarita pizza, chips and garlic bread and even had some space left for an ice cream afterwards. I smiled to myself as I thought of the look on Maud's face if she could see me cramming handfuls of fast food into my mouth. I drained the last dregs from my mega coke and decided to visit the toilet before I finished off the rest of my shopping. This was turning out to be a great day.

The toilets were at the rear of the restaurant and I had to carefully navigate around tables crowded with families and groups of friends on shopping trips. As I moved through the crowded tables my good mood mellowed slightly as I realised that last year I would have been part of one of these groups; shopping for presents with Mummy or with Georgina and Natalie. We'd be eating lunch and examining our gifts. It made me appreciate how much my life had changed. I hadn't realised how lucky I was. If someone had told me that this year I would be an orphan and excited at the prospect of shopping alone I wouldn't have believed them.

It was only now that I'd had a taste of freedom that I fully understood just how claustrophobic the Director's house was. I was already starting to dread going back. Who knew how long it would be before I had the opportunity to escape again?

The toilet was vacant so I stepped inside and locked the door. When

I turned around I gasped in shock; there was someone else in the toilet with me. I tried to shout out but a rough hand clasped firmly across my mouth preventing any sound from escaping. I clawed frantically at the hand. Then I heard the sound of a familiar voice.

'MaryAnn, it's me. It's Daryl,' the voice said softly. 'Please don't scream. I'm not going to hurt you. I promise.'

I locked eyes with my brother. 'If I take my hand away will you promise not to scream?' he asked.

I didn't have a lot of choice so I nodded and slowly he removed his hand. I gasped for breath and he took my arm and gently sat me down on the toilet seat.

'Take your time,' he said. 'You've had a bit of a shock.'

I gripped the edge of the toilet and breathed deeply, trying to stop my head from spinning. Daryl squatted down in front of me and I thought I saw him flinch slightly when he looked at my face. His hand moved up as if to touch my scar, but before he reached my cheek he pulled it away and instead clenched it tightly into a fist.

'Sorry to scare you,' he said. 'I had to find somewhere private to talk to you. I needed to make sure you weren't being followed.'

'Followed?' I echoed. My voice sounded hollow.

'Yes, by the Watch. They've been following you since you arrived at the mall this morning.'

So I hadn't been imagining it. There really had been someone following me. The Director had lied when he told me that I could go shopping on my own. He'd arranged for the Watch to escort me. I felt anger rising up inside me. All I wanted to do was go shopping on my own. I didn't need a babysitter.

'MaryAnn, are you listening to me?'

I realised that my brother was still talking to me and I stared blankly at him. Then the fuzz in my head slowly started to clear as I got over the shock of seeing him again. I realised that the Director and the Watch were the least of my problems. Squatting down in front of me was my brother. The last time I'd seen him was outside the Building of Light on the night of the charity ball; the night Daddy and Mummy had been killed.

I'd been thinking about this moment for a long time. Ever since the numbness of my parents' death had begun to fade, I'd started to wonder about Daryl and why he'd been outside the Building of Light on the evening of the explosion. Sometimes when I couldn't sleep I would play our last conversation over and over in my head, dissecting it in minute detail. I'd come to the conclusion that he had something to do with it. It was too much of a coincidence for him not to. Even though I tried. I just couldn't accept the Light's explanation that an energy convertor had accidently exploded and caused the blast. Somehow my brother was involved. I couldn't believe he would deliberately put our parents in danger, but I was sure that he knew something about it and he hadn't warned them.

Once I'd convinced myself of his involvement I became so angry, wondering how he could let them die like that. I'd fantasised about what I would say to him if I saw him again. I'd played out the conversation in my head hundreds of times. I'd imagined a scene where we would sit down and talk about his part in the explosion and then at the end of the conversation I would calmly hand him over to the Watch. I'd pictured myself walking away without a backward glance as he was led off in handcuffs to face his fate. Then I'd feel an overwhelming sense of relief that justice had been served.

In reality it played out a little bit differently. Acting purely on instinct and emotion I punched him hard in the face. I felt a sense of immediate gratification as he fell backwards and hit the bathroom floor with a resounding thud. Blood sprayed from a cut lip. Giving him no time to recover. I jumped on top of him, punching him over and over again.

'Christ,' he muttered thickly through his cut lip as he tried to defend himself.

The punches were aimed at his head and my three years of kickboxing stood me in good stead as I managed to get in a number of good blows.

Unfortunately I'd forgotten that after I'd grown bored of kickboxing and given up, Daryl had carried on his lessons until he'd won his black belt. After recovering from the initial shock of my attack he retaliated by flipping me face down onto the ground with my arm held painfully behind my back. If he pulled hard enough he could have broken my arm in two. However the pain only served to fuel my anger and I struggled against him.

'Stop it MaryAnn,' he hissed in my ear. 'You'll hurt yourself.'

I ignored his voice and instead continued to struggle, grunting hard against the pain as he bent my arm. I'd rather my arm be pulled right out of its socket than let Daryl win this fight.

'MaryAnn!' his voice was harsh now. 'Just calm down and stop struggling. I don't want to hurt you.'

'You don't want to hurt me?' I grunted. 'You're the one who's trying to pull my arm out of its socket.'

'Sorry,' he responded and I felt his weight shift slightly. My brother was so predictable. He'd forgotten all the fights we'd had when we were younger. He was always stronger than I was and could easily beat me in a physical fight, so I'd learnt to improvise. I knew he hated to hurt me, no matter how horrible I had been to him. I'd pretend that he was hurting me to make him feel guilty and then when he apologised and let me go I'd pounce on him and get my own back.

As I expected, he relaxed his grip on my arm and it gave me the opportunity I needed to turn over onto my back. I'd lost my glove but I didn't care. It gave me an advantage as I raked savagely at the flesh on his face with my finger nails. I felt a grim satisfaction as a prickle of red blood appeared along the broken line of skin.

Daryl winced and clasped a hand over the deep scratches, muttering something under his breath. He scrambled to his feet and grabbed a paper towel, dabbing tentatively at the line of blood.

I also clambered to my feet, rubbing at my aching shoulder. 'Why are you here?' I demanded as he wiped the blood away.

'I just wanted to make sure you were okay,' he said. 'That's all'.

'Do I look okay?' I jabbed at the scar on my cheek and he flinched in response.

'What about Mummy and Daddy. Do you want to check if they're okay? Because you know they're not. You know they're both dead, don't you. So instead of asking stupid questions that you already know the answer to why don't you explain how you were involved in this, because I know you had something to do with it. You knew about the explosion didn't you? I know you did.' The floodgates had opened and the words poured out of me like a torrent, I couldn't stop them. I was almost spitting with anger.

Daryl took a step back, his hands raised in front of him as if to physically block my tirade. 'I knew you'd be angry -'

'ANGRY! Are you kidding me?' My head felt like it was about to implode. 'You knew about the explosion didn't you and you didn't even try to warn Daddy or Mummy. You should be the one that's dead, not them. They were innocent and you let them die.' I was breathing hard and my fists were clenched at my sides as I put into words all the anger I felt towards him.

'I'm sorry,' he said. 'It was a bomb, we planted a bomb . . . that's what caused the explosion, not an energy convertor -'

'A BOMB!' I couldn't believe what I was hearing. 'You planted a bomb. You planted a bomb that killed our parents.' I spotted my glove on the floor and stooped down to pull it back on. I stuffed my hand into it angrily.

'I couldn't help them,' Daryl said. 'It was impossible.

'They were our parents! How could you leave them to die like that?'

'I came to warn you didn't I? You don't know how much I risked just doing that.'

'Well thank you,' I hissed at him vehemently. 'Thank you for risking so much to warn me, but that doesn't help Daddy or Mummy does it. They're still dead.'

'You were an innocent in all this. I couldn't let you die.'

'And Daddy and Mummy weren't innocent? They deserved to die. Is that what you're saying?'

'Our parents were members of the Light,' Daryl said. 'So no, they definitely weren't innocent.'

His response didn't make sense. 'What are you talking about?'

'You think our father was a good man?' Daryl asked. His question wasn't the response I was expecting, but I nodded vigorously. Of course Daddy was a good man. 'He was the Legislator,' I said.

'I asked whether our father was a good man, not what his occupation was,' Daryl responded.

'Daddy was the Legislator. He devoted his whole life to delivering justice. Of course he was a good man.'

'That's where you're wrong MaryAnn. The Legislate isn't about delivering justice. It's about power and intimidation. Our father was the chief enforcer in an organisation that has tortured and killed countless people.'

I couldn't believe what I was hearing. Daddy was one of the kindest most generous men I'd ever known. How could my brother say such terrible things about him, about his own father? It was disrespectful to his memory. 'You're lying! Why would you say such horrible things about Daddy?'

'I'm not trying to upset you,' he said. 'I just need to tell you the truth. There's so much you don't know . . . .' He paused for a moment as if he was searching for the right words. 'I know you must hate me,' he said, 'but please will you listen to what I have to say?'

'Listen to your lies, you mean?'

'I'm not here to tell you lies,' he said. 'I want to tell you the truth. There are things that have happened, that are still happening, that you know nothing about. I have so much I need to talk to you about.'

'Then talk,' I said. 'You have five minutes before I call the Watch.' I jabbed at my watch as I spoke.

To my surprise Daryl shook his head. 'No, not here. We don't have the time. If you stay in here for too long then the Watch will become suspicious and I don't want you to get into trouble.'

'You don't want to get caught, you mean.'

'No really, MaryAnn, you don't realise how dangerous things are at the moment. You need to be careful.'

'Why would I need to be careful? I haven't done anything wrong.'

'Maybe not, but the Director has you on a pretty tight leash. He's keeping you as close to him as he can.'

'He doesn't have me on a leash,' I protested.

'I've been trying to contact you for months and this is the first time you've been out on your own. I'd say that was a pretty tight leash wouldn't you?'

'He took me in after Daddy and Mummy died. I had nowhere else to go.'

'And you think he did that out of the kindness of his heart?'

'Of course! He was a friend of Daddy's and no-one else wanted me.'

Daryl scowled. 'The Director doesn't do anything out of kindness. There's always got to be a reason.'

'What other reason would he have to take his dead friend's teenage daughter into his home?' I asked. 'Apart from wanting to help me.'

'You don't think that he might have been hoping that I would contact you? There's a price on my head after all. I'd be quite valuable to him.'

'What do you mean, a price on your head? Now you're being ridiculous.'

'The Light put a price on all our heads after the bombing. They know I was involved. If someone saw us talking that night then they might also suspect you too.'

'Suspect me? But I didn't do anything. I tried to save them.'

'I know that, but the Director doesn't. It makes you look very suspicious. Talking to a Unionist minutes before the bomb went off.'

'A Unionist! I didn't meet any Unionists. I only met . . .' then the penny dropped.

'You're the Unionist?' I asked. My eyes widened with horror and I badly wanted him to deny it, to tell me not to be stupid and that of course he wasn't part of the Union.

Unfortunately he offered no such denial. He just watched me carefully without saying a word.

'I don't believe it,' I said. It couldn't be true. It was bad enough that there were rumours about him going Outside. I couldn't believe he would be stupid enough to join the Unionists. 'I don't believe it,' I whispered again. 'Why would you join the Unionists?'

'Because I told you, things are not what you think. The Light isn't good. We have to stop them. I'm just sorry that you're implicated in all this now.'

'I'm not implicated in anything. I didn't do anything.'

'Maybe not, but people have died for much less, believe me. I think the Director suspects that we've been in touch and that's why he's been watching you like a hawk. He's hoping to lure me out in the open, waiting for me to make contact with you -'

'He doesn't watch me like a hawk,' I interrupted.

'Really!' Daryl raised his eyebrows in response. 'So you're free to leave his house whenever you want? Take today for instance, it was easy for you to persuade him to let you go shopping on your own?' There was a question in his voice and I suspected he already knew the answer.

'I . . . I . . . well maybe he's concerned about my safety. He said there've been curfews across the whole Neighbourhood since the explosion, or bombing or whatever it was.'

'Since the bombing the Watch have been detaining and interrogating people across the Neighbourhood.'

'There've been no broadcasts about detentions, or interrogations -'

'That's because you've been isolated from it all in your ivory tower. Real life is passing you by little sister and you're missing it all.'

'Hardly,' I replied. 'I did spend four weeks in the hospital learning to walk again. That's about as much reality as I can handle at the moment thank you very much.'

I saw Daryl visibly wince and I was glad, because the comment was meant to hurt him.

'This is about more than just you and I,' he said. 'There's so much more at stake. I just want you to listen to what I have to say because now it involves you too. I just want you to understand.'

I was still angry, but I was shocked to find that there was a small part of me that wanted to listen to him. Maybe it was because he was all that I had left. Maybe having a murderous scumbag brother was better than having no brother at all. I couldn't believe I was still listening to him even though it would have been the most reasonable thing in the world just to walk away. I think that maybe I was curious. I wanted to know what could possibly have changed my placid, easy going brother into a Unionist. A terrorist who had bombed and killed his own family and who seemingly showed no remorse for any of it.

Most of the things he'd said hadn't made any sense to me, but there was one comment that had raised a red flag in my brain. Was the Director really keeping me on a tight leash? I wanted to laugh off the comment. The Director was a good man, he'd taken me in and cared for me when I had no-one else. But somewhere deep down inside I couldn't shake the feeling that there was at least some truth in what

Daryl had said. Over the last few months I'd become a virtual recluse. I'd blamed my seclusion on Maud and her awkwardness in social situations, but the truth was that the Director ruled his house with an iron fist. I remembered how hard it was to get permission to go on this shopping trip. At the time it had seemed right that I should ask his permission to leave the house, but now I was free, well it seemed a little ridiculous. I couldn't imagine my parents ever expecting me to ask permission just to go on a shopping trip to the Hub.

I understood that the Director wanted a companion for Maud and it was logical that I be tutored at home rather than going to school. I'd thought it was my decision to withdraw from society, to cut myself off so I could heal and get over losing my parents. In reality there had been little opportunity for me to actually leave the house over the last few months. If the Director had arranged for the Watch to escort me around the mall then that was definitely an intrusion of my privacy.

Also if Daryl was telling the truth about the bombing, and I suspected he was, then why would the Director tell people that it had been caused by an energy convertor. He always preached the value of honesty and integrity above all else. Yet he seemed to have lied to everyone.

I felt an all too familiar wave of dread and claustrophobia wash over me as I contemplated returning to the Director's house and it was this that persuaded me to do something I really wasn't planning to do . . . I heard myself agreeing to meet with my brother again.

I hadn't expected to feel the instant rush of excitement or for my heart to race quite so much as I agreed to the meeting. Just having a reason to escape the confines of the Director's house again, even if it was risky, was enough to make me agree to the proposal. I realised that I was interested in what Daryl had to say, but I also wanted to enjoy another taste of freedom.

Daryl smiled when I told him I would meet him again. When

he also told me that I wouldn't regret it, I wasn't quite sure that he was telling the truth. I expected that I was going to live to regret my decision very much. This was probably the most stupid thing I would ever do in my whole life, but even that didn't dampen my commitment and in reality I didn't have a lot to lose. My parents were dead, my old life was gone and I faced every day feeling truly miserable. So what if this was a terrible mistake, did it really matter?

'Do you want to meet here?' I asked. 'I could ask the Director for permission to go on another shopping trip.'

'No we don't want to raise his suspicions. Our meeting has to be secret. It's not safe for me to spend time in public places.'

'So what are we going to do?' I asked.

'You remember the playground we used to go to all the time when we were little?'

'Yes, East Park,' I replied, remembering my last visit to the park with Reese. It seemed like a million years ago.

'That's the one. Remember the tree we used to climb?'

'The tree you used to climb,' I replied. 'The last time I tried to climb it I had to be rescued by the park keeper when I got stuck up there and couldn't get down.'

Daryl grinned and for a moment the tension left his face and he looked years younger. He almost reminded me of the brother I thought I had lost four years ago. 'I remember,' he said. 'You screamed so loudly that half the Neighbourhood came out to look. I told you not to climb the tree. You should have listened to your older, wiser big brother.'

I resisted the temptation to stick my tongue out at him, remembering just in time that we weren't those children anymore. Too much had happened for me to feel comfortable joking with him. I sobered up immediately and, as if he could read my thoughts, the smile slid from his face too and his manner instantly became brusque and businesslike.

'There's a hole in the tree trunk,' he said. 'I'll leave some information for you in the hole. It'll have details of our meet up. Do you think you'll be able to get to the park later this week to collect the information?'

'I don't know,' I said. I realised I would have to find some way of getting out of the Director's house again.

'MaryAnn,' his tone was sharp. 'Stop being so stubborn, this is important.'

'I'm telling the truth,' I protested. 'The Director keeps me on a pretty tight leash remember. It'll take some planning to get out of the house.'

Daryl frowned. 'Okay, do you think you can do it?'

'I arranged this shopping trip didn't I?

This comment made him smile. 'I have faith in you,' he said. 'If anyone can get out of the Director's house it's you. You've always been very resourceful.'

I got the impression that our meeting was over so I put my hand out to open the door and made to leave. 'I should be going, before anyone gets suspicious – is there anything else?'

'Just be careful,' Daryl said quietly. 'I'd hate for anything bad to happen to you.'

'It already has,' I responded. I just had time to see the look of pain that flashed across his face before I let the bathroom door slam behind me. I tried not to feel bad about my parting shot, he deserved it.

I made my way back through the restaurant to my table and sat down heavily in my seat. I looked nervously around the other tables to see if anyone was watching me. Everyone in the restaurant seemed pre-occupied with eating plates of pizza, drinking mega cokes and chatting loudly with family and friends. I breathed a sigh of relief before remembering that if Daryl was telling the truth then I hadn't been very successful in spotting the Watch following me all morning. I realised they could be anywhere. Silently observing me from the shadows. Involuntarily I shivered at the thought that people could be watching me without my knowledge. It put my nerves on edge and I realised I wanted to be as far away from the restaurant as I could possibly be. I tugged at the collar of my shirt. The mall felt stuffy and I had the desperate urge to rush outside and fill my lungs with fresh air.

I asked the waiter for the bill and as soon as I paid I hurried outside.

Mr Murray was sitting in the front seat reading his PortPad. He quickly stuffed the PortPad under the seat when he saw me approaching the car and got out to open the door for me. He seemed surprised that I'd returned so early – it was only just after lunch and he hadn't expected me back until later in the afternoon. I feigned tiredness and told him to take me straight back to the Director's house.

As it happened the Director had guests over for dinner that evening and as an adopted member of his family he expected me to be on hand to help Maud entertain them. By the time the guests left it was nearly midnight and I was exhausted. All I could do when I got up to my room was change into my pyjamas and fall into bed. I was asleep before my head even touched the pillow.

The next morning when I awoke the conversation with my brother was still running around my head. I replayed it over and over as I showered and dressed for breakfast. I was so preoccupied I even managed to stay under the chem rinse for the required amount of time.

I was in complete turmoil. One minute I convinced myself that my brother had been telling lies and I shouldn't see him again, the next minute my stomach churned with excitement at the thought of escaping the Director's house, and to my shame I was actually thrilled at the idea of spending time with my brother . . . I hated myself for that. If he was telling the truth he'd been involved in planting a bomb that killed Daddy and Mummy and yet I realised I missed him and wanted to be with him again. I reasoned that it was because he was the only family I had left, but I hated the way that it made me feel.

CHAPTER 6

East Park

A week later I found myself wandering around East Park with Maud, Miss Chambers, our Biology tutor, and the Watch.

Miss Chambers was a squat robust woman. Her hair was always pulled back into an untidy bun and I thought that her round rosy features would have benefitted from a little bit of makeup, just to even up the tone a little bit.

Miss Chambers loved the outdoors and had been talking about a field trip for some time. The only obstacle was the Director, who preferred to keep Maud as close to home as possible. It was easy to convince Miss Chambers about the field trip to the park, the Director was much harder.

After dinner he liked to retire to his study for a couple of hours to read his beloved books. He had quite a collection of rare and first edition books and they were his pride and joy. I reasoned that if I intercepted him outside his study he would be keen to get rid of me and it would be easier to convince him to agree to my request. My instinct had been right. I could feel the Director's impatience the moment I called out to him. Throughout the conversation I noticed that he kept stealing furtive glances at his study door while pretending to give me his full attention. As I expected he dismissed the idea of the field trip straight away. It took some determined persuasion on my part, including an argument about how much Maud would benefit from being in the fresh air, before he relented and agreed that we could go on the trip, as long as the proper security arrangements were in place.

Despite the security presence, which I was scared might hamper my plan a little, I was feeling quite pleased with myself by the time we arrived at the park. Miss Chambers was outfitted from head to toe in safari beige. She wore hiking boots, combat pants and a beige jacket that fastened down the front with military style buttons. She looked like someone who was preparing to slay a rampaging elephant rather than take a field trip to the local park with two teenage girls.

After we arrived at the park she handed Maud and me a series of worksheets which contained a list of flower and plant specimens that we needed to collect. It felt a little like a treasure hunt. A scary treasure hunt where I could be discovered, rounded up and then taken to the Square of Light and shot as a traitor. 'No pressure then MaryAnn!' I muttered to myself.

The tree was at the far end of the park. I thought it might look suspicious if I walked straight over there so instead I played it cool, or as cool as my nervously beating heart and sweaty palms would allow. After spending an hour diligently collecting most of the specimens on the worksheet, Maud and I circled the boat pond until I had the tree in my sights.

'I think that tree is an oak,' I pointed in the general direction of my brother's tree in what I hoped was an offhand way. 'I'll get a sample of its leaves and you can look for a weeping willow.' To my relief Maud nodded eagerly. I was scared that she would see the guilt in my eyes and become suspicious, but she seemed totally fooled by my attempts to enthusiastically join in with the field trip.

'I think there's a weeping willow over there.' I pointed in the opposite direction. Maud eagerly headed off in the direction of my finger.

I approached the oak tree slowly. My chest was tight and I felt a little light headed. I realised I was holding my breath. 'Breathe, you idiot,' I reminded myself. The last thing I needed was to faint before I'd even picked up Daryl's message.

I took a number of deep breaths and let them out slowly. After a few minutes I felt a lot better and I continued my approach towards the tree.

I carefully glanced around, but no-one appeared to be paying attention to what I was doing. I pulled out a tree identification guide from my backpack and pretended to study it intently. I could see a grey uniformed member of the Watch standing close by, his gun was raised in a protective stance and the visor of his grey helmet glinted brightly in the winter sun. Thankfully he didn't appear to be paying any attention to me. Instead he was focussed on Maud. The Watch's primary objective was to protect Maud and to keep her safe, not to worry about what I was doing.

I circled the tree carefully. The branches jutted out from the trunk and I could see the hole very clearly. I leant my worksheet up against the trunk and pretended to write on it. As I did so my hand darted quickly inside the hole. I grasped something cold and plastic, pulled it out and stowed it safely in my pocket, my eyes fixed determinedly on my worksheet.

Once the package was safely stowed away in my pocket I glanced around nervously, but no-one seemed to be paying me any attention.

I started to walk away from the tree, then I remembered I hadn't taken a leaf sample. I snipped one off carefully and dropped it in my specimen bag.

I felt elated. I'd done it, I'd really done it.

'You got it?' a voice interrupted, causing me to almost jump out of my skin.

I turned to find Maud standing behind me a questioning look on her face.

My palms started to sweat and my voice caught in my throat. 'Got what?' I whispered.

'The leaf,' she asked. 'From the tree.' Her brow furrowed in concern. 'Are you alright? You look ever so pale.'

I smiled at her, using all the self-control I had to stop myself from sagging to my knees in relief . . . *she was talking about the leaf.* 'Yeah I got it,' I said. 'It's right here.' I indicated the bag in my hand. 'I'm feeling a little bit tired though, do you think it's nearly time for home?'

Maud nodded in response. 'Miss Chambers sent me to collect you.'

The journey back to the house seemed to take forever. I was so excited that I could barely sit still. All I wanted to do was to lock myself in my bedroom so that I could open the package. Unfortunately I had to go straight back to the classroom with Miss Chambers and Maud so that we could study the specimens we'd collected.

The time dragged by incredibly slowly and Miss Chambers told me off a number of times for not paying attention. I mentally scolded myself. I had to be careful that I didn't raise any suspicions. After that I tried to give the lesson my full attention until we were dismissed for lunch.

As always we went straight to the dining room where lunch was laid out for us. The Director ate his midday meal at the office so lunch was normally a much more informal affair than our evening meal. I ate all the food on my plate, barely tasting it, eager to finish so I could escape to my room. Maud chattered enthusiastically about the field trip. She'd clearly enjoyed her time outdoors. I made sure I nodded in all the right places so she didn't seem to notice my preoccupation. After what seemed like an eternity lunch was finally over.

'You want to go and watch Day2Day?' Maud asked. 'I have the

next episode on playback. I saw the trailer this morning and it looks very exciting.'

Day2Day was Maud's favourite soap. The cameras followed a family of Celeb Alphas twenty four hours a day. It was fun to watch, and definitely one of the better soaps on TV. Maud was obsessed with the programme; she watched it whenever she could. When she wasn't watching the programme she was discussing what had happened, what might happen next and looking up facts on her PortPad. I wasn't sure whether I could cope with an hour of family feuds and arguments so I told her I was feeling sleepy and needed a nap before afternoon lessons.

Maud's face fell and she looked disappointed. I felt incredibly mean, but all I could think about was reading the note from Daryl. 'Maybe we can go for a swim or something later,' I said. 'After lessons this afternoon.'

Her face brightened at the suggestion. 'Great,' she said. 'Actually I feel a bit sleepy too. Maybe I'll go and lie down for a bit.'

We left the dining room and, fighting the urge to bolt straight up to my room, I walked steadily and carefully up the stairs and along the corridor. Once I entered my bedroom I locked the door and pulled the plastic envelope out of my coat pocket. My fingers were trembling as I fumbled with the zip. Inside there were two pieces of paper, one looked like a map while the other was a piece of lined writing paper.

I opened up the lined writing paper first. I read the contents quickly, but it was gibberish, just a lot of numbers. I was really disappointed. I wondered whether this was all some kind of trick. I turned the paper over in my hands; the back of the letter was blank. Why would Daryl send me a page full of nonsense?

I stared at the piece of paper for a long time until I remembered a game Daryl and I used to play as children. We'd pretend we were part of the Watch, leaving messages for each other in a secret code so we could catch imaginary Unionist rebels.

I rummaged through my bookcase for a copy of Harry Potter and the Chamber of Secrets. It had been one of my favourite books as a child. I remember that I made Mummy read it to me over and over again. The author had written three books before the virus broke out. The second one had always been my favourite. If Maud really had recreated a perfect replica of my bedroom then it would be somewhere on my book shelves. Cursing that I wasn't more organised and arranged my books in alphabetical order I eventually found it wedged between a volume of the Encyclopaedia Britannica and a copy of Charlie and the Chocolate Factory.

I pulled the book from the shelf and opened it. Daryl and I had made up the code so that each string of numbers represented the page, the sentence and the word and letter needed to decipher the code. We'd both been very proud of our ingenuity; the code meant nothing to anyone else unless they had a copy of the book. I'd loved the book so much when I was younger that I'd carried it with me wherever I went. So it had been the natural choice when we'd been selecting which book we should use.

It took me some time to work through the message as it was quite long, but when I'd eventually decoded it, it read:

'Family picnic spot, midnite, ten Dec
Tunnels under house
Access from library (C plan)
Press loose panel next to special book collection
Follow tunnel to trap door
Head to rendezvous
B careful

I opened up the other piece of paper and found that it contained a plan showing a series of tunnels running under the house. I couldn't believe it. I'd explored the house at length and had never seen any evidence of tunnels. It was all very cloak and dagger. I giggled when I read the letter again. *'Rendezvous'*. That was so like Daryl. When we were children he'd loved playing at being the Watch. I remembered that he'd dreamt of becoming one of them, catching the bad guys and putting them in jail, just like Daddy. I'd spent most of my childhood in handcuffs.

How strange that it was Daryl who had grown up to be the bad guy.

I re-read the letter and checked the code a couple more times just to make sure I hadn't missed anything, then I hid both pieces of paper inside my jewellery box and locked them safely away. The meeting was in three days so I had a few days to plan how I was going to get away from the Director's house.

Over the next three days I spent most of my free time planning my escape. When the tenth arrived I was almost hysterical with nervous energy. At breakfast I had to force the food down my throat. I knew I couldn't afford to raise any suspicions so I had to carry on as normal.

I'm not sure how I got through my classes, but somehow I made it to four o'clock. Maud suggested a swim before dinner and I thought it would be a great way of burning off some of my excess energy. I think I swam a mile, maybe even two. Maud had given up and left the pool a long time before I finally hauled myself out of the water; my arms and legs almost numb from the exertion.

The next hurdle was to keep my nerves under control long enough to get through dinner without raising the Director's suspicions. Despite my best efforts, dinner was awful, I could feel each mouthful of food sticking in my throat as I chewed and swallowed it down. After what seemed like hours my plate was cleared and dinner was over. Maud and I played cards until nine thirty and then I excused myself and went to bed.

Maud tired easily in the evenings and was usually asleep by ten. The Director was out visiting friends so I had plenty of time to get back to my room and make preparations. If I had to be at the meeting point by midnight I'd have to leave the house at eleven as it was about an hour's walk to the picnic spot.

I washed up and changed into a pair of dark black jeans and a green boat neck top with long sleeves. I wasn't sure what clothes you were supposed to wear to a secret rendezvous, but the hours of spy games I'd played with Daryl had taught me that black and green were probably the most suitable colours for being inconspicuous.

I sifted through my shoes looking for something appropriate to wear. For the first time in my life I cursed my love of heels. All my shoes were cute with at least two or three inch heels. I pulled out box after box and rejected them all. Just as I was starting to feel desperate I came across a pair of flat pumps; the shoes I'd worn for my date with Reese. I grimaced as I held them in my hand remembering that Reese had thrown up all over them. I sniffed them tentatively but they didn't smell of vomit, someone must have cleaned them. I had no other shoes in my wardrobe that I could walk any distance in so I had no other option but to wear them.

I grimaced again as I pulled them on but was thankful that they still fit perfectly. I flicked through my wardrobe and found a black jacket that belted around the waist and pulled it on. I checked myself out in the mirror. *Very GI Jane,* I thought. At least I looked the part, even if I didn't feel quite so confident.

Sneaking out of my bedroom was surprisingly easy; with Maud in bed and the Director out at a function the servants were all taking some time off. I tiptoed down the stairs to the library. The library was located at the rear of the house. It was a large room complete with wooden panelling, stone floors and a large open fire place. The walls of the room were covered with rows of old style paper books.

At one end of the room was a large glass book case that housed the Director's special collection of first edition books. A number of these were very valuable and were kept under lock and key for the *'Director's eyes only'*. Maud had warned me not to touch any of the books; they were the Director's pride and joy. As a self-confessed book worm the cabinet had piqued my interest, but I'd purposely kept away from it, not wanting to anger either the Director or Maud. Now I advanced towards the forbidden cabinet.

Daryl's note had mentioned a loose panel so I felt around tentatively until a panel wobbled under my touch. I was partly ready for the whole thing to be a hoax, expecting that I would press the panel and nothing would happen. I gave it an experimental push and jumped back in surprise as a hollow thwacking sound came from behind the panel. The noise seemed to echo loudly around the sleeping house and I peered behind me nervously, scared that someone would hear the noise and come rushing in to investigate. The last thing I needed was for someone to find me hovering next to the Director's beloved book collection.

I caught the faint grinding sound of machinery and then the panel moved noiselessly aside. I squinted into the hole that had appeared in the wall and could see steps leading down from the threshold. It was pitch black inside and I couldn't see anything beyond this. I hadn't brought a torch with me so I pulled out my mobile phone and flicked it on. The dim light from the phone showed a dank and dark corridor. I shuddered at the thought of stepping in. *You could always turn back*, a little voice in my head suggested. It sounded sensible to me. How I wished I could follow its advice. It would be so easy to simply close the panel and head back upstairs to my warm cosy bed.

As I stepped into the tunnel I noticed there was another lever on the other side of the panel. I pulled it and the panel slipped noiselessly back in place and the comforting view of the library disappeared. I shuddered, it was surprisingly damp in the tunnel and I could feel the moisture starting to cling to my skin.

'Okay! Pull yourself together MaryAnn. The Hunters are made of stronger stuff than this.' I whispered into the eerie darkness. I sounded confident, but my stomach clenched tightly in anticipation. With what I like to think of as a *'grim resolve'* I travelled down the tunnel using the light from my phone to guide me.

I noticed a number of other tunnels leading from the main passageway, but I ignored these and kept diligently to my path. The tunnels gave me the creeps and in my state of heightened nervous tension I thought that I heard noises coming from some of them. Not just random noises either, a number of times it almost sounded like an animal howling in pain. I knew it was my overactive imagination and that the howling must be the wind, but nevertheless I shivered every time I heard a noise and resisted the overwhelming temptation to turn around and run back to the library and to the comfort of my bed.

Somehow I managed to remain doggedly on my dark and murky path and was overcome with relief when I reached a trap door at the end of the tunnel. I exited out into the cold evening air. The exit to the tunnel was located in a clearing just a few metres from the walls that surrounded the Director's house. There was no moon and it was pitch black outside, so I was sure that no-one could see me from the house.

I decided that it would be safer to stay away from the roads and instead hike over the hills to the rendezvous point. I reasoned that taking a route over the hills meant I was unlikely to meet anyone else and I would have less chance of being discovered.

Unfortunately when I'd visited the picnic spot with my parents we'd always travelled in the car and so I only had a vague recollection of how to get there over the hills.

CHAPTER 7

Boundary

The journey to the rendezvous was dreadful. I'd spent so much time making sure I looked the part that I'd forgotten to bring essentials with me like a hat and scarf to keep out the cold. I also didn't have a torch so had to rely on the dim light from my mobile phone again.

As I stumbled along a rough country track I cursed my lack of planning. By the time I arrived at the rendezvous my trousers and shoes were coated in mud and my hands were blue with cold. Any excitement I'd felt at the beginning of the journey was gone and now I was just cold and miserable. I was also regretting overexerting myself in the swimming pool earlier in the evening as my legs were growing increasingly heavy and felt like lead weights.

It had taken me longer than expected to reach the rendezvous point and I was twenty minutes late when I arrived at the top of the hill. I scanned the darkness nervously. It was pitch black and I couldn't see my brother anywhere. I was freezing cold and put my hands to my mouth to blow some warmth into them.

I wondered whether Daryl had given up waiting for me, or indeed if he had even shown up at all. I heard the distinct snap of a twig behind me. I turned and was blinded by a bright light. My hand flew up to shield my eyes.

'Hey Daryl, turn off the light, you're blinding me.'

'You MaryAnn?' asked a rough accented voice that I didn't recognise. The sound of the stranger's voice filled me with dread. Had the Director intercepted the letter from my brother and sent the Watch to lie in wait for me?

'Who are you?' I stammered.

'Are - you - MaryAnn?' the disembodied voice repeated. The tone was more insistent this time. Each word pronounced slowly and carefully.

'Yes,' I managed to squeak. I prayed that it wasn't the Watch. How would I explain this to the Director? I was probably breaking a million laws. Girls like me didn't last very long in jail.

'You alone?' the voice asked. The light was still directed into my eyes.

'Yes,' I squeaked.

If he was a member of the Watch surely he would have arrested me by now.

'Who are you?' I asked again.

There was no responding answer, but whoever was out there in the darkness directed the light of the torch away from me, leaving my eyes dancing with vivid yellow spots.

'This way,' the voice said. 'Follow me.'

I remained rooted to the spot. Did this person seriously think that I was going to blindly follow him into the darkness? 'Not till you tell me who you are,' I called after him.

I thought I heard the stranger sigh, although it could just have been the wind. 'Daryl sent me to collect you,' the stranger said. 'Come on. We can't stay here, we have to keep moving.'

'Not till you tell me why Daryl didn't come to meet me himself.' I wasn't going anywhere with this stranger until I understood what was going on.

This time the sound of a loud sigh was unmistakable. 'Daryl said you might be difficult.'

'Difficult?' I protested. 'I'm not being difficult, but I'm not going anywhere with you until you tell me where he is.'

'Daryl had some business to take care of, so he asked me to meet you instead.'

'But I don't know who you are. How do I know you're telling me the truth?'

'For crying out loud. We're already late and I really don't have time for this,' the stranger muttered under his breath. The next comment was obviously directed at me. 'Look, would I be standing out here freezing my bollocks off if I didn't need to, if I wasn't doing a favour for your brother?'

'There's no need to be rude . . . or crude,' I added. 'I'm just surprised that Daryl isn't here to meet me. That's all.'

'Well if you've had enough time to get over your surprise then maybe you'll follow me.' There was no mistaking the sarcasm in the stranger's voice. Before I had time to respond I heard the crunch of rock and gravel as he walked away from me, taking the illumination from the torch with him. I found myself standing alone in the pitch black and I decided that following this stranger was probably better than being alone in the dark.

I started to follow him but it was so dark without the illumination from the torch that my foot caught on something and I tripped over, falling clumsily onto the wet ground.

'For crying out loud,' the voice ahead of me muttered. The beam from the torch changed direction and moved towards me. It stopped directly in front of me as a pair of large hands grabbed me under my armpits and pulled me roughly to my feet.

I brushed at my clothes, trying unsuccessfully to get rid of the thick mud that was smeared across the front of my jacket.

'You able to walk?' the stranger's tone was sarcastic. 'Or do you need me to carry you over the nasty bumpy ground?'

'No need to be rude,' I replied. 'I fell over, that's all.'

'Christ knows how I ended up with this job,' the stranger muttered under his breath. 'Daryl owes me big time for this.'

'Hey,' I responded. 'If it's a problem then I'll go back home.' The threat would have been much more effective if I hadn't tripped over again and found myself sprawled out across the floor for the second time that evening.

This time the stranger tutted loudly and then pulled me to my feet again. 'Follow me,' he growled, 'and try and keep on your feet will you.'

I stumbled after him in the dark until we arrived at a large truck. I waited expectantly by the passenger door, but the stranger ignored me and climbed into the driver seat.

'Are you getting in?' he called out. I was taken aback when I realised that he wasn't going to open the door for me. I climbed inside, not sure what to make of his rudeness.

As I settled back in my seat I gave a yelp of surprise as I felt hot fetid breath on the back of my neck. I turned and found myself staring into a pair of bloodshot brown eyes. The eyes stared at me unblinking for a moment, and then a large pink tongue shot out and licked me wetly across the side of my face. I gave a shriek of horror.

'Bad boy,' the stranger said as he leant over and gently pushed the creature away from me.

I wiped at my face frantically trying to clean away the slobber. 'What was that?' I asked.

'It's just my dog, Flash Gordon. Flash, say hello to MaryAnn.'

The dog gave a low woof, almost as if he was giving me a doggy greeting.

I peered into the back of the truck squinting against the dark, curious to see what the dog looked like, but I could only make out an indistinct form. There weren't any dogs in the Neighbourhood. At school we'd been told that people used to keep them as pets. After the virus all pets had been banned from the Neighbourhood as there wasn't enough food for them and they spread disease.

I dug into my pocket and pulled out an antiseptic wipe, scrubbing furiously at my face.

The stranger infuriated me by smiling. I could see his teeth glinting in the darkness.

'Don't worry, Flash Gordon's a nice clean dog. You won't catch anything from him.'

I eyed the stranger dubiously. If he owned the dog then he would tell me it was clean wouldn't he. He wouldn't want to admit to owning a dirty disease ridden dog.

I continued to scrub at my face, praying fervently that I hadn't been infected by something horrible. 'However clean he is I'd appreciate it if you kept him away from me.'

'Whatever you want,' the stranger responded as he switched on the engine and slowly we began to move forward.

'Lights,' I prompted.

'Not yet,' he responded. 'I want to make sure we haven't been followed.' The ground was rough and the truck lurched wildly from side to side. I had to cling to the seat so that I wasn't thrown around the cab. I heard Flash Gordon scrabbling around in the back frantically trying to remain in his seat.

We drove for about ten or fifteen minutes before the man switched on the lights. The beam illuminated the cab and for the first time I was able to study my companion properly. I was taken aback to find that he wasn't a man at all, he was just a boy. He was probably only a few years older than I was. He was big though and his blue jumper was stretched tightly across his broad shoulders. His short blonde hair was plastered across his forehead and I thought he could almost be attractive if he paid a bit more attention to himself, maybe cleaned himself up and wiped the scowl from his face.

I didn't have any more time to think about my companion's beauty regime as the truck suddenly picked up speed and I was almost thrown out of my seat as it lurched forward. I heard the dog yelp from the back seat.

'Careful,' I complained. 'Can't you slow down a bit?'

My companion's scowl deepened. 'We're already late for the meeting. If you'd been on time then maybe we could have taken the gentle scenic route.' He turned to the back seat. 'Flash, quit making all of that racket.' The dog stopped yelping immediately.

I decided right there and then that I hated the boy. He was so rude. I'd just spent an hour hiking through the countryside in the freezing cold to get to the stupid rendezvous point and he was being mean because I was twenty minutes late. I opened my mouth to tell him what I thought of his manners, but he scowled at me again and I surprised myself by thinking better of it. I snapped my mouth shut, choosing to glare at the side of his head instead.

At first I tried to make polite conversation, but the boy mostly responded with monosyllabic grunts so I soon gave up. I realised that he must be one of those rude teenage boys who hadn't fully developed his social skills. I'd met others like him at school; misfits and loners who lounged around on chairs at the back of the cafeteria scowling at any girl that walked by.

When we came to a standstill I looked around with interest, but it was pitch black outside and I couldn't see anything.

'Are we here?' I asked.

'Not yet but we can't take the truck any further. We have to cross on foot,' the rude boy said as he pulled a backpack out from under his seat.

'Cross what?' I asked, puzzled by his response.

'The Boundary,' the rude boy replied offhandedly as he rummaged around in the bag.

Time seemed to slow down as I stared at him in horror. I must have misheard. 'Cross the Boundary?' I queried. My mouth was dry and my voice came out as a hoarse whisper.

The rude boy looked up from his backpack. 'Yes, of course we need to cross the Boundary,' he said.

I searched his face looking for something that would tell me that he was joking, but there was not a hint of humour in his expression. He just continued to stare at me. I tried to swallow, but it was difficult because my mouth was so dry.

'You want me to . . . to go Outside?'

'Well of course,' the rude boy sounded puzzled. 'That's where Daryl is. He's waiting on the other side of the Boundary.'

Something was crushing the breath out of my lungs and I felt slightly faint. 'No-one mentioned crossing the Boundary,' I squeaked.

The rude boy frowned again. 'You sound weird,' he said. 'What's wrong with you? Daryl didn't mention that this would be a problem.'

'A problem,' I responded. I had to fight the urge to ram my head between my knees. 'You're asking me to cross the Boundary and go Outside and you didn't think it would be a problem? Are you completely mad?'

'Erm, I don't think I'm acting like the mad one here -'

'It's electrified . . . the Boundary. If we touch it we'll die.'

Unexpectedly the rude boy laughed loudly.

I was so annoyed that I forgot how afraid I was. 'You think this is funny. Did you and Daryl make up this little joke just to laugh at me? Bringing me out to the Boundary and putting me in danger.'

'It's not a joke. I'm just laughing at how naïve you are. The Boundary borders the whole Neighbourhood. Do you know how much power it would take to electrify it all?'

I was bewildered at his response. Everyone in the Neighbourhood knew that the Boundary was electrified. It was the only thing that kept us safe from the Echo. Without the Boundary they would overrun the Neighbourhood and steal our food and homes.

I tried to explain this to the rude boy, but infuriatingly he just carried on laughing. 'Do you honestly believe everything that the Light tells you?'

Again his response bewildered me. 'Of course I believe them,' I said. 'Why would they lie?'

This last sentence caused the rude boy to laugh even harder. 'Daryl never told me you were so funny. You're hilarious. Why would they lie? Classic, really classic.'

I wasn't sure why this boy was laughing at me. Did he really expect me to cross the Boundary? I glared at him fiercely and his face became serious.

'This area of the Boundary is perfectly safe, it isn't electrified. We cross it all the time.'

When I didn't respond he sighed. 'Look either you trust me and come with me, or I take you back. It's your decision.'

'Trust you! I don't even know you.' My head felt woozy and I couldn't think straight. He was asking me to make a decision. To stay within the safety of the Boundary or to go Outside and face whatever dangers were lurking in the darkness. How could I be expected to make a decision like that? I'd never been across the Boundary. In fact I'd never even thought about crossing it. Never wanted to see what was Outside. Never wanted to leave the Neighbourhood.

'You need to make a decision MaryAnn. I can take you back if you want me to.'

'I don't know what to do.'

'Well we can't sit here all night. You want me to take you back?' The engine grumbled into life.

'No,' I said as he started to disengage the handbrake. 'Don't.'

He let go of the handbrake. 'You want me to take you to see Daryl then?'

'No,' I said. 'Yes. I don't know . . . .' I trailed off helplessly.

'Make up your mind, which one is it? You have to make a decision, either we go and see Daryl or I take you back. It's a simple choice.'

'I can't, I can't make the decision. It's too much. I . . .'

'MaryAnn, I don't have time to debate this with you. You have to choose now.'

My brain was scrambled, I couldn't make a decision. I really couldn't.

'MaryAnn, what do you want to do?'

In a moment of complete madness I made my decision. 'Okay, I'll go with you.' I tried to sound resolute, but I couldn't quite keep the quaver from my voice.

The rude boy nodded in response. He seemed calm and composed, totally unaware that I'd just made one of the biggest decisions of my life. If we were caught at the Boundary then we could both be executed. That was if we were lucky enough to escape being fried to death first. I wasn't even going to think about the Feral Echo that lurked on the Outside waiting to infect and eat me.

The rude boy said that we needed to camouflage the truck and he pulled some netting material from the back seat. When he climbed out of the cab he busied himself covering the truck with the netting. Again he didn't bother to open the truck door for me, so I had to let myself out. I couldn't understand his behaviour. He was obviously not Alpha, so I wasn't sure why he was breaching protocol. I didn't want to confront him out here in the darkness as I wasn't sure how he would react. I decided to wait until I found Daryl. He could deal with it. This boy was his friend after all.

Once the rude boy had finished covering the truck he indicated that it was time to go.

I took a number of deep breaths to steady my nerves. 'Okay,' I responded. I tried to make my voice sound as casual as possible. Like I crossed the Boundary every day.

The Boundary rose like a ghostly spectre in the distance and I could feel my heart begin to hammer rapidly as we approached it. I was reminded of a nightmare I used to have of being electrocuted on its wire fence. When I was eight my class had been taken on a mandatory school trip to the Boundary. I remembered the day very vividly. On arrival we'd all been ushered into a damp hut where we were given a lecture by the Watch about the importance of the Boundary. They told us how the Boundary had been erected by the Light to keep the Neighbourhood safe from the Echo, who hadn't been immunised against the Sandman Virus.

Boundaries had been erected around each of the three Neighbourhoods to protect them from the Outside. The Watch had shown us a broadcast of the Echo trying to climb over the Boundary. We'd watched in horror as they'd fried to death on the electric fence. I can still remember the image of their smoking blackened corpses bouncing off the fence as thousands of volts coursed through their bodies. If that wasn't horrific enough, the Watch had taken us to the fence and demonstrated how effective the Boundary was by throwing rats at it. The smell had made me retch. My teacher told me that it was the smell of cooking flesh and before the virus people used to eat cooked animals all the time, especially for breakfast. That made me feel even worse. I was grateful we only had synthetic meat to eat in the Neighbourhood.

My mouth started to water as I thought of the blackened corpses and I clasped my hand across it to stop myself from throwing up. I noticed that the rude boy was already at the Boundary and I hurried to catch up, fervently hoping that the next smell to waft over the fence wouldn't be the smell of my roasting flesh.

CHAPTER 8

Outside

As I approached the Boundary I was stunned to discover that it looked broken and poorly maintained. Some of the fence posts were leaning at an angle and the wire was torn and ripped. Constructing the Boundary had been an astounding feat of engineering. I'd seen broadcasts about it and it had never looked broken and beaten, as it did here. The Light said that the Boundary was key to our survival, that it kept us safe from the Outside.

'I told you didn't I!' the rude boy said as I approached the fence. 'The Light can't afford to maintain the Boundary so they just concentrate on the areas that are closest to the Hub. Hardly any of it is electrified anymore.'

'If it's not electrified why haven't we been overrun by the Echo?' I asked.

'What do you mean?'

'If the Echo know that the Boundary isn't protected why haven't they invaded the Neighbourhood to steal our supplies and spread infection?'

I felt the boy stiffen beside me. 'Have you thought that maybe you don't have anything that the Echo want?' His tone was calm and measured, but I sensed that I'd angered him in some way.

I couldn't understand the reason for his anger. Everyone knew that the Echo were dangerous and desperate to invade the Neighbourhood. I'd seen broadcasts of what had happened to other Neighbourhoods when the Echo had overrun the Boundary. It had been horrible. The Echo were feral animals who couldn't be tamed. The Watch had a constant battle to keep us safe.

The rude boy had crouched down over the fence and was working at a hole with his fingers. 'Here,' he beckoned towards me. 'This should be big enough to crawl through.'

I crouched down next to him. 'You first,' I responded. If we were going to fry then I definitely wanted this boy to go before me. The boy grinned as if he understood my hesitation.

I jumped as he gave a loud whistle. A blur of yellow and red appeared beside us. It was Flash Gordon; he came to a halt as he reached the boy. I was able to study him by the light of the torch and I took in every inch of him. I could see that he was a large sandy coloured dog, lanky legged with a close cropped coat and oversized ears. He wore a red and white checked bandana around his neck. When the boy indicated the hole the dog crouched low, his stomach skimming the grass, and scrambled through it. Once he was safely through to the other side the rude boy followed without hesitation. He faced me through the wire mesh of the fence. 'Your turn,' he said.

I took a deep breath, squeezed my eyes shut and crawled quickly through the hole. I crouched low making myself as small as possible so that no part of my body would touch the fence. I'd seen the dog and the rude boy make it through safely, but I was scared the power might come back on at any minute.

In just a few seconds I was on the other side of the Boundary. I was Outside and I'd just violated one of the strictest laws in our Legislative Code. If I was caught then I would be severely punished. My whole body was trembling, but I couldn't tell whether it was from the cold night air or from cold naked fear.

'Come on,' the boy said impatiently. He was already on his feet and heading away from the Boundary. 'Stop dawdling, we need to hurry.'

'Alright,' I muttered as I clambered to my feet. Didn't he realise that this was the most dangerous thing I'd ever done in my life and that I needed time to recover?

I followed the rude boy until we arrived at another truck. This one was also camouflaged. The boy pulled off the netting and stowed it away before whistling for Flash Gordon, who immediately bounded onto the back seat. He climbed into the cab and started the engine. This time I didn't even bother to wait for him to open the door for me.

We set off again and drove across the wilderness until finally the vehicle came to a halt. I looked out of the window, but could see nothing beyond the dim light thrown out by the headlights. 'Out,' the boy commanded.

'Can I have a please with that?' I muttered to myself. If he heard my comment he chose to ignore it and instead jumped out of the cab.

I had two options; either remain in the truck and sulk (this actually seemed an attractive option) or get out, find Daryl and make him explain exactly what was going on. For a moment I did consider refusing to leave the car to see how the rude boy would react. However I expected he would just manhandle me out onto the grass, so reluctantly I chose the latter option. I clambered out of the passenger door, resigned to the fact that he wasn't going to assist me.

Once I was outside I looked around with interest. There was a clearing to my left. Within the clearing I could just make out the outline of a building.

The rude boy was busy petting Flash Gordon who was shuffling excitedly at his feet when a figure materialised from out of the trees. I was startled to see that he had a gun and it was aimed directly at us. I raised my hands high above my head as I'd seen people do in the old film broadcasts that Daryl used to love to watch.

'Will, it's only me,' I heard the rude boy say. The dog gave a whine of pleasure and threw himself at the boy. The boy, Will, squatted in front of the dog and scratched him behind the ears. Flash Gordon wriggled in delight.

Will turned and shouted into the trees, 'Max, Jake, it's okay, you can come out. It's Peter, Peter Mallory.'

Two other figures appeared out of the trees. They had guns too, but I was pleased to see that they weren't aimed at us. I hesitated for a moment watching them warily. When it looked like we were in no danger I slowly lowered my hands down to my sides.

The three gunmen took no notice of me. They didn't seem infected so were definitely not Echo, I thought they might be Delta. I wondered what these people were doing out here, why weren't they on the other side of the Boundary, safe in the Neighbourhood?

'You're late,' Will greeted the rude boy; Peter they called him.

'Not my fault we're late,' Peter complained. 'I was on time, she wasn't.' He jerked his thumb back at me.

I folded my arms across my chest and took a deep breath, but didn't retaliate.

'Yeah, well Patrick's worried. He thinks something might have happened to your precious cargo.' This time it was Jake who spoke. I noticed that the word '*precious cargo*' came out as a sneer. It seemed that, like my companion Peter, these people didn't want me here either. I was tempted to turn on my heel and walk away, but I realised that I didn't have a clue where I was and had no way of getting back to the Boundary, never mind the Director's house. If these people were Delta then they were out of order talking to me like this.

'We should hurry,' Peter said as he set off towards the building.

I hesitated for a moment, angry that he hadn't made the boys apologise for being so rude. 'Come on,' he called back impatiently.

He was already at the entrance to the building so I hurried across the grass to catch up with him. He opened the door to the building and stepped inside. I followed and waited for a moment on the threshold. When nothing happened I looked up, perplexed. I couldn't detect any of the machinery normally associated with a HealthScan. I was contemplating whether I should just step inside when a hand darted out of the entrance, grabbed the front of my jacket and pulled me over the threshold into the dark hallway beyond.

'What about the HealthScan? It's not working.'

'We don't have scanners here,' Peter responded.

I was horrified. 'But it's against the law not to have a scanner.'

'That's your law, not ours. No-one has a scanner on this side of the Boundary.'

I didn't really understand what he meant by '*your law*'. The Light made all the laws and everyone had to have a scanner. I was surprised that the owners of the house hadn't been arrested by the Watch.

I cautiously stepped into the hall. At the end of the corridor there was a large wooden door. Light seeped under the threshold and I thought I could hear voices coming from the other side. Before I had time to wonder what type of people would be in a deserted house in the middle of nowhere, Peter pushed the door open and stepped inside. I cautiously followed.

The room buzzed with the hum of voices which stopped as soon as I entered. I observed a large number of people standing around in small groups. I felt self-conscious when I noticed they were all staring at me. I shyly surveyed the group trying to locate my brother. As always when I met new people nowadays their first reaction was to look at my scar. I could feel it begin to burn hotly under their collective gaze and my hand flew protectively to my cheek. I blushed red imagining what everyone in the room must be thinking about my damaged face. I felt uncomfortable meeting new people. My scar was always the centre of attention and I hated it when people openly stared at it. Even if most of them were too polite to mention it.

Daryl extracted himself from one of the groups of people and strode towards me.

'MaryAnn you came.' There was obvious relief in his voice. He bent down to stroke Flash who was staring up at him with a look of complete adoration, his pink tongue flopping lazily out of the side of his mouth.

'You didn't think I'd come?' I questioned as he turned his attention back to me.

'I wasn't sure. I thought you might change your mind.'

He looked over at Peter. 'Thanks for bringing her here safely.'

'Oh, the pleasure was entirely mine,' Peter responded sarcastically.

Daryl considered him for a moment, and then smirked at me. 'It seems like you both hit it off.'

I screwed up my face in disgust and I thought I heard Peter make a noise that sounded not unlike a snarl.

There were footsteps in the hall outside and the door to the room creaked open bringing with it a draft of cold air. A man entered the room and Daryl's face broke into a wide grin. The man was very tall and slim, with short blonde hair that was almost military in style. In fact it wasn't just his hair but also his bearing that hinted at some military experience. His presence filled the room commanding everyone's immediate attention.

I struggled to hide my astonishment when he embraced Daryl in a friendly hug. Once they parted the man greeted Peter and then stared expectantly at me. Daryl turned to me with an air of anticipation.

'MaryAnn. I want to introduce you to our Uncle Patrick.' I detected a certain amount of pride in his voice.

I thought I'd misheard him at first. 'Uncle?' I questioned. 'We don't have an uncle. Daddy and Mummy didn't have any brothers or sisters.'

Daryl nodded, his eyes were ablaze with a curious excited light.

'Yes our Uncle Patrick,' he said. 'He's our father's brother. I only found out four years ago.'

My uncle smiled and held out his hand. I looked at it, confused. Did he expect me to shake it? I had gloves on, but still I didn't know him well enough. He quickly withdrew his hand and gave a small bow instead.

'Sorry, I've been away from the Neighbourhood so long that sometimes I forget about your customs. His voice was low, but with a strength behind it that made me think that he was in charge of this group of people.

He quietly surveyed me. 'I'm so happy you're here,' he said. 'Daryl has told me so much about you.'

I couldn't believe that this man was my uncle. Daddy would have told me if he had a brother.

'Well I know absolutely nothing about you,' I responded, making no apology for my rudeness.

'MaryAnn,' Daryl remonstrated. 'That was really rude.'

My uncle held up a hand to quieten him. 'It's okay Daryl, MaryAnn has every right to be cautious, and this must be a real shock for her.' His dark blue eyes studied me intently for a moment and I felt myself redden under his gaze.

'Why did Daddy never mention that he had a brother?' I asked the stranger.

My uncle cleared his throat. He seemed uncomfortable. 'Erm . . . well, your father and I, we had certain ideological differences so we parted company a long time ago.'

'Ideological differences, what does that mean?'

'What he means,' Daryl interrupted in a bitter voice, 'is that our father believed that it was acceptable to torture and kill people and Patrick doesn't.'

I didn't understand his response, 'What are you talking about Daryl? Daddy didn't kill people and he certainly would never torture anyone.'

This comment was greeted by a murmur of noise from the people gathered in the room. I looked around bewildered. 'Daryl is that what you've been telling these people, that Daddy tortured and killed people? You know that's not the truth. He was the Legislator, not a killer. Why would you say such horrible things about him?'

Daryl was about to respond when my uncle reached out and placed a warning hand on his shoulder. 'Quiet Daryl,' he said. 'We've spoken about this already. Remember what a shock it was when you found out about your father. MaryAnn has to come to terms with this on her own.'

'Come to terms with what! Daddy was one of the kindest, gentlest men I ever knew. He wouldn't hurt a fly. He barely raised his voice to me my whole life. How can you say such horrible things about him?' I was incredibly angry that Daryl could say such awful things about Daddy and that these people seemed to believe him.

'MaryAnn,' my uncle said. 'This is going to be very difficult for you to hear, but the father you knew; he wasn't the same person that we know. Most of the people in this room have suffered at the hands of your father.'

I don't know what I'd been expecting from this meeting, but it certainly wasn't this.

'It's true,' Daryl said.

'Suffered,' I responded. 'What do you mean? How did they suffer?'

'Do you know what a Legislator is?' Daryl asked me.

'Of course, the Legislator is responsible for law and order,' I said. 'He arrests and prosecutes criminals.' I faltered a little as I suddenly realised that I wasn't quite sure what work Daddy actually did. I'd never really paid much attention to his job.

'Prosecutes criminals,' Daryl said. 'Is that what you think?' He sounded angry.

'See over there,' he pointed to a girl with corkscrew curls, the bottom half of her face covered in a vivid red burn. 'Our father's handiwork,' he said. The girl's hand rose self-consciously to her face and for a moment she reminded me of myself when people stared at my scar. My hand moved up to touch my own ruined face.

Daryl pointed to a short bearded man on crutches. He had a leg missing. 'More of our father's handiwork.'

The man glared at me, unsmiling. Next he pointed to a tall emaciated looking woman. 'Our father made Cindy a widow.'

He extended his finger again, but I didn't want to hear any more.

'Stop it,' I said. 'Why are you telling me lies?'

Daryl ignored me and continued. 'See Tony -' he pointed to a man with dark hair . . . but I didn't want to listen to any more lies about Daddy. I wasn't sure what was wrong with Daryl. I suspected he might have been brainwashed.

'Is that why you brought me here?' I interrupted. 'You hated Daddy so much that you wanted to tell lies about him. You thought that you could make me hate him too?'

Daryl tried to respond, but I shook my head.

'No, stop it. I don't want to listen to any more of your lies.'

'Daryl!' my uncle interrupted. I detected a warning note in his voice.

Daryl ignored him and instead spoke directly to me. 'You have to hear this. You need to know the truth about our father.'

I shook my head, wanting desperately to block out his voice. I couldn't believe that I'd come all the way here for this.

'Daryl. Stop it now.' My uncle's voice was firm and I detected a hardness to the tone. He was a man who expected to be obeyed.

This time Daryl heeded the warning and scowled in response as he thrust his hands roughly into the pockets of his grubby jeans.

'This was a mistake,' I said to no-one in particular. 'I want to go home.' I was aware of the waver in my voice.

My uncle stepped forward blocking my view of Daryl. He looked down at me. 'I'm sorry that this is hard for you,' he said, 'but we need you to listen to us.'

'Listen to you being mean about Daddy,' I interrupted. 'When he can't defend himself. You should respect his memory.'

Again this was followed by a low murmur from the people gathered in the room. My uncle slowly scanned the room and the silence that followed was deafening.

He faced me again and it was the look of pity on his face that scared me more than anything else. I'd seen a similar look on the face of the doctor at the hospital before he told me that my parents had died.

'MaryAnn,' he said gently. 'I know this is hard for you but you need to stay and listen to what we have to say.'

I shook my head. 'I don't want to stay if you're going to say horrible things about Daddy.'

'I understand,' he said, 'but if you leave now then you'll never know the truth.'

'Daddy was a good man,' I said. 'That's all the truth I need to know.'

'Alright, let's make a deal. If you stay and listen to us, then we'll let you have the opportunity to tell us about your father, about the man you knew. Does that seem fair?'

I hesitated, considering his offer. It was tempting. I couldn't bear the thought that all these people hated Daddy so much. I wanted to make them understand what he was really like. How charming and funny he was. How he had been so dedicated to his job and kept the Neighbourhood safe from the Echo.

'Does that seem fair?' my uncle repeated.

'I suppose.' Suddenly the lateness of the hour combined with the tension in the room manifested itself in an enormous fatigue that hit my body like a fist. My knees sagged and if it wasn't for the swift movement of my uncle I would have dropped to the floor. He grabbed me under one arm and I was so weary that I didn't even recoil at his touch.

'I think we'd better sit down,' he said as he pulled out a chair. I didn't resist as he pushed me down into the seat. He sat down next to me at the head of the table. My brother took a seat to my right and Peter sat opposite him. The remainder of the people found a place at the table or on one of the sofas that dotted the room.

My uncle addressed the group. 'My niece, MaryAnn, is here of her own free will and I expect you to treat her with the utmost courtesy and respect. Does everyone understand?'

'We don't care what this spoilt brat has to say,' a man shouted from further down the table. 'I'm not interested in listening to her.'

'If that's how you feel Tom, then you're welcome to leave the meeting. That goes for anyone else who isn't willing to do as I ask.' A few people exchanged glances but no-one moved.

My uncle studied me for a moment. 'MaryAnn, some of the things that you're about to hear are going to be unpleasant but I ask that you try and listen with an open mind. Can you do that?'

'I suppose,' I said.

'That's all I can ask. That's all any of us can expect.'

I waited anxiously, unsure what was going to happen next.

'I know you've heard some pretty terrible accusations about your father this evening. I want you to know that we aren't just saying these things to make you feel uncomfortable, we have evidence.'

'What type of evidence?' I asked.

'We'll talk about that later,' my uncle said. 'First I want to understand how much you know about the Legislate. The organisation that your father controlled.'

'The Legislate is the department for justice,' I said. 'They control the Watch and the Law Courts. They're responsible for finding and prosecuting criminals. It was something that Daddy was very passionate about.'

'And the Echo?' my uncle asked.

'Well they're also responsible for managing the Echo threat,' I said. 'To keep the Neighbourhood safe.'

I was startled to hear angry murmurs from the people around the table. I regarded them carefully. 'The Legislate keep us all safe from the Echo,' I explained.

The murmurs grew louder and people glared at me with open hostility. I looked uncertainly at my uncle, not sure what I'd done wrong.

'Would it surprise you if I told you that most of the people in this room are what you refer to as Echo,' he said.

It took a moment for my poor fatigued brain to process this new piece of information. At first I thought I'd misheard. 'What do you mean?' I whispered quietly.

'These people,' my uncle waved his hand around the room, 'are all Echo.'

I surveyed the room in horror. 'Echo?' my voice was faint.

'Yes, every last one of them.'

'But . . .'

'But they're not savages,' my uncle finished my sentence for me. 'That's what you've been told isn't it?' he asked. 'That the Echo are mindless savages who spread disease and infection.'

I was too busy trying to process this new piece of information to respond to his question. I was aware of Peter, his green eyes studying me silently across the table. 'You!' I asked. 'Are you an Echo too?'

'No, I'm lucky enough to be Delta.' There was a bitterness in his tone that I couldn't understand. Surely he should be pleased that he wasn't an Echo. Delta were respected as legitimate workers in the Neighbourhood.

I scrutinised the table and literally cringed in disgust. My stomach heaved and my hands flew to my mouth. I was sitting in a room surrounded by Echo. It was too horrific to contemplate. My ears started to buzz and I felt slightly faint.

'MaryAnn, are you okay?' I heard Daryl's voice as if it was coming from a great distance. When I didn't respond I heard my uncle tell him to go and get me a glass of water.

I was aware of a glass being thrust into my hand with an instruction to drink. I slowly sipped at the water and after a few moments I felt calmer and my head cleared a little.

'Are you okay?' my uncle asked.

'Am I infected?' I squeaked. I realised that I wasn't quite sure how the disease was spread.

I was taken aback when my uncle smiled. 'You haven't been infected with anything MaryAnn. It's all lies. Whatever you heard in the Neighbourhood, the Echo are people just like you and I. They're not animals.'

'But at school, the broadcasts. I've seen them. They attacked innocent people and . . . they ate them.'

'The footage from the shopping centre. The people trapped inside?' my uncle asked.

'Yes that's it,' I nodded emphatically. 'They were infected with the Sandman Virus and they went mad. The broadcast called it the living death.'

'Those broadcasts are all lies,' my uncle said. 'Lies cobbled together from old movies and fake footage. None of it is true. The Sandman Virus didn't turn people into bloodthirsty maniacs. It was called the living death because those who were infected slowly lost control of their bodies. They sank into a coma and wasted away; died from starvation. A truly horrific way to die, certainly; but nothing to do with creating the savage creatures that you describe.'

'But how could the broadcasts be fake?' I asked.

'It's no coincidence that the Alphas, the people who could afford to pay for the vaccination, were the rich and the powerful in society. The very people with enough money to pay for fake footage.'

'But it seemed so real,' I protested.

'You don't think that an actress, who is talented enough to earn two million credits per movie, couldn't perhaps use those talents to fake a broadcast and make it seem real?'

'Why would the government fake the virus?'

'They didn't fake the Sandman Virus. That was very real. The mortality rate was seventy percent and it devastated the population. Countless people died in the first few months of the disease and we feared that the population would die out if a cure wasn't found. The medical services were overwhelmed and stretched to breaking point.

Then the Cure was discovered by the Light Foundation and suddenly there was hope, we were saved, or so we thought. Unfortunately the vaccination took time to develop. The disease was spreading so quickly that there wasn't enough time to inoculate the whole population. This meant that the Cure became a powerful tool. It was the wealthy and influential, those who were given an Alpha or Bravo designation, who could afford to buy the Cure and were given the chance to survive.

Once the immunisation programme commenced the government were able to focus on rebuilding what was left of society. In only a few months the economy had been decimated. Overseas trade was almost non-existent and the harvest had been left to rot in the fields which meant that Britain was on the brink of famine. The government realised that they no longer had enough resources to support the entire population. If the remaining population were immunised then they would all need to be fed, clothed and housed. That's when the Light developed the idea of the Neighbourhoods. They called it the *'Select Neighbourhoods Project'*. They created a safe haven for the rich and powerful. Of course this new community also needed nurses, teachers, builders; skilled workers who would be able to keep the Neighbourhood functioning. So a decision was made to immunise the Delta designation, those people with desirable skills. Once the Neighbourhoods were fully operational Alphas, Bravos and Delta retreated behind the safety of the Boundaries, leaving the Echo to their fate. The government hoped that they would die out quickly and quietly.'

'No that's not right,' I interrupted. 'The Echo were already infected. Driven mad by the disease. They were a danger to themselves. The government couldn't let them into the Boundary because it wasn't safe. So they had no option but to leave them Outside.'

'A lie,' my uncle said.

'Why would the Light lie?' I responded.

There was a harsh laugh from Peter. 'Because that's what people like that do. They lie to protect their own power. If you're terrified of the Outside then you're less likely to question what's really going on. They can do whatever they want because they are protecting you, keeping you safe from the monsters lurking on the other side of the Boundary.'

'But if it's all a lie, why haven't I heard about it before. Why hasn't anyone challenged the Light?'

'Lots of people have challenged the Light,' my uncle said. 'People from both sides of the Boundary, but the Legislate are skilled at making sure the truth remains hidden. Other people profit from keeping quiet so they don't question what's going on right under their noses.'

'After the people retreated behind the Boundary, what happened to the Sandman Virus?' I asked.

'Things were pretty bad for a long time after the Boundary was erected, but in the end the Sandman Virus ran its course. The last case of the virus was over fifteen years ago. So you won't catch the disease from anyone here or for that matter anyone on this side of the Boundary. If you take a look around the room you'll see that we all look healthy.'

It was true the people did look normal. When I'd first entered the room I'd realised that they couldn't be Alphas or Bravos because there was a look of poverty about them, but I'd assumed they were Delta. Possibly my uncle's servants, but definitely not Echo.

'These people don't look like Ferals,' I agreed.

There were angry shouts from around the table and my uncle flinched. 'Please don't use that word.'

'Ferals?' I queried. 'Why not?' I was perplexed. 'What's wrong with the word Feral? We use it all the time in the Neighbourhood.'

'These people are my family and my friends and they are definitely not feral.'

'It's easier for you people to think of us as animals isn't it?' Peter interrupted.

'I wasn't calling you an animal,' I said. 'It's just a word that we use. It doesn't mean anything.'

'You call these people Ferals and you don't think it means anything,' he looked at me in disgust.

I shifted uncomfortably in my seat, not sure what I'd done wrong. My uncle must have seen my confusion because he ordered everyone at the table to be quiet.

'Feral is a word that we don't use on the Outside,' he said. 'Using terms like Feral makes it easier to dehumanise the Echo. Turns them into animals and if they aren't considered human then it's easier for the Light to exploit them without fear of consequence.'

'How are the Ferals . . . or Echo,' I quickly corrected myself, 'being exploited? We don't need anything from them; we have everything we need inside the Boundary.'

'Can I ask you a question?' my uncle asked. I nodded in response, eager to do anything to change the mood in the room, which despite the muted silence still felt hostile to me.

'Where does your food come from?'

The question took me by surprise. As far as I knew it came from the supermarket like everyone else's food.

'The food you eat inside the Boundary,' he repeated patiently as if talking to an idiot. 'Where does it come from?'

'We grow our own food,' I said. 'We have market gardens on the edge of the Neighbourhood. Daddy said that before the virus farmers used to raise animals for meat and milk, but there's not enough space for us to do that now so we use synthetic alternatives instead.'

'You think that growing a few vegetables in a market garden provides enough food to feed everyone in the Neighbourhood?'

I shrugged. It wasn't something I'd thought about before. There was always plenty of food to eat; we'd never experienced any shortages.

'You can't feed the whole Neighbourhood with the food you grow. The Light has been supplementing it with food they stockpiled before the Virus. In the beginning when the Boundary was erected the Light used to send the Watch to nearby towns and villages to scavenge for food and supplies. That's why the Echo used to riot, because the government stole the only food they had and now it's happening all over again. After the virus the Echo survived by taking over deserted farms and growing their own food. At first it was hard, crops failed regularly and people starved. Now communities have built up around these farms and people are no longer hungry. Unfortunately the Neighbourhood stockpiles are running low and the Light are facing a food shortage.'

'And they're stealing our food,' the man called Tom shouted angrily.

'And calling it taxes,' said the woman with the burnt face. 'Taxes for what? They don't give us nothing.'

'So we're facing starvation again because the harvest is being taken to feed the people in the Neighbourhood,' my uncle said.

'We offered to trade some of the food,' the man Tom said, 'but they refused and then stole everything we had. Anyone who argued was shot.'

I couldn't believe what I was hearing. The Light took care of us. We had our own resources in the Neighbourhood, there was no need to steal food from the Echo.

My uncle must have seen the doubtful expression on my face because he said, 'You don't believe me?'

'I just can't believe that the Light would steal from the Echo.' I managed to stop myself before I added that no-one from the Neighbourhood would eat food grown by the Echo for fear of contamination or disease.

My response was greeted with a stony silence. The silence seemed to expand and fill the room, making me feel increasingly uncomfortable. 'If there were food shortages in the Neighbourhood surely someone would have reported it . . . it'd be all over the Portal,' I said.

This time it was Peter who spoke. 'Isn't the Minister for Media also the owner of the Portal?' he asked.

I nodded. I'd met Mr Greenberg, the Minister for Media, at a number of Daddy's parties, he was always very nice to me. Georgina said that he knew absolutely everyone.

'What does that have to do with reporting food shortages in the media?' I asked.

'If you were the Light and you wanted to stop people from finding out about something what would you do?'

A light bulb switched on. 'Oh! You'd control the information that was reported on the Portal.'

'Precisely,' Peter replied.

I looked at my uncle. 'If what you say is true then I'm sorry that the Light has been stealing food. I really am, but I don't understand what this has to do with Daddy. If he was alive then I'm sure he'd have done everything he could to stop it. He believed in justice. He wouldn't have let this happen to you. He wouldn't have wanted anyone to starve.'

This time I wasn't surprised when my response was met with angry jeers from around the table. A few people even laughed out loud. It seemed that every time I mentioned Daddy or the Legislate I received the same response.

'Unfortunately our experience of the Legislate and your father is a little different to yours,' my uncle said as he glared at the people around the table.

'Your father . . . my brother was always a very ambitious man. He was devoted to the Light and to the Legislate, especially the power that came with his position.'

'So Daddy had ambition. It doesn't make him a bad person.' I felt that I had to defend Daddy against all of these people. Why did they think that ambition was such a bad thing?

'In this case unfortunately it did.'

'How is Daddy any different to you?' I interrupted. I could feel my face flush with anger. How dare this man criticise Daddy's ambition? 'Daddy might have been in charge of the Legislate, but don't you lead the Unionists? Doesn't that make you ambitious too?'

My uncle gave me a hard look. 'I lead the group through circumstance rather than choice,' he responded. 'I have no interest in power. I'm only interested in justice.'

'But so was Daddy,' I argued. 'That's why he joined the Legislate.'

'The Legislate has never been interested in justice. It was created as an organisation of control; to supress people who threatened the authority of the Light.'

'That's not true,' I protested loudly.

'We have evidence,' my uncle responded.

CHAPTER 9

Union

My uncle signalled down the table. 'Can you pass me the file please?' A file was placed in front of him and he picked it up and turned it over in his hands.

'This folder contains evidence,' he said, 'but I need to warn you that it's going to be very difficult for you to look at.' The expression on his face scared me a little and I swallowed hard. I took a deep breath and mentally shook myself. I was just overreacting to the tension in the room. All I'd heard so far was hearsay; there was no evidence to prove that Daddy had done anything wrong.

He opened the flap of the envelope and pulled out a sheaf of papers. He carefully placed them face down on the table in front of me.

'Take your time,' he said.

There was an expectant hush in the room as I turned over the first picture. I instantly wished I hadn't. With my stomach heaving I silently leafed through all of the photos, each one was more grotesque, more horrific than the last. In all of them I could clearly see Daddy. Some of the images were so disturbing that I couldn't take them in. Instead, as I would soon come to realise, my brain simply filed them away in a safe place to torment me with later.

'These have been doctored,' I whispered weakly. 'They aren't real.'

Uncle Patrick gave me a look of sympathy. 'You know that these haven't been doctored,' he said. 'You know deep down that it's your father in the photographs.'

The images blurred in front of me. 'It can't be true,' I said hoarsely. 'They've been doctored, I know they have. Daddy would never do things like this . . . the things in these photographs are horrible and Daddy was a good man.'

'You need to read the rest of the evidence,' Daryl said as he pulled a piece of paper from the bottom of the pile. It was an order for torture with Daddy's signature on the bottom of it. I recognised it right away, the ornate way that he scripted the H, the flourish he added to the R for Richard. On top of this he laid a copy of a death warrant and once again I noticed Daddy's signature scrawled across the bottom of the page.

My hands were shaking as I picked it up and read it.

'If Daddy signed a death warrant, then there must have been a good reason for it,' I whispered faintly.

'It was my father's death warrant.' I recognised the voice. It was Peter. I didn't look up. I couldn't bear to meet his eyes.

'These could still be forgeries.'

'But they aren't,' Uncle Patrick said. 'You know they aren't.'

I didn't want to listen to my uncle. He seemed so sincere, but I wanted to believe that he was lying. My gut on the other hand screamed that he was telling the truth, that Daddy was the monster that everyone thought he was. Somewhere deep inside there was the realisation that I'd known that Uncle Patrick was telling the truth from the very beginning. Why else would I have stayed and listened when I could have walked out of the room hours ago? There was something about the way that people acted around Daddy. At parties there was always a space around him, like people didn't want to get too close. At home I remembered how tense and nervous the servants were whenever he was in the room. I'd always thought it was respect, but now I realised that it wasn't respect at all, it was terror. People were terrified of Daddy.

'What do you want from me?' I asked weakly. 'You must have shown me these pictures for a reason.'

There was a strained silence around the table and I waited expectantly. Then Uncle Patrick shocked me by telling me that he wanted me to join them, to become a Unionist. I was taken aback. It was the last thing I'd been expecting. It had been a long night and I was tired so it took me a while to fully comprehend what he was asking. When I understood what he wanted I shook my head slowly. 'I can't join you,' I said.

'Why not?' Daryl sounded confused.

'Isn't it obvious?' I replied.

The blank look on his face told me that it wasn't obvious to him. I scanned the faces in the room and it seemed that no-one else understood either.

'Because you killed them. You were responsible for killing my parents, weren't you?'

Daryl immediately recoiled at the question.

'You did, didn't you. All of you were responsible for planting the bomb in the Building of Light?'

A tense silence followed my comment and I noticed that no-one in the room was able to maintain eye contact with me. The silence was only broken when Uncle Patrick slowly nodded his head and confirmed my suspicions.

I stared at Daryl in disbelief. 'You expect me to join you, even though you killed our parents?'

'We had no choice,' Daryl ran his fingers anxiously through his hair. 'We didn't want to plant the bomb,' he said. 'We haven't attacked the Neighbourhood in a long time. We keep watch over the

Light, interfere with Watch patrols, spread disinformation, but we haven't attacked them. Instead we've focussed on building up our own communities. When they started to steal our food and our people began to starve we had no choice, we had to make them sit up and listen . . . force them to stop. They had to understand that we aren't going to take it anymore.'

'Stealing your food was wrong, but there's always a choice. You planted the bomb and it killed our parents. How could you just leave them to die like that?'

Daryl flinched as if I'd slapped him across the face, but I refused to let go of my anger. Something deep inside me wanted to make him suffer, make him feel some of the pain I'd felt over the last five months. 'You've shown me evidence that our father was a torturer and a murderer, but how are you any different? You're definitely our father's son.'

A pained expression played across his face and in the candlelight he took on the haggard appearance of someone much older than his nineteen years. 'Don't say that.' His voice was rough. 'I'm nothing like our father.'

'You murdered innocent people at the party.'

'No-one at the party was innocent,' a voice yelled from further down the table.

'But I was,' I directed my response towards the unknown voice. 'I didn't know what the Light was doing. Yet you would have killed me along with everyone else.'

'This is a war MaryAnn,' my uncle said. 'We can't always choose who lives and who dies.'

'The party was full of Alphas and Bravos,' Daryl said. 'They don't care about us, so why should we care about them?'

'So you believe that because they were Alphas and Bravos they deserved to die.'

Daryl nodded. 'They have everything and they leave the people on the Outside with nothing.'

'But what about the Delta?' I asked.

My brother frowned. 'What about the Delta?'

'There were Delta servants at the party, some of them were killed too. Don't you care about them either?'

'The Delta casualties were unfortunate, but in a conflict there's always collateral damage,' my uncle said. There was something hard and uncompromising about his expression.

I shook my head in disgust and glanced around the table, but no-one seemed quite able to meet my eyes. I suspected that not everyone at the table placed as little value on the life of Delta as my uncle appeared to. 'The Light believes that people in this room deserve to die because they are Echo. So doesn't that make you just as short sighted as they are?' I asked.

'It's not the same,' my brother protested.

'Isn't it?' I asked. 'It sounds the same to me.'

'You have an interesting philosophical argument,' Uncle Patrick interjected, 'but sometimes in a war you have to make difficult choices.'

'I understand the difficult choice you made. It made me an orphan and left me with a permanent reminder of that night too.' I touched the ragged scar on my cheek. 'Is this any different to what my father did to you . . . or you?' I pointed at the lady with the burns and the man who had lost his leg. 'It seems there are monsters on both sides of this fight.'

My statement was followed by a stunned silence. I noticed that Daryl had turned a sickly shade of green and he stared at me open mouthed. I was shaking, barely holding myself together. I just wanted to get out of the room and away from these people.

'You don't understand at all,' Uncle Patrick said. 'You don't understand how important this is.'

'But I do,' I said. 'I understand what you're doing and why you feel you need to do it. I just don't agree with your methods and that's why I can't join you. I can't be part of a group that murders people in cold blood.'

'But if you aren't part of the group then . . .'

I interrupted Uncle Patrick. 'You don't have to worry. I might not be part of the group, but I'm not going to tell anyone about this. Your secret is safe with me.'

'We can't trust her,' a voice shouted angrily from further down the table.

This comment was greeted by an ominous silence and I felt a growing unease. If these people didn't trust me to keep their secret, then what would they do? Would they kill me? For a moment I wished I'd lied and pretended to join the Unionists. Once I'd escaped back to the safety of the Director's house then I would be safe from them. The irony that the Director's house had suddenly become my safe haven wasn't lost on me either.

'I think we can trust her,' said a voice that I recognised from across the table. I looked over at Peter, stunned. He was the last person that I'd expected to come to my defence.

'Now she knows the truth I don't think she'll tell anyone about us and I don't think she'll betray Daryl.'

Peter was right. I wasn't sure I could ever forgive Daryl or my Uncle Patrick for taking my parents away from me, for making me an orphan and for ruining my life, but they were the only family I had left and I knew I could never give them up to the Light.

'He's right,' I said. 'I can't be part of your group, but you can trust me to keep your secret.'

'But you don't understand the value you could bring?' Uncle Patrick responded. 'You're in a unique position to help us. You're living with the enemy. You could be of real value to us.'

'I'm sorry.'

'So instead you'll sit on the fence while people are oppressed and killed every day,' Uncle Patrick sounded angry. His eyes were hard and his intensity scared me a little.

'I'm really sorry,' I repeated. 'But I can't join you.'

'And that's your final decision?' Uncle Patrick responded.

'Yes it is.'

'MaryAnn.'

I turned to Daryl. I desperately wanted him to understand, but I knew he wouldn't. 'I'm sorry Daryl, but I can't join you and you won't change my mind.'

The mood in the room was horrible. People were angry, Daryl was disappointed, and I could tell that Uncle Patrick was frustrated with me. I just wanted to leave this place so I could go home, climb into bed and forget all about this horrible night.

'It's getting late,' Uncle Patrick looked at his watch. Maybe after you've had a good night's sleep things will be a little clearer.'

'I'm sorry but I don't think they will.'

'I'll take her home if you want,' Peter volunteered without even being asked. Again he took me by surprise. The last thing I expected was for him to offer to drive me home.

Uncle Patrick got to his feet. 'Daryl and I will see you to the car,' he said curtly as he exited the room. I followed without a backward glance, Peter and Daryl bringing up the rear.

It was still pitch black outside and freezing cold. I shivered violently and Uncle Patrick took off his jacket and placed it over my shoulders. I pulled it around me, grateful for the residual body heat that radiated from it.

When we arrived at the truck I handed the coat back to Uncle Patrick and he opened the door for me. Daryl hesitated by the open window. He started, as if to say something, and then stopped. He shuffled on the spot for a brief second, his hands stuffed into his trouser pockets. 'Look after yourself,' he said gruffly before turning away and walking back to the farmhouse.

'I'll take care of him,' Uncle Patrick assured me as we both stared at his retreating back.

I gave him a thin smile in return.

'You'd better get going; you need to be home before it gets light.'

Peter had already climbed into the driver's seat. Flash Gordon was leaping around excitedly in front of the truck.

'Remember if you change your mind we'll be waiting for you,' Uncle Patrick said as the car spluttered into life and we slowly pulled away from the farmhouse.

We drove in silence but I didn't care, it was easier not to talk. When I shivered from the cold Peter turned up the heater in the cab and then pulled a blanket out from under his seat and threw it onto my lap. I wrapped the blanket gratefully around me. Peter was full of surprises. First he'd defended me in the meeting and now he was being kind to me. I couldn't quite work him out.

After we'd swapped trucks at the Boundary I must have fallen asleep because the next thing I remember Peter was waking me up.

He hadn't driven me back to the rendezvous point, but instead had parked in a clearing a short distance from the Director's house. I was relieved that I didn't have to tackle the strenuous hike across the hills. I was so weary I think I would have just curled up in a ditch and fallen asleep . . . probably dying from hypothermia in the process.

'Thanks for driving me back,' I said.

Peter shrugged, 'I promised Daryl and Patrick that I'd get you home safely.'

'Are you going to be okay?' I asked. 'What if someone discovers you in the Neighbourhood?'

He pulled a card out of his pocket and flicked it with his forefinger.

'It's okay, I have a work permit.'

I was too tired to ask how he'd gotten the permit. I was about to get out of the truck when he said, 'You know Patrick and Daryl didn't mean to hurt you. They thought they were doing the right thing.'

'You think that planting the bomb and killing those people was the right thing to do?' I asked.

'It was a difficult choice. Sometimes you have to choose duty over family, especially when your family . . .' he trailed off, seemingly unsure how to continue.

'Especially when your family are torturers and murders,' I added helpfully.

He nodded self-consciously, 'Yeah something like that.'

The way he couldn't quite meet my eyes made me realise something. 'You didn't agree with the bombing did you?'

He still refused to look at me.

'Did you?' I prompted.

'The group are a democracy. I agreed with the majority vote,' he said.

'But you didn't agree with the decision?' I persisted.

He paused for a moment and then shook his head. 'No, I didn't.'

'But you're still a Unionist, even though you didn't agree with the bombing?'

'The Unionists are my family; they took me in when I had nothing. I owe them my life. Daryl and Patrick were right about the Light, they have done terrible things. I might not have agreed with the method, but I'm loyal to the cause. Once you have had a good night's sleep you might see things differently too.'

'I don't think so.'

'Your choice. If you do change your mind, just remember you can leave a message for me in the tree at East Park and I'll make sure it gets to Patrick and Daryl. Now you should go before it gets light.'

The house was deserted; everyone was asleep so I was able to make it through the library and up to my bedroom without being discovered. I fell asleep straight away and woke a few hours later to find Maud hovering over my bed.

'Time to get up sleepyhead,' she said. 'Your alarm's been going off for fifteen minutes. I can't believe it didn't wake you.'

My head felt like it was full of cotton wool. 'I didn't sleep very well last night,' I mumbled. I'll get up in a minute.'

'Breakfast is in thirty minutes. Don't be late.'

'Huh Huh,' I grunted in response and then closed my eyes again. I heard the door click shut as she left the room. I knew I had to get up but my brain was still heavy with sleep and didn't want to wake up just yet, didn't want to face the truths that I'd learnt the night before.

Eventually I was able to gather the strength I needed to pull myself together and slowly climb out of bed. I scrutinised myself in the mirror and groaned. My hair was mussed and I had massive bags under my eyes. I looked like I hadn't slept for a week.

I struggled through the rest of the day trying to shake off the melancholy that enveloped me.

I had my first flashback at lunchtime. I was digging into a mound of mashed potato when a forgotten image surfaced from somewhere deep within my subconscious. I gasped loudly enough to make Maud glance up from her meal. Fortunately I was able to convince her that I'd just swallowed a mouthful of hot food.

The next flashback came during biology when the tutor handed me a scalpel to dissect a piece of tree bark. I turned it over and over in my hand in horror. This time Maud was too preoccupied with the lesson to notice that anything was wrong.

If the flashbacks weren't debilitating enough, two days later the dreams started. Horrible dreams of my father covered in blood standing over my bed, his arms dripping with gore as he grasped desperately at my bedding, begging me to believe in him. I woke from each dream in a cold sweat with a strangled scream in my throat. Soon I was finding any reason not to sleep. I'd force myself to stay awake till the early hours of the morning reading a book, writing in my diary, even doing school work! Anything to keep the dreams away.

Maud commented on the dark rings under my eyes and worried that I was coming down with something. The last thing I wanted was a visit to Isolation so I lied and told her that I was just missing my parents. As I'd expected this made Maud feel uncomfortable and she left me alone with my thoughts. I felt cruel, but it was only a white lie, I reasoned. In a way I *was* mourning my parents. Mourning the loss of the parents I thought I knew and coming to terms with the people they really were.

CHAPTER 10

Truth

I was slowly going insane. I desperately needed to talk to someone about the nightmares, about the things I'd seen in the photographs, but I was completely alone. Whenever I thought about this it made me cry because I realised that in any other circumstance I would have turned to my parents for comfort. Now my parents were the cause of my nightmares.

After four nights with very little sleep and the nightmares slowly turning my brain to mush I realised that I had to do something. My father was appearing in my dreams pleading with me to believe in his innocence, yet I'd so easily accepted his guilt based on evidence from the very people who had killed him. I needed to uncover the truth for myself.

I had to find out more about the Light and needed to understand the real purpose of the Legislate. I suspected that I would find this information in the Director's study. The only problem was that he kept the door locked at all times. Even Maud didn't have a key.

I spent the next few days planning how I could get into his study. I found a hiding place in the hall where I could observe the room. I watched and waited for an opportunity to present itself, but after three days I gave up. The Director never left the room unlocked.

On the third evening, after I'd given up watching the study and I lay in bed fighting sleep, I remembered something important. I jumped out of bed and pulled out the map Daryl had sent me. The tunnel I'd used to escape the house had taken me from the library to the exit outside the grounds, but I'd noticed that there were other tunnels drawn on the map too. These tunnels ran underneath the whole of the house. I traced the length of these tunnels with a fingernail; casually observing that I was long overdue for a manicure. My heart leapt a little when I saw that one of the tunnels seemed to end directly under the Director's study. This meant that there might be an exit from the tunnel directly into the study. This could be my way in.

I decided to explore the tunnels the following evening. After dinner I excused myself and went back to my room. I waited impatiently until everyone had gone to bed and then pulled on my GI Jane outfit. I reasoned that it was much better suited to indoor exploration than to outdoor activities. This time I remembered to pack a torch.

I had no problems sneaking out through the trap door in the library. I consulted the map by the light of the torch and studied the maze of passages and tunnels under the house. I noticed that a number of these were intersected by a thick blue line but I wasn't sure what it meant as there was no key.

The tunnel I'd used to escape from the Director's house was highlighted in red. It was one of the narrower tunnels and located right at the very edge of the map. I travelled along this passageway and when I arrived at the first intersecting tunnel I took a detour to explore it further. I was disappointed when it came to a dead end and noted that the thick blue line was drawn right across the end of this tunnel.

The next tunnel proved a little more interesting and led into a series of narrow tunnels. I was careful to keep track of the route I was using so that I wouldn't get lost. To my disappointment each of these ended in a thick brick wall too. I began to suspect that the blue line on the map represented a wall or dead end. If that was the case then there was no way I could reach the Director's study.

When I arrived at the last tunnel I was damp and cold and the enthusiasm I'd felt at the beginning of my trip was starting to wane. I travelled the full length of the tunnel and again was disappointed when it came to another dead end. I checked my watch and found that I'd been in the tunnels for over an hour. It was bitterly cold and my feet were frozen stiff. As I stamped my feet hard on the ground to encourage a bit of warmth back into them I noticed a large grated vent fitted into the bottom half of the wall. I crouched down to take a closer look. There was a light breeze blowing through the opening in the vent and I could make out a faint light coming from the other side. I pulled at it experimentally and it came away easily in my hands.

When I moved the grate aside it left a hole in the wall that was big enough for me to crawl through. I poked my head and torch through to the other side and saw a much wider, but shorter, tunnel. Curious, I crawled through and advanced towards a weak light. I was intrigued to find that the illumination was coming from a series of electric wall lights that lined the whole length of the tunnel. Unlike the derelict tunnels that I'd just exited, these looked well maintained and cared for.

I consulted the map. If I took the first left turn it should take me in the direction of the Director's study. As I reached the turning I froze, thinking I heard voices in the distance. I strained to listen, but there was nothing. I was imagining things.

Further down the tunnel I stopped again, this time I was definitely sure I'd heard voices. It sounded like there was someone up ahead of me. There was a wooden door carved into the wall to my right. I pressed my ear to it and when I was sure there was no noise coming from inside I opened the door and stepped into a small room.

The room was empty and looked like it was used as an office. It was functional rather than ostentatious, with a wooden desk and simple office chair. At the opposite end of the room I noticed a pair of double doors. I noiselessly padded over and opened them. Behind the doors was a large stationery cupboard. I pulled out some sheaves of paper and noted that they had the Director's personal seal on them. I was confused, why did the Director have an office under the house when he had a perfectly comfortable study above ground and an office in the Building of Light too?

I explored the room, leafing through a stack of papers piled high on the desk. I was hoping to find something that would help me understand a little bit more about the Light. At the bottom of the pile I found a plain brown folder and opened it curiously. I gasped loudly and had to hold onto the edge of the desk to steady myself. The file contained photographs. I forced myself to look through them, even though the contents made me feel sick. I studied each one carefully, this time there was no question about my father's guilt.

I replaced the file, taking care to put the papers back exactly as I'd found them. I was just about to leave the room when I froze. There was a voice outside the door. The door handle started to turn and I looked around frantically for a place to hide. I clambered into the only safe place I could think of . . . the stationery cupboard. There wasn't a lot of room inside the cupboard and I crouched on the floor wedged uncomfortably between two large reams of paper. My heart was beating wildly and I could feel a cold prickle of sweat start to make its way down my back.

The doors to the stationery cupboard weren't very thick and I could make out two distinct voices in the room beyond. One voice sounded male with a high reedy tone. The other voice was female; it was more nasal with a clipped, almost officious, tone. I heard a chair creak loudly as if someone had just taken a seat. I strained to listen to the conversation.

'You wanted an update on the prisoner?' the reedy voice said.

The female voice responded with an affirmative.

'We captured him earlier today. He's in one of the cells waiting to be interrogated. He put up quite a fight so we had to suppress him.'

I heard the female laugh at this. 'You always did enjoy suppressing prisoners,' she said.

'He won't be causing any more problems, you can be sure of that. Nice and quiet he was when we left him.' This comment was followed by a high reedy laugh.

'So you think he's a Unionist?' the female asked.

'No. I think he's just a protester. We'll find out more once we get the chance to interrogate him further. I'm sure we can persuade him to talk. I have a few new techniques that I've been dying to try.' I gave an involuntary shudder at the tone of the man's voice. 'Do you need me for anything else?' the high reedy voice asked.

'No. We're finished here. You can go and see to the prisoner.'

I heard the creak of the office door as it opened and then closed. Someone had left the room, but I could still hear noise in the room beyond. There was nothing I could do but stay in the cupboard and wait for the person to leave.

I tried to get comfortable, but there wasn't a lot of room and after a while my legs began to cramp painfully. As the minutes ticked by the ache in my legs became unbearable. Just as my calves were practically screaming with pain and I'd had to mash my lips tightly together to stop myself from moaning in agony I heard the creak of a chair. I held my breath and crossed my fingers. The door creaked loudly and then I heard it slam shut. I waited for a few moments to make sure that the room was definitely empty and then clambered awkwardly out of the cupboard, my legs screaming in protest.

I gave myself a few moments to rub some feeling back into my legs before letting myself out of the office. I checked my watch. It was late and I needed to go back to the house. It wasn't safe in the tunnels. Especially now that I knew there were other people in here.

As I crept back along the tunnels I must have taken a wrong turn because I ended up at a series of empty metal cages that I hadn't seen before. The air quality had changed and the stale musty smell I'd grown used to was replaced by a strange new metallic tang. The smell seemed familiar, but I couldn't recall what it was. I followed the scent trying to find its source and found myself outside a thick wooden door where the smell was stronger than ever. There was no noise coming from inside the room so I pushed at the door experimentally and was pleased to find that it was unlocked.

As I stepped inside I almost fell backwards as the stench hit me. The metallic tang was stronger and was now infused with the smell of stale sweat and something else . . . my mind searched for a reference; urine. The room smelt like a toilet. More than that, it reeked of death.

I was so busy gagging at the smell that my brain couldn't process what was inside the room. Slowly as I came to my senses the full horror hit me and my legs gave way so that I staggered, grabbing at the doorway for support. My attention was drawn to the blood and gore stained chair in the middle of the room. It had once been metal but now it was crusted with blood. The arm, leg and head restraints were equally gore ridden and I could see tiny bits of skin and hair hanging from them.

I noticed a blood soaked table and saw that it contained a number of bloody implements; I recognised a saw, a chisel, and a screw driver before I looked away. I clasped my hand to my mouth, the contents of my stomach threatening to make an appearance. I was desperate to leave the room and get away as quickly as possible, but my legs were like lead, refusing to move as quickly as I wanted them to. I slipped on something, it was a dismembered ear, glistening with blood. I squealed in horror, pulled the door shut and then ran for my life.

My brain must have switched into autopilot. Within what felt like a few moments I'd reached the door to the library, but I couldn't remember crawling back through the grating or pulling out my torch to find my way through the unlit tunnels.

I pushed the lever and exited through the panel. In my haste to escape the tunnels I forgot to check if anyone was inside, but fortunately the library was empty.

I ran from the room and tore through the house to my bedroom. As soon as I was safely inside my room my legs gave way and I slithered down the full length of the door onto the floor. I hugged my knees, shaking uncontrollably. My heart was hammering against my chest and I was so close to hysteria that I didn't even notice the person sitting on my bed silently watching me. It was the loud creak of the bed springs that caught my attention. As if in a fog I saw Peter standing over me. In slow motion he knelt down in front of me and said something that sounded like my name. His voice was coming from somewhere far away. I stared at him numbly and continued to shiver uncontrollably. I felt a pressure on my arm. He was shaking it. He looked concerned. I heard him ask if I was okay. I started to laugh at the absurdity of the question, of course I wasn't okay. I was slumped on my bedroom floor shivering violently and probably having a heart attack.

The laughter became a sob and then I was crying uncontrollably.

'Shush,' he whispered in my ear. 'Someone will hear.' Even through the fog of emotion I could detect the note of panic in his voice. But I couldn't make myself stop.

Peter wrapped an arm around my shoulder and crushed my face tightly against his chest, I expected this was an attempt to drown out the noise rather than to make me feel better, but I didn't care. I wrapped my arms around his waist and howled loudly. I cried until my chest felt torn and ragged and all that was left were loud hiccupping sobs. In the end when even the hiccupping had finished I pulled away from Peter and leant my head back limply against the wall.

Peter pulled a handkerchief from his pocket and handed it to me. I could feel him watching me as I wiped my face, waiting for an explanation. I closed my eyes in an attempt to block him out.

'Are you going to tell me what happened?' he asked softly.

I shook my head. I couldn't talk about it, not to him, not to anyone. 'It was nothing,' I said hoarsely.

'Really!' his tone was disbelieving. 'Something obviously upset you, unless you're in the habit of breaking down into hysterics over nothing?'

My eyes flew open. It sounded like he was mocking me. It was too much. It gave me the energy I needed to push myself to my feet and stumble to the bathroom.

I heard him get up and follow close behind. I could feel his presence in the bathroom doorway as I splashed handfuls of cool water onto my face.

'Was it something really bad?' he asked. This time there was no mocking tone in his voice.

'Was it something bad?' I repeated quietly. Then I pictured the dismembered ear, the congealed blood smeared across the floor, the skin hanging from the metal chair. I made it to the toilet just in time to throw up. I heaved loudly until my stomach was empty.

Peter remained in the doorway watching impassively as I stood up and grabbed my toothbrush. I took a long time brushing my teeth, steadying myself, preparing myself for the questions I knew would come once I'd finished. The look on Peter's face told me that he was expecting answers.

After I'd rinsed my mouth he spoke again, 'I want you to tell me everything that happened.' His voice might have been soft, but there was no mistaking the determined tone.

I picked up a towel and tried to push past him back into the bedroom. He didn't yield.

'MaryAnn, tell me what happened.'

'I need to sit down,' I said weakly. 'Please,' I added when he still didn't move out of my way. He considered me for a moment and then stepped aside.

I crossed the room and sat down on the edge of my bed. Peter took a seat in the chair next to me. He leant forward placing his hands in his lap and waited expectantly. His eyes didn't leave my face for a second.

'I went down into the tunnels,' I said after a few minutes of silence.

I saw the look of surprise on his face; whatever he'd been expecting I don't think it was this. He considered me for a moment. 'That was stupid. What if you'd been caught?'

'I know,' I interrupted. 'Believe me, I know exactly what would have happened if I'd been caught.'

'What do you mean?' his eyes narrowed curiously.

'I saw . . . I saw . . . .' I found that I couldn't find the right words to describe what I'd seen. 'There was a room. In the tunnels . . .' I tried again. 'It was . . . .' My voice cracked. The horror of the room threatened to resurface again and I clasped my hand across my mouth as I struggled to maintain control.

'It's alright MaryAnn,' I heard Peter say quietly. 'I think I know what you saw.'

'You do. You've seen it too?'

'No, but I've heard stories about it. All the Unionists have. The Legislate take prisoners there to extract confessions. They're usually very successful.'

'It was horrible.' I shivered. 'The blood, the smell . . . there was an ear!' I clutched at the edge of the bed to steady myself. When I looked up Peter was watching me, waiting . . . what was he waiting for? . . . did he want more details?

'Please don't make me describe it to you,' I said. 'I just want to forget about it.'

'If only it was that easy,' he said flatly. There was a faraway look in his eyes and for a moment he seemed to be talking to himself. Then he frowned and shook his head, 'Forgetting,' I mean. 'If only we could forget things so easily.'

I gave an involuntary shiver. My whole body was drained of energy and I felt incredibly cold. My teeth started to chatter loudly and even when I clamped my jaw tightly shut it wouldn't stop.

Peter picked up a blanket from the end of the bed. 'I think you might be in shock.' He wrapped the blanket around my shoulders. 'You need to keep warm.'

I pulled the blanket tightly around me. I was still shivering loudly, but was glad for the extra warmth.

'Why did you go into the tunnels?' he asked.

I considered this for a moment and decided I should be honest with him. 'I thought I might be able to find a way into the Director's study. I wanted to find some evidence that would prove Uncle Patrick was wrong about my father.'

'And you found it?' he asked.

'No,' I murmured, my voice barely audible. I expected Peter to make a sarcastic comment about being right all along but he didn't. I noticed that he couldn't quite meet my eyes though. I expect he couldn't bear to look at me, the daughter of a torturer.

I realised that he hadn't explained what he was doing in my room. My heart quickened with panic. 'Are Daryl and Uncle Patrick alright?' I asked.

He seemed confused by the question. 'Yes of course.'

'Then why are you here?'

'Oh! I'm here to fix the toilet.' He pointed at the badge on his overalls. 'SanTech,' he said. 'The Director had an, erm, unfortunate blockage in his plumbing and I'm here to fix it. We offer a twenty four/seven service to our important clients and The Director is the most important . . . day or night we're here to service his every need.'

'You work in Sanitation?' I crinkled my nose in disgust.

'It's the easiest way to move around the Neighbourhood unnoticed. SanTechs are practically invisible. No-one wants to get close to us.'

'So you just happened to be here this late in the evening and you thought you would pop into my bedroom to say hello?' I queried.

'No, the blocked toilet was what I like to call a happy accident. I have an invitation for you from Patrick. He thought you might want to celebrate Christmas Eve with your family.'

I was a little taken aback. I hadn't even thought about Christmas, even though it was fast approaching.

'He still thinks he can persuade me to join the Union?' I asked.

Peter shrugged, 'I don't know, he just asked me to deliver the message.'

'Do you think I should go?'

'It's up to you. If you want to spend time with your family, then you should come.'

After the horrors of the evening I realised that I wanted to be as far away from the Director's house as possible. That I wanted more than anything to be with my family again.

'But how would I get away without anyone noticing?'

'The Director and his daughter always attend the carol service at the church every Christmas Eve. After the concert they come home, have dinner and go to bed early. You should be able to get away once they're safely tucked up in bed.'

'How do you know all this?' I asked. 'And how did you know that the toilet would be blocked today?'

'I have my sources,' Peter responded mysteriously, but wouldn't tell me anything more even when I pressed him for details.

'Would I have to go back into the tunnels?' I asked, although I feared that I already knew the answer to my question.

'I'm afraid so,' he said.

'I don't know whether I can. Not after tonight.'

'It's the only way,' he said. 'You don't have to go back to the room. You just have to go to the clearing outside of the house where I dropped you off last time. I promise I'll be there to meet you. You'll be perfectly safe.'

'Safe!' I murmured. I wasn't sure that I would ever feel safe again. Not after the events of the last few days. My life seemed to be on a downward spiral taking me on a slow trip to hell. I swallowed hard and considered my lack of options. 'Alright,' I said reluctantly. 'I'll do it.'

'Great, I'll meet you at ten thirty,' he said. 'You have to make sure you're on time, you can't be late. It'll look suspicious if I have to wait around for you.' He glanced down at his watch and muttered a curse. 'Damn. I've been here too long. I need to go.' He got to his feet. 'You going to be okay?' he asked.

'Would it make a difference if I said no?'

He gave me a questioning look. 'What's that supposed to mean?'

'You still have to leave even if I'm not going to be okay, so why bother asking the question.'

Peter gave me a strange look. 'Anyone would think that you didn't want me to go,' he said as he patted me on the shoulder. 'You can get through this. You know you can.' He moved towards the door. 'I'll see you on Christmas Eve. Remember, don't be late.' I heard the door click shut behind him as he left the room.

I sat for a few moments on the edge of the bed, fighting the tightness that gripped my chest. I'd feared that this would happen as soon as Peter left. The moment I was on my own the blackness descended. I was totally alone, in danger and living in the house of a monster. Fear gripped me and although I was breathing heavily I couldn't get enough air into my lungs. I ran to the window and threw it open, hanging my head outside and taking frantic gulps of cold air. After a long time when I was able to breathe again I finally closed the window and climbed shivering into bed.

The pressure on my chest had released but this didn't stop the hollow gnawing feeling that crawled around in the pit of my stomach. Thankfully I was so tired that sleep came quickly and saved me from the full impact of the loneliness and desolation that usually followed an attack.

CHAPTER II

Caves

Christmas Eve announced itself with a dramatic storm that roused me from a fitful sleep. I climbed out of bed and crossed my room to curl up on the window seat to watch the storm rage outside.

When I was very young I'd been terrified of storms, especially the thunder. I'd hide under my bed with my hands over my ears so that I couldn't hear the boom of each thunder clap. I'd be scared, but certain that my father would come and rescue me. He'd retrieve me from under the bed and take me back to his room. My parents would let me sleep in their bed, taking it in turns to tell me funny stories until the storm had passed by.

Now each thunder crack reminded me that I didn't have that safety net anymore and my father wouldn't be coming to rescue me. The realisation that I was completely alone caused the all too familiar quickening of my heart. I knew that if I didn't fight for control that I would be engulfed by the blackness and the absolute certainty of my impending death. My ears would be buzzing and I would be fighting hard for each breath. These attacks had become a frequent occurrence since my parents' death. Sometimes they came without warning, but most often they would arrive when a memory resurfaced and I remembered that my whole life had been built on a lie and I was alone. The attacks forced me to confront the bleak hollow reality of my life.

This time I was determined not to succumb to the blackness. This wasn't how I wanted to start my Christmas Eve. I remained huddled on the window seat forcing myself to focus on the vivid flashes of light that cut across the pale morning sky. I counted the length of time between each crash of thunder. Keeping my brain occupied really helped and as the storm wore itself out my breathing also returned to normal.

The storm was replaced by a drizzling rain and I watched as it streaked down the window pane, knowing that soon I would have to get up. It had been a week since I'd gone into the tunnels and each day I'd had to face the Director, knowing that our great and fearless leader was nothing more than a cold blooded torturer. He might look like he'd stepped out of a photo shoot, but he was drenched in as much blood as . . . as much blood as my father. I shuddered. *Stop it* I mentally reprimanded myself. The Director as a killer was something I was coming to terms with. My father, on the other hand, well that was a different matter altogether.

There was a quiet knock at the door and I jumped.

'Are you awake?' a disembodied voice asked.

It was Maud.

'Come in,' I said, glad to have a distraction to take my mind off my sombre mood. Even the prospect of Maud fussing around was better than remaining alone in my room wallowing in miserable reflection.

Maud crept into the room, she was still in her pyjamas and her hair was tousled from sleep.

'Did the storm wake you?' I asked. I noticed that her eyes were puffy and red and it looked like she'd been crying.

'I hate storms,' she said by way of explanation. 'They scare me.' She sat down beside me on the window seat.

'No more storms now,' I said. 'Just rain.'

'It's not very Christmassy is it?' she said. 'The rain makes it look so miserable outside. I wish we had some snow.'

The rest of the day turned out to be a typical winter's day without even the promise of snow and when we arrived at the church for the Christmas service, at seven o'clock, it had been raining all day so we had to wade through puddles of water. The Director wasn't religious, but after the virus many people in the Neighbourhood had turned to God and, not wanting to alienate this section of his public, he'd encouraged religious practice to continue. He even appeared to endorse it with regular visits to church.

At the end of the service I could hardly bear to watch him as he smiled and gave a friendly bow to each member of the congregation. After a conversation with the vicar we left the church and arrived home at eight thirty. We ate a light supper before Maud and the Director retired to bed.

I waited impatiently in my room, flicking through my wardrobe trying to find something appropriate to wear. As I didn't need to trek across the wilderness this time I decided I could wear something nice to the party. I pulled out a few dresses, the type of party dresses I would normally wear. I rejected them almost immediately as I still had to hike over the Boundary. A pair of trousers was the best option. I chose a pair of wide legged black trousers and a red silk top. I also pulled a new pair of boots out of their box. The boots were made of a soft black material and had a flat heel. They buttoned up the side finishing just above the ankle. I'd ordered them on the Portal in preparation for the party. I thought they were perfect; smart, but very functional.

Once I'd showered and changed I pulled on a clean pair of gloves and made my way down to the library. As I approached the secret panel my insides knotted and I had to fight the urge to turn and run. I needed to distract myself so I decided to mentally work through my wardrobe and count all my shoes. I owned so many pairs that I thought it would be a good way to take my mind off the tunnels.

One: my blue shoes with the glass wedge heel. They gave me a blister every time I wore them, but they looked so cute with a pair of shorts and vest that I simply couldn't resist them.

Two: a pair of strappy silver sandals covered in sparkling diamanté. Handmade and given as a Christmas present last year by Georgina and Natalie. I remembered that I'd jumped up and down with excitement when I'd received them.

The panel slid open and I stepped through.

Three: a pair of red stilettos, so high that they almost made me feel tall.

The corridor was dank and musty. Was I just imagining the metallic smell of blood in the air?

Four: purple crushed velvet with a picture of a pink cat sewn across the toes. Adorable, and the subject of much admiration from my friends when Diana Temple had started a 'cute animal' clothing trend across the Neighbourhood last year.

Despite the cold air in the tunnel I was sweating profusely.

Five: midnight blue Mary Janes. Small heel and perfect with jeans.

I'd made it to thirty four: gold dusted, peep toe sandal, bought for last year's spring dance, when I exited the tunnels. I stopped for a moment to breathe in the chill evening air and let out a sigh of relief. Who would have thought I'd be so thankful to be standing outside in the wet drizzling rain.

Now I was safely out of the tunnel I felt the butterflies in my stomach slowly flutter into life. Soon I would be on my way to see Daryl and Uncle Patrick.

I headed to the clearing to meet Peter and tried to keep tightly to the shadows. I almost jumped out of my skin when someone tapped me on the shoulder.

'Don't sneak up on me like that. You scared the life out of me,' I hissed as my heart nearly exploded out of my chest.

Peter ignored my complaints and pointed towards a waiting truck. 'Your carriage awaits,' he said. He even opened the door for me this time.

Peter seemed distracted and lost in thought as we journeyed towards the Boundary. I glanced over at him a few times and tried to engage him in conversation, but he answered in monosyllables. Eventually we came to a halt under the cover of a large hill with the Boundary visible in the distance.

'Time for another adventure across the Boundary,' he said. His tone was light hearted, but when I glanced over at him I saw that his face had a tight closed look.

Despite my better judgement I asked him if he was okay and he gave a non-committal shrug. 'Fine,' he said flatly.

I wasn't convinced. 'You don't seem fine.'

'It's nothing,' he responded sharply. 'Nothing that I want to talk to you about, anyway.'

I bristled at his tone. 'Well that's a bit rude. I was only trying to be friendly.'

He gave a brittle laugh. 'You think I'm rude because I don't want to wail about my problems to anyone who'll listen,' he said.

I stiffened. He was talking about the other night in my room. He was making fun of me. 'Well I'm sorry if my wailing offended you. It was just bad timing that's all. It won't happen again.' I flung open the car door and jumped to the ground.

'I didn't mean it like that. I wasn't talking about you. What you saw must have been awful. It was a stupid comment. I'm sorry.'

I ignored him, stalking off in the direction of the Boundary.

'I don't want any drama,' he shouted after me.

'You'll get no drama from me,' I called back over my shoulder as I continued towards the Boundary. I was grateful that he couldn't race after me as he had to stay behind and camouflage the truck.

The Boundary looked as battered and broken as it had the last time I'd crossed over. I squatted down to find the hole in the wire and without a pause I clambered through to the Outside. I was amazed at how easy it was this time. Now that I realised there was nothing bad waiting for me on the other side I wasn't the least bit scared about leaving the Neighbourhood.

I found a flat dry rock and sat down and waited for Peter to finish camouflaging the truck. He arrived about ten minutes later and climbed through the hole in the wire.

'You could have helped,' he grumbled.

I held out my newly manicured nails, the polish visible through the clear material of my gloves. 'What if I'd chipped a nail,' I said snippily. 'I know how much you hate me wailing over nothing.'

'For crying out loud, that wasn't what I meant.' He threw his hands up into the air as he stormed away from me across the wet grass in the direction of the new truck. 'You might just be the most irritating person I've ever met in my whole life. You think that the world revolves around you and your problems.'

I sprang up from the rock. 'No I don't,' I protested as I jogged along beside him. 'I don't think the world revolves around me. You started this by being rude.'

'I think you started this by prying into my personal life.'

'So asking you if something is wrong counts as prying does it?'

We'd reached the truck and he yanked at the camouflage covering with a loud grunt. He struggled to pull it off the truck and again I refused to help.

When he'd removed the cover he rolled it up into a ball and stuffed it into the boot. Then he stormed around to the driver door and

147

yanked it open with such force I was surprised it didn't come off in his hand. He climbed inside and stared stonily out of the window, waiting until I climbed in beside him. Once I'd closed the door he handed me a strip of black cotton. 'Put it on,' he said.

I turned it over in my hand, puzzled.

'It's a blindfold. You have to wear it.'

'Why do I have to wear a blindfold? I didn't have to wear one last time?'

'It's just a safety precaution. Last time we took you to a safe house. It's somewhere we won't use again. This time we're taking you to our home. Patrick insists that all visitors wear one.'

'Well that seems stupid. You can trust me. I'm not going to tell anyone.'

Peter sighed, 'MaryAnn, can you just humour me and put it on. Please.'

I opened my mouth in protest, but he interrupted me with a wave of his hand. 'You've seen the room in the tunnels. It doesn't matter whether you plan to tell anyone or not. If the Light captures you, they'll make you talk. You won't be able to keep this a secret. The less you know the better.' He gave me a hard stare.

Well that made me feel a whole lot better. 'Brilliant,' I muttered. 'Now rather than just dreaming about the room I can actually imagine myself being tortured in it. Thanks for that image.'

Peter didn't respond but sat with his arms crossed silently waiting for me to put on the blindfold. I didn't want to argue anymore so I wrapped it around my eyes and tied it in a knot at the back of my head. The blindfold was made out of thick material and allowed no light to penetrate.

'Good girl,' I heard Peter mutter sarcastically.

'Don't patronise me,' I growled, and even though I couldn't see his face I knew that he was smirking at me.

I could hear the rain outside as it bounced noisily off the metal roof and the wipers scraped loudly across the windscreen. After a short while the road surface changed, we were no longer driving on grass, but seemed to be on a tarmac road.

'How much longer?'

Peter shushed me. 'This is a really bad road and I need to concentrate. Otherwise we could end up taking an unexpected trip down a couple of hundred meters of hillside.'

After hearing that comment I was extremely grateful to be wearing the blindfold.

Eventually the truck came to a standstill.

'You can take off your blindfold.'

I pulled the piece of cloth from my eyes and found that we were parked in front of a large rock face. As we clambered out of the truck two figures melted out of the shadows. They were both female and carrying large guns that were pointed right at us.

'It's okay,' said Peter. 'It's only me.'

'Peter?' one of the girls asked.

'Who else,' Peter responded.

'Who's that with you?'

'Patrick's niece, MaryAnn.'

They both gave me an appraising look as they approached, but neither of them spoke to me.

'We okay to go in?' Peter asked. 'Or do you ladies want to give this excellent specimen of manhood a full body search first.' He spread his arms wide and winked at them both.

Both girls giggled loudly. 'Well Peter, if you didn't just go and put me off my Christmas dinner,' one of them said.

'Ladies you wound me,' Peter said with a raised eyebrow. 'You really don't know what you're missing.'

'And hopefully we'll never find out,' one of the girls responded. She indicated the rock face. 'I think you should get inside before you miss the party. Uncle Patrick won't be happy if his niece misses the festivities.' They both looked pointedly as me.

'Duty calls,' Peter sighed. 'I suppose we'd better get inside, but if you two ladies change your mind then you know where to find me.'

Both girls giggled in response. 'Hopefully we'll never be that desperate,' one of them threw over her shoulder as they both melted back into the shadows.

'This way,' Peter said and jerked his thumb towards the rock. This time I was prepared and I pulled a torch out of my coat pocket. As we approached the rock the illumination from my torch exposed a small opening.

Beyond the opening there was a narrow tunnel. Peter crouched low and set off down the passage and I followed closely behind.

Eventually we came to a flight of thick stairs that were cut into the rock and obviously manmade. Peter descended the steps, taking them two at a time. I scrambled after him breathing hard as I struggled to keep up. The steps were wet and green with slime and I had to tread carefully so I didn't slip. As we neared the bottom the air grew damper. It reminded me of the tunnels under the Director's house and I shuddered both from the cold and the feeling of dread that came over me whenever I was reminded of them.

At the bottom of the staircase I was surprised to find an underground river. It was wide, wide enough to accommodate the three or four rowing boats that were tied up to a jetty protruding from the steps. Lanterns hung from the walls and they shed a weak light down the waterlogged tunnel. Peter clambered onto the boat closest to the jetty.

'Get in,' he said, as he pulled out a pair of oars.

The boat was rocking alarmingly and there was no real handhold to steady myself. I clambered gingerly over the side of the boat, trying to take care not to fall . . . too late, the boat gave a heave to the left and I lost my balance, sprawling ungainly across the seat. I thought I heard a snigger from Peter.

I pulled myself upright, the bottom half of my trousers were soaked through from the water on the boat. 'You could have helped,' I said.

'I suppose I could,' came the reply as he held out his hands for inspection, 'but I might have chipped a nail.'

'Ha ha ha, very funny.'

'Besides, seeing you fall over at every opportunity adds a little bit of extra fun to our field trips, don't you think?'

I resisted the urge to punch him in the head and instead I decided to take the moral high ground.

'Take a seat,' he said. 'I'd hate for you to fall over and hurt yourself again.' This comment was followed by something that sounded suspiciously like another snigger and my fists clenched at my sides. Taking the moral high ground was proving to be very difficult.

I tried to make myself as comfortable as possible on one of the hard wooden seats as we journeyed down the weakly lit passageway. I looked around with interest. 'Where are we?' I asked.

'It's an old lead mine,' Peter replied, puffing heavily from the effort of rowing. 'I don't think they ever mined much lead, but it makes a great hiding place.'

The boat meandered along the passageway. Its whole length was lit by weak lights. I noticed that the lanterns had been replaced by electric lights, but I couldn't understand where the power was coming from. When the passageway widened I felt a current tug at the bottom of the boat. There was a landing stage built into the rock and Peter steered the boat towards it.

When he'd moored the boat he offered me a hand but I made a point of ignoring it as I stumbled out after him.

Peter gestured for me to follow him. 'Great, more dark, dank passageways,' I muttered to myself as I followed closely behind. Again Peter set a brisk pace and I struggled to keep up. He obviously knew these caves very well as he navigated them with complete ease.

This passage was wider than the last and the rock face was a few feet above my head so there was no need for me to crouch or bend uncomfortably.

We exited the tunnel into another much larger cavern. A mix of electric lights and candles flickered around the base of the cave shedding light upwards. In the dim light I couldn't make out the roof of the cavern, but I could see large stalagmites jutting upwards from the rocky ground glistening wetly in the half light. It was breath-taking.

'It's stunning isn't it?' said a voice beside me. Peter had a torch in his hand and was shining it at the stalagmites. I was silent as I took in the full beauty of the cave. 'It's amazing,' I said. 'I've never seen anything like it before.'

I caught the distinct smell of wood smoke and noticed that a number of fires flickered around the cavern. Small groups of people were gathered around each fire chatting loudly. I heard the strum of a guitar and the low sound of a carol being sung; *Silent Night*.

As I took in the full beauty of the cave Uncle Patrick and Daryl appeared beside me.

'MaryAnn, you're here,' Uncle Patrick cried. 'Merry Christmas.' His arms extended in welcome and I took a quick step backwards in horror. He hesitated, arms outstretched. There was a moment of awkwardness between us, and then he smiled and gave me a small bow. 'We should probably stick to the standard Neighbourhood greeting until we get to know each other a little better,' he said. I shuddered a little when he hugged Peter, clapping him hard on the back. Hugging was so unsanitary. It wasn't illegal but was definitely frowned upon in the Neighbourhood.

'This place is incredible,' I said, staring around the cave. 'Is this where you live?'

'Yes, this is our home,' Uncle Patrick said. We have everything we need, a school, a hospital, a market . . . . It's like an underground town. You want to look around?'

I agreed eagerly.

'Well, let me take you on the grand tour,' he said. 'You want to come?' Uncle Patrick asked Daryl and Peter. My brother shook his head. 'No, I have to check on the arrangements for the Christmas Eve party.'

'Yeah I'm busy too,' said Peter. Although he didn't venture any more information about what he might be doing.

'This way,' Uncle Patrick guided me through the large cavern. It took an age to make our way out of the cavern as we were stopped every couple of minutes by people wanting to wish Uncle Patrick a merry Christmas. He introduced me to all of them, and didn't seem to notice the wary smiles that I received in return.

We exited the cave and entered another tunnel. This tunnel led into another massive cavern. This one was also full of people and my senses were assaulted by an array of smells. Some I recognised: baking bread, the sweet smell of honey intermingled with the deep acrid aroma of coffee; others were unfamiliar to me. I sniffed the air appreciatively.

The cavern comprised a series of thick ragged terraces, roughly carved into the grey rock, which rose up through the whole height of the cave. Many of the higher terraces were lined with what looked like large wooden booths. Above each booth brightly coloured banners hung from the rock. I squinted to read the ones closest to me: 'Barry the Butcher, Purveyor of Fine Meats', 'Coffee n go', 'Capri Pizzeria'.

'Are those shops?' I asked.

'Yes, we call this the Market,' Uncle Patrick said and I caught a hint of pride in his voice. 'This is where people come to shop, to meet friends. It's the heart of our little community.'

'It's remarkable,' I was lost for words. The Market contradicted everything I'd learnt about the Echo. They were not ignorant, feral animals living in filth and squalor. They had a built a real community in this cave.

'You want something to eat?' Uncle Patrick asked.

My stomach rumbled in reply and he smiled. 'Let's go and get a sandwich.'

He led me upwards through the terraces to a booth with a sign outside that read *'Bun in the Oven'.*

'Can we have two cheese sandwiches?' Uncle Patrick asked the flamed haired woman behind the counter. Her name badge identified her as Cheryl. She wore a bright pink smock decorated around the collar with delicately embroidered flowers. The smock was covered by a sensible white apron.

The woman took out two large brown rolls, slit them lengthways and stuffed them with cheese and tomato. Then she wrapped them in brown paper and handed them across the counter to Uncle Patrick. He dipped into his pocket and Cheryl put up a hand in protest. 'You know your money's no good here. It's on the house.'

Uncle Patrick started to protest but the woman's mouth set in a determined line. 'It's on the house.'

'How can you expect to make any profit, if you give away free food?'

'No-one gets free food,' she replied with a warm smile. 'Except for you.'

Uncle Patrick returned the smile and then introduced me. 'This is my niece MaryAnn.' He turned to me. 'Cheryl's been with us for about ten months now, isn't that right?'

'Yeah, came over here with my husband, decided to join the Union after the Light raided our farm and took our crops. Thought we would starve over the winter, but we found a home here and even managed to set up our own business.'

'And doing very well I see,' said Uncle Patrick.

'Yeah, we have lots of business at the moment. People are always hungry.'

'You going to the Christmas meal?' Uncle Patrick asked.

'Yeah, closing up in an hour. Brian volunteered to help set up the tables, he's down there somewhere.' She pointed vaguely down towards the floor of the cavern where I could see a hive of activity. Tables were being dragged into position, floors were being swept and candles lit.

'The Christmas Feast has become a bit of a tradition. We like to get everyone together each Christmas Eve to celebrate,' Uncle Patrick explained as he handed me a sandwich. 'Although soon we won't have enough room to accommodate everyone, this is going to be our biggest Christmas yet.'

I took a bite of my sandwich and my mouth exploded. It was absolutely delicious. I'd never tasted cheese like it before. It was thick and creamy with a sharp tang. My mouth watered and I took another huge bite.

'You like it?' Uncle Patrick asked.

My mouth was so full of bread and cheese that I couldn't reply so I simply nodded emphatically.

'It's made from real cow's milk, not synth milk like the cheese in the Neighbourhood. We have our own herd of cows.'

I'd learnt about real cheese in school but this was the first time I'd ever tasted it. There wasn't enough space to farm cows in the Neighbourhood so the scientists had created a synthetic substitute for cow's milk. As I found out now it was a pale imitation of the real thing.

The sandwich commanded my full attention as I followed Uncle Patrick out of the Market and into another tunnel. He told me that we were heading to the school. Before we reached it we arrived at an intersection. There was a big red cross painted on the whitewashed walls of the cave. I stared at it in horror. 'Is that the . . . ?' I couldn't even bring myself to say the word.

'The hospital,' Uncle Patrick finished for me. 'Yes it is.'

I shuddered with revulsion. 'Are there sick people there?' I whispered.

'Don't worry, it's not part of the tour. I know how the Neighbourhood feels about disease. So we'll keep away from the hospital. Come on, the school is this way.'

I followed behind Uncle Patrick, slightly taken aback at the offhand way in which he spoke about the hospital. In the Neighbourhood when anyone mentioned the hospital or Isolation it was in hushed, quiet tones.

It took only a few minutes to reach the school, which comprised a series of interconnecting caves; each one equipped with tables and stools.

'Each cave is a classroom,' Uncle Patrick explained. 'We're lucky enough to have a number of teachers in our group, so all the children get an education.' He pointed at a chalk board on the wall. 'We don't have enough power for fancy new technology so we've had to revert back to some old fashioned techniques. It might be low tech but it seems to work well. We also have a nursery,' he said leading me into an adorable cave decorated with colourful wall hangings of animals and trees.

'We expect every member of the Union to work and contribute to our community so we offer childcare for all the parents,' he explained. Next, Uncle Patrick took me to the living quarters. If the previous caves had been amazing, then the living quarters took my breath away. We entered a massive cavern, the biggest I'd seen. A wide river snaked its way around the edge of the cave and floating on top of the water was a line of brightly coloured wooden boats. I pointed them out to Uncle Patrick.

'They're canal boats,' he said. 'Some of the families live on them. Other people live in the rock.' Similar to the Market this cavern was also terraced. Scattered along each terrace was a mass of brightly coloured tents and shelters. The place hummed with life as people chatted loudly in small groups.

I noticed that this cavern was also lit with dim electrical lights. 'You have power here?'

'We use the water from the river to make electricity,' he said. 'It doesn't provide a lot of energy but it allows us to light the entrance tunnels, the main living areas, the hospital and the nursery.'

'Do all the Unionists live in this cave?' I indicated the tents and barges.

'Mostly it's just families who live here. Our Ops Teams move around a lot so we have a number of safe houses around the country that they use.'

'It's fabulous.' I stared wistfully around the cave. 'It must be a great place to live.' I thought of the quietness and sterility of the Director's house and how isolated it made me feel. No-one would ever be lonely here, living in this cave surrounded by all these people.

'It is,' Uncle Patrick said, 'but sometimes it can be a little, erm . . . too hectic. People live side by side twenty four hours a day so there's very little privacy. Sometimes it's a little claustrophobic.'

'Still you've built a home here, in the caves. It's astonishing what you've managed to achieve.'

'It's not that remarkable really,' Uncle Patrick said. 'When the Light isolated themselves behind the Boundary they abandoned hundreds of creative and talented people Outside. People who were able to come together and create all of this,' he indicated the cavern, 'from nothing. The Light preaches that these people are Ferals, yet the very people they chose to discard have worked together to build a community. What's truly remarkable is the absolute stupidity of the Light and that they deemed these people to be worthless.'

His passionate speech was interrupted as a speaker crackled into life. 'Merry Christmas, ho ho ho,' a deep voice boomed out around the cavern. 'The Christmas Feast will commence in fifteen minutes.'

'We should probably head back,' Uncle Patrick said as he led the way out of the cave.

CHAPTER 12

Celebration

We arrived back at the Market to find it bustling with activity and noise. Uncle Patrick bumped into a small group of people chatting by the entrance. I immediately recognised them; they'd been at the farmhouse during my first meeting with the Unionists. Uncle Patrick exchanged warm hugs before he turned to me. 'MaryAnn,' he said, 'let me formally introduce you to some of our Stewards.'

'Stewards?' I queried.

'Our Union leaders. This is Brandon Rivers, Robert Lawson and Leah Carter.' The men both smiled warmly. The woman, Leah, surveyed me through narrowed eyes before quickly leaving the group, murmuring a vague excuse about finding her brother. I was a little confused, she seemed to have taken a dislike to me but I wasn't quite sure why. Brandon and Robert exchanged a long glance as she left but Uncle Patrick didn't seem to notice that anything was wrong.

'How many Stewards are there?' I asked.

'There are six Stewards; some of them live in the caves, the others are living in the community as part of our outreach programme. We always have at least two or three Stewards living outside the caves. It helps raise our profile, but also provides a contingency in case any of us are captured. It means the Union will still have leadership.'

'So how do you decide who's a Steward?' I asked.

'We hold elections,' Brandon said. His voice was surprisingly deep and I noticed for the first time that his eyes were a startling shade of blue; clear and bright like ice crystals. He wore a black waistcoat which I thought might even be real leather; he was the very essence of cool. I remembered boys at school who had tried, and failed, to carry off the look that he wore with ease. I felt myself blush as he addressed me and wondered absently how old he was.

'Every three years the Union members get to decide on their leadership,' he continued.

'Even you?' I asked Uncle Patrick. 'They have to vote for you too?'

He nodded, 'We're a democracy. Everyone has the opportunity to vote for their leaders.'

'Not like the Light,' Robert said. 'How long has the Director been in charge . . . ten . . . fifteen years?'

'It's easily been fifteen years,' Brandon purred. 'Remember the old Director, he didn't last very long. He was only in office a few years before he had that heart attack.'

I found it hard to imagine the Neighbourhood under the control of anyone other than the current Director. He'd been in power for as long as I could remember. The idea that the Union chose new leaders every three years seemed totally alien to me. How could normal people possibly be expected to decide something so important?

'So you've only been the leader for three years?' I asked Uncle Patrick. He appeared so comfortable in his position that it seemed to me like he'd been doing it for a very long time.

Brandon clapped Uncle Patrick on the back. 'Patrick's been our leader for nearly nine years,' he said as he flashed me a disarming smile. 'Every time we hold an election he's voted right back in. The opposition never stand a chance.'

A loud gong sounded out around the Market. 'Looks like it's time to take our seats,' Uncle Patrick said as he interrupted the conversation. Brandon and Robert clapped Uncle Patrick warmly on the back, nodded goodbye to me and headed towards a crowded table. I watched Brandon stride away, admiring the perfect fit of his jeans, then reluctantly I followed Uncle Patrick as he steered me in the opposite direction through the crowds towards a table at the head of the cave. I saw that Daryl and Peter were at the table carefully studying a map.

'Put that away,' Uncle Patrick said as he took a seat opposite them. 'It's Christmas, let's celebrate.'

'Ho ho ho,' Peter grinned as he folded up the map and stuffed it into his trouser pocket.

'You enjoyed your tour?' Daryl asked.

'It's incredible. I can't believe you built all of this.'

'It's not finished yet,' said Peter excitedly. 'Next year we want to expand the stores, improve the kitchen and maybe build a gym.'

'You haven't been given approval for the gym yet,' Uncle Patrick said.

'But we need to keep our teams in tip top physical condition,' Peter argued.

'Hmmm,' Uncle Patrick didn't sound convinced. 'There's plenty of physical work to do if people want to keep fit.'

'Work, work, work,' Peter protested. 'That's all you ever think about.'

'Yeah, what about fun? We need some fun around here you know, Patty old boy,' Daryl grinned across the table at him.

Uncle Patrick scowled. 'I'm not against people having fun,' he said, 'and don't call me Patty. It's Patrick or sir.'

'Yes sir,' Peter and Daryl responded in unison before giving Uncle Patrick a mock salute.

Uncle Patrick greeted the salute with another scowl and then squinted quizzically at them both. 'What on earth have you both got on?'

That's when I noticed the jumpers they were both wearing. Daryl's was bright red, a fat Father Christmas plastered across the front.

Peter's jumper had the face of a reindeer splashed across the front of it. Its red nose contrasted garishly with the bright blue of the wool.

Daryl pulled at the bottom of his jumper. 'It's great isn't it? Murray knitted them.'

'We love 'em,' said Peter. 'It's the best present I ever got.'

Uncle Patrick shook his head in despair.

'Don't worry Patrick,' Daryl grinned. 'I'm sure you haven't been left out. I expect Murray made one for you too.'

'Yeah I think he has a nice green one he made especially for you. It has a cute little elf on the front of it,' Peter sniggered.

'You'll look great in it,' Daryl laughed. 'Green's a very good colour on you.'

'Goes with your eyes,' Peter finished.

'Be careful,' Uncle Patrick warned. 'It may be the season of goodwill but I can still change the rota and put you both on guard duty this evening.'

Peter and Daryl both looked horrified. 'You wouldn't,' Daryl breathed.

'Try me,' Uncle Patrick responded. He surveyed the room. 'Where is Murray?' he asked.

'He sent his apologies. He's on duty and can't get away,' Daryl said.

'It's a real shame,' said Peter. 'He absolutely loves Christmas.'

'He's here with us in spirit though,' Daryl said pointing at Peter's lurid blue jumper.

The conversation was interrupted by a scrabbling sound and a sandy coloured head popped up above the top of the table.

'Flash!' Daryl exclaimed. 'Where have you been?'

'He's been begging for scraps in the kitchen again,' Peter said. 'Look, he's got gravy all over his whiskers.'

With a single bound, Flash Gordon had leapt onto the vacant chair next to Peter. He licked Peter's hand as he tickled him under the chin.

The dog looked completely ridiculous with a pair of reindeer antlers on his head and his chequered bandana replaced by a woollen scarf.

'Even Flash is getting into the Christmas spirit,' Peter said. 'Look at the new scarf that Murray knitted for him.'

'Why does a dog need a woollen scarf when he's covered in fur?' I asked.

Daryl glanced at me in mock despair. 'MaryAnn, Christmas is not just for people, dogs celebrate it too.'

The Christmas meal was a revelation. I discovered a totally different side to Peter. It was obvious that he had a very close bond with Daryl. They laughed and joked and finished off each other's sentences like an old married couple. They recounted some hilarious stories about botched missions and near misses and I found myself laughing more than I had in a long time.

The first course arrived as soon as we took our seats. It was vegetable soup. Despite the sandwich I'd eaten only a short time ago I was starving again. The soup was great and I emptied my bowl.

The bowls had been cleared away and I was laughing at a story that my brother was telling about a pack of Alsatian dogs that had chased Peter through the woods during a patrol. It was horrifying and shouldn't have been funny, but Daryl and Peter told it in a way that was so hilarious that I was laughing hard enough to make my sides ache. My attention was drawn to a man who was strolling towards our table with a massive platter in his hands. He placed the platter down on the table in front of me.

'What's that?' I croaked, pointing at its contents.

Peter considered me curiously. 'What's wrong with you?'

Uncle Patrick understood straightaway. 'It's a turkey,' he said.

I felt a bit light headed. 'A turkey,' I whispered. 'You mean it's a bird, a real live bird?'

Peter was still staring at me curiously. He raised a questioning eyebrow at Daryl. 'I don't think the bird's alive MaryAnn, in fact it looks pretty dead to me.' He poked at it with his fork as if to emphasise his point.

'Remember, there are no animals in the Neighbourhood,' Daryl explained. 'So they only eat synth meat.'

'Oh yeah,' Peter responded. 'Of course, I always thought that was a bit weird.'

'Weird!' I whispered faintly. 'You think it's weird that we don't eat flesh. It's . . .' I struggled to find the right words to explain how I felt. 'It's barbaric and disgusting.'

Peter smirked and then he leant across the table and ripped a leg off the turkey. He tore off a chunk of meat with his teeth and smacked his lips with exaggerated relish.

'Tastes blooming lovely though,' he said through a mouthful of food.

I grimaced as he chewed the flesh with such obvious pleasure.

'Peter!' Uncle Patrick warned. 'Stop teasing her. It's not fair. Eating flesh is repulsive to people in the Neighbourhood.'

I looked away from Peter determined to ignore his teasing and addressed Daryl. 'So you eat flesh now?'

Daryl nodded a little sheepishly as he leant over and helped himself to a slice of meat.

'You look a little bit pale MaryAnn,' Peter said through another mouthful of flesh. He was somehow able to grin and eat at the same time.

'Ignore Peter,' Uncle Patrick said, shooting the boy a poisonous look. 'You don't have to eat the meat. There are plenty of vegetables and roast potatoes too.'

The table was loaded with vegetables and potatoes and they were all delicious, but I was relieved when the meal was finished and the remains of the bird were cleared away. After the turkey was removed the dessert was served. It was a Christmas pudding with an excellent real milk custard. I had two helpings it was so delicious.

The meal was concluded with mince pies and elderflower wine. Peter brushed some crumbs off the front of his jumper and excused himself. 'Got to go and get ready for my star turn,' he said. 'Back soon.'

'Where's he off to?' I asked as he left the table.

'You'll find out soon enough,' Daryl responded mysteriously.

The wine was excellent and I was on my second glass and feeling a little bit fuzzy headed when I heard a blast of loud music. I watched in amazement as a full brass band exited the tunnel into the Market. The band was playing Rudolf the Red Nosed Reindeer and everyone in the cave began to clap and stamp their feet loudly in time to the music.

The band was followed closely by a large sleigh which lurched unsteadily on top of four giant wheels. At the front of the sleigh were twelve wooden reindeer with space between for a person to fit inside so they could pull the sleigh along. Seated on top of the sleigh was a very large, very jolly Father Christmas.

'Ho ho ho Merry Christmas,' his voice boomed out around the cavern. 'I'm here to see all the good boys and girls.'

The children in the room squealed loudly and as the sleigh came to a halt in the middle of the cavern they clambered around it in excitement.

Father Christmas was perfect. He was fat and jolly and all the children adored him. They fought to take turns to sit on his knee and shouted excitedly when he handed them a present. Despite the white beard and large protruding belly there was something familiar about him, but I couldn't recognise what it was. Then Father Christmas looked over to our table and winked at my brother, who blew a kiss back in return.

NO it couldn't be!

'That isn't Peter is it?' I asked Daryl.

'Yeah, he does this every year to entertain the kids.' There was an amused smile on this face. 'He made the sleigh himself. He works on it all year around, makes a lot of the toys as well. The kids adore him.'

'I can't believe it,' I said. 'He always seems so . . .'

Daryl glanced across the table at me. 'He always seems so what?'

'Well so rude and irritable all the time,' I said.

Daryl was quiet as he considered this for a moment. I remembered the way the girls had reacted to Peter outside the cave and Daryl's silence told me all that I needed to know.

'He only behaves like that with me, doesn't he?'

Daryl shook his head. 'He's my best friend and a really good guy. Everyone likes him.'

'Well I don't,' I said. 'I think he's horrible.'

'You shouldn't be so hard on him,' Daryl said. 'Our family hasn't exactly been kind to him.'

'But he likes you. You're his best friend.'

'We've been through a lot together and he knows I had no love for our parents or for the Light.'

'But I still don't understand why he hates me so much.'

'I think you're being a bit dramatic MaryAnn. I don't think he hates you . . . and . . . well, you can be a bit difficult sometimes.'

I felt a flash of annoyance. 'Difficult! What's that supposed to mean?'

'Well, sometimes you can be a bit full of yourself. It's not your fault,' he added quickly when I scowled at him. 'It's the burden of being an Alpha. It makes you believe that you're privileged in some way and that other people are here to serve you.'

'I do not,' I said indignantly. 'I do not think I'm privileged and I don't expect other people to serve me.' I was so annoyed my voice had risen an octave or two and a few people stared in our direction.

I saw Peter glance over at us briefly.

Uncle Patrick made a shushing noise. 'It's Christmas. This isn't the time for petty family arguments.'

I flushed with embarrassment. 'I just don't think I'm full of myself,' I hissed across the table at Daryl.

'Really!' he hissed back at me. 'So you didn't treat Peter like a servant when you first met him?'

'No of course not,' I said indignantly. Then I paused as I remembered my annoyance at Peter when he didn't open the car door for me, how frosty I'd been towards him. How I'd planned to complain to Daryl. I blushed a deep shade of red.

'I thought so,' Daryl whispered back.

'He told you?' I asked.

Daryl shrugged non-committally. 'No, but I guessed something was wrong when he arrived at the farmhouse in such a foul mood. He was also furious that you were twenty minutes late to the meeting. That type of behaviour can get people killed. He risked his life to meet you and you treated him with complete disregard.'

I was appalled. I hadn't meant to put him in danger. 'I didn't realise.'

'It's not the same on the Outside MaryAnn. Being an Alpha doesn't mean the same as it does in the Neighbourhood. You shouldn't expect special treatment here.'

I considered his comment, feeling slightly ashamed at my behaviour.

'I know it's a lot to learn,' Daryl's tone was kinder now. 'It was hard for me when I first left the Neighbourhood too. You'll get used to it.'

'I feel dreadful,' I said. 'Now I understand why he's been so unfriendly towards me.'

'I don't think Peter meant to be unfriendly. He really is a nice guy,' Daryl continued. 'I know that Christmas is a difficult time for him and he's been a little bit on edge lately.'

This piqued my curiosity. 'Why is Christmas a difficult time for him?'

'Four years ago, about a week before Christmas, the Watch raided his family's dairy farm. Peter's family are Echo but Peter was tested Immune and reassigned Delta. The Watch arrived to take him away but his family refused to hand him over. They took his father into custody and shot the rest of the family. Peter escaped because he was dropping off gifts at a neighbour's farm and the Watch couldn't find him. He arrived home to find his family tied up in the kitchen, shot through the head.'

I stared at Daryl in horror. 'I didn't know,' I breathed, trying to imagine what it must have been like for Peter to arrive home and find that his whole family had been murdered.

'He doesn't talk about it much,' Daryl said. 'Not even to me. He came to the Union and asked Uncle Patrick for help to find his father, but it was already too late.'

'He was already dead,' I whispered. 'Our father signed the death warrant.' I remembered the piece of paper Uncle Patrick had shown me at our last meeting.

'That's when he decided to join the Unionists,' he continued. 'It was the same year that I met Patrick and ran away from home. I thought Peter would hate me after what our father did to his family. But he didn't, even though other people were suspicious of me and gave me a hard time, Peter never did.'

'It was because he felt that you were in the same situation. You'd both lost your families. Maybe you'd lost them in different ways, but you were still on your own,' Uncle Patrick interrupted.

'I never thought of it like that,' Daryl said as he gave Flash an absentminded pat on the head.

'Peter has a talent for understanding other people and putting himself in their shoes. He saw that you were suffering in the same way he was and so he became your friend.'

Daryl was thoughtful for a moment. 'Yeah, that sounds like something that Peter would do,' he said.

I observed Peter with a newfound respect. I wasn't sure that I would be able to behave in the same manner: dress up as Father Christmas and act so jolly if my family had been murdered at Christmas. At least it explained his behaviour earlier in the evening, the reason why he was so quiet on the journey to the caves and why he hadn't wanted to talk to me about it. I wouldn't have wanted to discuss it with anyone either.

The big meal and the elderflower wine were beginning to make me feel drowsy and I slumped into my chair with my eyes half closed. I was contented just to be here with my family and let their conversations wash over me.

Peter had finished handing out presents and returned to our table. He'd changed back into his jeans and garish Christmas jumper and was laughing loudly at a joke Daryl had just made. A band had taken to the raised platform at the bottom of the cavern and some of the Unionists were dancing. I noticed that Brandon was on the dance floor, his arms wrapped around a pretty blonde girl.

'This is the best Christmas ever,' I murmured. 'I love being here with all of you.'

'What did you say?' Daryl glanced over at me.

'I said, it's the best Christmas ever and I love being here with you all.' My words slurred slightly.

Daryl smiled. 'You're drunk,' he said. 'Who knew my little sister couldn't hold her drink.'

'Stop making fun of me,' I murmured. 'Can you believe that I thought that this was going to be the worst Christmas ever and that I would be alone? But here I am with all of you and it's been better than I could ever have imagined.'

There was a silence around the table and my uncle frowned slightly.

'You know you're not alone MaryAnn.'

''S not true,' I slurred. 'I'm alone most of the time.'

Even in my drunken haze I realised I was bringing down the mood of the party and I didn't want to ruin the evening. 'It doesn't matter though.' I forced a smile. 'I'm used to it now and I'm fine. It's not so lonely anymore. Not now I have my family.'

Uncle Patrick leant forward and held my gaze for a moment. 'Things will get better,' he murmured. 'I promise.'

'I know they will,' I whispered back.

The band struck up a folksy happy tune and Daryl grabbed my hand. 'Come on. I love this song. Let's dance?' Before I had chance to respond he'd dragged me to my feet and we were whirling around the dance floor. Most of the steps were unfamiliar so Daryl had to teach them to me and soon I was able to keep time with the music without disgracing myself too much. As soon as the song ended the band struck up another tune, this time the song included a fiddle and a harmonica. The music was fast and furious and Daryl twirled me round and round the dance floor until my head was spinning and I was breathless. He seemed to know all the songs and sang and whooped along to the music.

This was much more fun than the dancing in the Neighbourhood; everyone together in couples, happily holding hands and swinging each other around the dance floor. In the Neighbourhood everyone would keep their distance. Somehow together but physically separate.

Once I'd grown used to holding onto Daryl's hand I began to relax and enjoy myself. Each song seemed to be filled with hope and expectation and the promise of a better future . . . or maybe that was just the elderflower wine talking.

The band played their final song and as we left the dance floor an expectant hum filled the room.

'I think they're expecting a speech,' Peter said.

Uncle Patrick got to his feet and a hush descended across the Market. He surveyed the room with a warm smile.

'Unionists, Stewards, friends and family,' I felt a flush of happiness as he glanced in my direction when he said '*family*'.

'I'm happy to be spending another Christmas with you all. Each year as I stand before you, I look out across the room and see our numbers growing and our movement increasing in strength. I'm proud to be part of this brave group of people who want to stand up and fight against the oppression of the Light and to say NO MORE . . . no more to hunger and no more to oppression.

The Light call us Ferals and demonise us, but as I stand here before you all, I see no demons, I see only mothers, fathers, sisters and brothers working side by side to build a better future and I'm proud to call myself one of you.'

The crowd gave an appreciative roar.

'And so we celebrate another Christmas Eve and soon we will move into a new year, but we cannot leave this year without looking back over our losses and remembering at this important time the people who can't be with us. Our fallen comrades who made the ultimate sacrifice to keep us safe. I have their names here and I want to read them to you so we can reflect on each life, given in bravery, sacrificed to our great cause.'

He pulled a folded piece of paper out of the top pocket of his shirt and in a clear voice began to read out a long list of names. I noticed a number of tears among the Unionists and for a moment I felt a pang of jealousy that they were able to openly mourn their losses among their friends. This was something I could never do. Any feelings I had for my parents had to be buried deep inside. It's easy to mourn the brave and the good, but what about the monsters, the killers? My eyes prickled with tears and someone pressed a glass firmly into my hand. 'Drink,' Peter whispered as if he had read my mind.

I accepted the glass from him and took a large gulp of wine. There was an explosion of warmth in my stomach and I instantly felt a little better. I gave him a smile of thanks.

'To a year filled with hope and freedom,' Uncle Patrick concluded his speech, raising his wine glass high in the air.

'And free from bloody taxes,' called out a voice from among the crowd. Everyone laughed warmly and then raised their glasses high in the air. 'Hope and freedom,' they chorused loudly.

When the shouting had receded the band struck up a tune and soon the cavern was ringing with voices. I didn't recognise the tune. Peter told me that it was an old protest song and that a long time ago the Union had adopted it as their anthem. I listened to the Unionists sing the chorus:

'The Union forever
defending our rights
Down with the Light,
all Echo unite
With our brothers and our sisters
from far across the land
There is power in the Union.'

I'd never heard people singing with such passion before and for a moment it almost brought a lump to my throat. As the song came to an end the Unionists stamped their feet loudly in appreciation and the band took a final bow before leaving the stage. All around us people began to get up from the tables and rowdily leave the cavern.

'I think it's time to get you home MaryAnn,' Uncle Patrick said. 'It's getting late and we need to make sure you're safely back in the Director's house before dawn.'

I realised the night had to come to an end, but even so my heart dropped a little at the thought of leaving my family. I'd had such a great evening I didn't want to go back to the Director's house.

Uncle Patrick must have sensed the change in my mood because he asked if he could hug me goodbye. I was pleased that he still had enough respect for the Neighbourhood traditions to ask my permission and the wine must have lowered my inhibitions because I agreed to his request. I'd barely responded with a nod when he grabbed me into a fierce hug. It was a long time since anyone had hugged me like that and for a moment I recoiled in shock, but soon I was able to relax a little and even found that I enjoyed it.

'Everything's going to be fine,' he said patting me gently on the back. 'We'll see you soon.' He pushed me away from him and held me at arm's length so he could look me in the eyes. 'Won't we?' There was a question in his voice.

I realised that it was my decision. If I wanted to see Uncle Patrick and Daryl again then the next step was up to me.
I didn't even hesitate. Of course I wanted to see them again. After this evening I couldn't imagine going back to my empty life at the Director's house, but I had to be clear about one thing. 'I want to see you again, but I won't join your group,' I said. 'I haven't changed my mind about that. I can't be a Unionist.'

'I can't say I understand your decision, but I can accept it,' Uncle Patrick said. 'For now.'

'We'll need to find some way to stay in touch,' I said.

Uncle Patrick rummaged in his pocket and extracted a white envelope which he handed to me. 'A little Christmas present,' he said.

I opened the envelope and found a thin chip inside. I cradled it in the palm of my hand and waited for an explanation.

'We use the Portal to communicate with our operatives working inside the Neighbourhood. The chip will allow you to access our Portal site. We use a public site so we don't raise any suspicions. We hide on one of the pages and leave coded messages for each other.'

'It's easy once you get the hang of it.' Peter explained. 'You just need to make sure the chip is inserted into your PortPad so you can read the encrypted Contacts.'

'I'm Luke Skywalker,' Daryl said, making the whooshing sound of a lightsaber.

'What?' I responded, confused at the sudden change in direction of the conversation.

'Yoda I am,' said Peter with a grin.

'You're not making any sense, either of you.'

'They're our code names. We took character names from Star Wars. We thought it would be cool,' Daryl said.

Uncle Patrick rolled his eyes. 'Not my idea,' he responded. 'Using the Portal to hide messages was Daryl's brainwave. We were able to boost the signal so that we could piggyback off the Neighbourhood's bandwidth. I left Daryl and Peter to set it up – unsupervised,' he grimaced as he said the word unsupervised.

'Your code name is Ewok,' Daryl said. He was barely suppressing a smile.

'Ewok! I don't even like Star Wars,' I protested. 'Why can't I choose my own code name?'

'What, from one of those stupid reality shows you like so much?' Daryl sniggered.

'Or maybe one of those stupid makeover shows,' Peter taunted. 'I bet you like those too?'

Daryl gave Peter a high five. 'You're right on the money my friend; she loves all of those dumb shows.'

'Well at least I'm not wasting time watching old films from years ago that no-one even cares about anymore,' I complained. 'You weren't even born when that film was made.'

'Well there haven't been any proper films made since the Virus so our viewing is pretty limited. We had to go *old skool*. Anyway we see it as our contribution to keeping quality media alive. Sticking up two fingers to celebrity shows that actually make watching paint dry seem interesting,' Daryl said.

'We did have another name for you,' Peter said.

'Really! Was it better than some stupid furry creature from a boring old sci-fi film?'

Peter swooped down low and placed his hands protectively over Flash Gordon's ears. 'Hey let's have a little less negativity about furry creatures shall we? You'll upset Flash.'

The dog peered up at me with a mournful expression.

'You said you had another code name for me?'

'Yeah,' Peter sighed wistfully, 'but Patrick vetoed complete pain in the a -'

'He's joking, he's joking,' Daryl said quickly as I stepped towards Peter with my fist clenched. 'Anyway we think Ewok is the perfect code name for you.'

'Yeah, because you're always so cute and cuddly,' Peter winked at me.

I chose to ignore both the comment and the wink. I wasn't going to let him antagonise me any further. 'What about Uncle Patrick?' I asked. 'What's his code name?'

'Ah, Uncle Patrick, there's only one character he could be isn't there? . . . Obi Wan.'

Uncle Patrick shook his head sorrowfully. 'As I said previously I had no hand in this, I left it entirely up to Daryl and Peter. Now of course I curse my naivety.'

'Come on Uncle Patrick, Obi Wan is a bona fide Jedi Master, how cool is that? It's an honour to be named after him.'

'If you weren't two of my best operatives I'd have had you locked in a cell by now,' Uncle Patrick growled.

'So the Portal site you hide out on is a Star Wars fan site?' I asked.

'Oh no, nothing as cool as that,' Daryl responded. 'It's a sci-fi website. We have a number of operatives in the Neighbourhood and they all work in coded units based on sci-fi films. It's a work of genius if I do say so myself,' Daryl said with a hint of pride in his voice. 'The Watch will never figure it out.'

'Yes, indeed a real work of genius,' Uncle Patrick interrupted sarcastically. 'Now if you've finished congratulating yourself I think it's about time that MaryAnn was heading home. It's going to be light soon.'

'Why does no-one ever appreciate my genius,' Daryl complained dejectedly.

'Most genius isn't appreciated until after you're dead mate . . . I'll make sure you get a good eulogy,' Peter joked.

Daryl made a gesture that would have got him grounded if we had been at home. Peter laughed loudly and then addressed me. 'You ready?' he asked. Reluctantly I told him that I was ready to go.

Uncle Patrick hugged me again and I didn't mind so much that he didn't ask permission this time. 'Take care MaryAnn. Just be careful with the chip. It should be safe, but we never know which sites the Watch are monitoring so only post a Contact when it's absolutely necessary.'

Next it was Daryl's turn to pull me into a tight hug and despite myself I squeezed him back just as tightly. 'I don't want to let you go,' he whispered into my ear. 'I can't bear the thought of you living with those people.'

I pulled away from him. 'It's okay,' I responded, trying to sound offhand. 'They treat me well, you know they do.'

Peter interrupted, 'Come on, we need to be going. It'll be light soon.' After giving Flash Gordon a quick pat, Peter ushered me out of the cave and back onto the boat. This time I managed to climb on board without falling over and Peter gave me a short round of applause. I joined in with his good humour by giving a small curtsey.

I yawned all the way back up the river and when we exited the cave into the frigid morning air my legs felt like lead. Once we were in the truck I settled into my seat and closed my eyes. 'Wake me when we get to the Boundary,' I mumbled before falling fast asleep. There was no need for the blindfold this time.

It seemed like only a few seconds later when Peter was shaking my arm and telling me to wake the hell up.

'Charming,' I muttered as I clambered out of the cab, but somehow I didn't mind the fact that he was teasing me. I stumbled wearily to the Boundary and Peter politely held the wire open for me.

'I didn't know you had such good manners,' I said as I scrambled through to the Neighbourhood.

'You're so clumsy that after a few drinks of wine I'm worried you'll accidently bring down the whole Boundary and with it destroy the last remnants of civilisation,' he joked. 'So I'm not just helping you, I'm actually saving humanity.'

CHAPTER 13

Rebellion

As the truck drew closer to the Director's house I tried in vain to hold on to the happiness I'd felt in the cave. As my mood began to sour I had to resist the almost overwhelming urge to grab the steering wheel and force Peter to turn around and drive me back to my family.

'You okay?' Peter glanced over at me.

I painted a smile on my face. 'Fine,' I said. 'Just fine.'

He cocked an eyebrow in disbelief. 'Really,' he said. 'Are you telling me the truth?'

I tried to give a non-committal shrug. 'Yes,' I said, hoping he couldn't detect the waver in my voice.

There was a short silence as I stared out of the window blinking furiously, angry that my eyes were beginning to water. I didn't feel fine at all.

'I don't believe you,' Peter interrupted the silence. 'I don't think you're fine at all.'

'Can we not talk about this? I have to go back to the Director's house. So it doesn't matter whether I'm fine or not. It doesn't make any difference. This is just my life whether I like it or not.'

'Are you telling me that you'd rather live in the cave? Where you would have none of your things, none of your home comforts. You don't realise how hard it can be sometimes.' Peter sounded slightly incredulous and his tone made me angry.

'You think you know me,' I said, 'but you don't. You don't know what it's like living with the Director, knowing what the Light have been doing. I've seen that room remember. I know what's happening right under my feet and I still have to go back there and act like nothing's wrong . . . I don't know whether I can do it anymore.'

'Yes you can, MaryAnn.' His voice was firm. 'You'll do it because you have to. Everyone has to make a sacrifice and this has to be yours.'

I bit back a laugh. 'What you mean is that it's not such a great sacrifice is it, to live in luxury in the Director's house.'

'I didn't say that.'

'But that's what you were thinking.'

'Please don't put words in my mouth.'

'You just don't understand.'

'Of course not, how could I ever understand how you feel?' his tone was mocking. 'You're not that hard to read MaryAnn,' he said. 'I know how miserable you are. It's written all over your face.'

For some reason this comment irritated me more than anything else he'd said all evening. How dare he insinuate that he knew me, understood how I was feeling? 'It's got nothing to do with you,' I said huffily.

'I suppose it hasn't. I just thought you might want to talk about it.'

'What! Like you wanted to talk to me about what was bothering you earlier this evening.'

'That was none of your business.'

'Right! And this is none of yours.'

We finished the rest of the journey in silence. When we pulled up into the clearing close to the Director's house I made to climb out of the cab. Peter unexpectedly offered me an apology. 'I didn't mean to upset you,' he said. 'I just . . . I just don't like to see you so miserable. I wish you could come back and live with us if that's what would make you happy.'

'You mean that?' I asked. I was slightly incredulous.

'You're my best friend's sister,' he said offhandedly.

'You're almost family. Of course I want you to be happy.'

His apology was completely unexpected, but it seemed genuine so I took it in the spirit it was intended and I returned his apology with a grateful smile and a whispered 'Merry Christmas', before climbing out of the cab.

I watched him drive away and then I headed back into the tunnels. As I climbed into bed I remembered I'd meant to ask my uncle to explain his comment about Peter being reassigned Delta. I'd never heard that term before. As far as I was aware Echo was Echo and Delta was Delta. I'd never heard of anyone transferring between designations. It made a mental note to speak to him about it the next time we met.

I managed to grab a few hours sleep but was still tired when my alarm woke me. Despite my exhaustion I had to drag myself out of bed to face a full day of Christmas festivities in the Director's household.

We kicked off the day with brunch, which included a number of invited guests specially selected by the Director. I'd eaten a massive meal only a few hours earlier so wasn't particularly hungry but managed to force down some scrambled eggs with cheese. I'd never noticed how little taste there was to the synth cheese. It tasted nothing like the real thing. It made me wonder what real eggs actually tasted like too.

Following brunch we all retired to the formal drawing room where the Christmas tree was located. The tree was breath-taking. It was so tall that it reached the ceiling and had taken two whole days for the designer to decorate. It was styled in a red and gold theme with lights that weaved throughout its thick branches and twinkled in a number of complex patterns.

Presents had been arranged in piles around the tree and the Director had made sure there was a gift for everyone. He was at his most charming as he handed out the lavishly wrapped packages to his guests. He had a ready smile and well placed compliment for each of them. It seemed phoney and insincere to me, but I could see the other guests were completely taken in by his act. A number of the younger women even blushed and lowered their eyes to the ground when he addressed them directly.

The Director gave me a beautiful brooch decorated with red and green stones. I suspected that he hadn't purchased it himself but instead had arranged for one of his staff to buy it. My suspicions were confirmed when Maud opened her package and received exactly the same gift. She didn't seem upset at all and smiled in delight, thanking the Director profusely.

Maud had bought me a diary, to write down '*my thoughts*' she said. It was a nice idea but considering my situation I suspected that '*my thoughts*' could prove incredibly dangerous.

I'd bought Maud a jewelled compact mirror. I remembered that she had once admired mine and she didn't have one of her own. She was absolutely delighted with it.

It was early afternoon by the time we'd finished opening the presents and the Delta servants had cleared away the discarded wrapping paper.

The Director had arranged for carol singers to entertain us until dinnertime. I welcomed the break as it meant I could sit back and relax without having to make the effort of talking to anyone. My busy night was starting to catch up with me and I felt incredibly weary.

Dinner involved five courses and I found myself seated next to Dr Butters and Maud. Dr Butters was very drunk and his cheeks were flushed with wine as he jovially told us to call him Julian. After ten minutes in his company I began to understand why my father referred to him as a blithering idiot. At first I tried to make polite conversation, but he was practically incoherent and seemingly unable to finish a sentence properly. He would begin to tell a story only to lose the thread of the conversation completely and then break into a loud laugh, his white-blonde fringe flopping into his eyes. I was relieved that Maud was sitting beside me as she was better practised at polite conversation. A few times she caught my eye and we both giggled quietly behind our napkins.

From my seat I was able to observe the Director at the other end of the table. His guests seemed to be hanging onto his every word. Occasionally there would be a stifled giggle or a loud guffaw of laughter and all attention at the table would be instantly drawn to the Director, to whatever joke or funny story he was entertaining his guests with. It was difficult for me to associate this smiling, friendly and affable man with the monster I knew him to be. I wondered how his guests would react if his true nature was revealed to them. I expected that they wouldn't believe the truth of it.

After coffee and liqueur chocolates Christmas was over for another year and I was able to go to bed. I was so tired all I could do was check my jewellery box to make sure the chip was safely tucked inside before climbing into bed and falling into a deep untroubled sleep.

Once Christmas was over the snow arrived and we spent most of January under a coating of white powder. Life returned to normal and Christmas with my family seemed like a distant memory. The highlight of my week was logging onto SciFiGeek.com to see if there were any messages from Daryl and Peter; or Luke Skywalker and Yoda as they referred to themselves. Usually they left me a message at least once a week to let me know they were alright. I didn't dare leave a response, remembering that Uncle Patrick had warned me to post a Contact only in an emergency.

As January slipped into February and the snow turned into a horrible grey sludge, the Director began to make his annual preparations for Boundary Day on the twentieth of February. This was the biggest day of the year for our community and a Neighbourhood holiday. The day started with a trip to the church for a remembrance service followed by the Director's public address, which he usually gave from the balcony of the Building of Light.

Each year a massive crowd gathered in the Square of Light to listen to the Director as he gave an all too familiar account of the history of the Neighbourhoods and the 'Select Neighbourhoods Project'. His image was projected around the square on large screens.

In his address the Director spoke of the Heroes; the doctors who had given their lives fighting the virus. He praised the chemists who had developed the vaccine; the engineers who built the Boundary to keep us safe and the Watch who protected us and maintained law and order. After his address we all sang the Neighbourhood anthem before returning home for a dinner of thanksgiving.

A massive construction project had been underway over the last six months to repair the Building of Light after it was partially destroyed on the night of the party. The Director was keen to ensure that it was ready in time for the celebrations.

In the weeks leading up to Boundary Day I noticed an increased number of Contacts on the Portal. I began to suspect that the Union was planning something to disrupt the Boundary Day celebrations and it scared me. Until now I'd respected Uncle Patrick's request that I only post in an emergency but the increasing number of Contacts worried me. I tried in vain to discover what was going on but all my questions were met with an ominous silence.

Boundary Day was a frosty cold day, but thankfully there was no rain. The day started with a visit to the Church. I found it hard to concentrate on the remembrance service because I was so worried about my family and Peter.

Once we'd said a final prayer the service came to an end with a rendition of the Director's favourite hymn and I listened as his strong voice rang out across the church.

'Abide with me; fast falls the eventide;
The darkness deepens; Lord with me abide.
When other helpers fail and comforts flee,
Help of the helpless, O abide with me.'

We all trooped out into the cold afternoon air to find the Director's car was waiting for us. I instantly recognised the chauffeur, it was Mr Murray who'd driven me to the mall just before Christmas. He gave me a warm smile as he held the door open for me and I bobbed my head in acknowledgement.

The journey to the Square of Light took us only fifteen minutes. When we arrived the square was empty, but I noticed a large queue of people congregated at the entrance waiting to be let in through the gates. Maud said that she'd read on the Portal that people had been queuing since early morning to get a good position in the square.

We entered the building through the front doors and the Director's aides led us up to the 'ready room' which was adjacent to the balcony. While there was a lot of construction work taking place inside the Building of Light, the façade was still intact as was the balcony where the Director traditionally gave his address.

The Director spent an hour in wardrobe and makeup preparing for his broadcast. This gave Maud and me an opportunity to sneak onto the balcony and watch the people file into the square below. As they entered the square each person respectfully laid a rose at the feet of the 'Hero'.

When the Director was ready to begin his address he beckoned us back inside. It was traditional that he lead the procession out onto the balcony. He took a sip from a glass of water and then indicated that he was ready for the ceremony to commence.

We all paraded onto the balcony and Maud and I took our positions in chairs to the left of the Director. My seat was at the very front of the balcony so I had a good view of the square below. I nervously examined the crowd and fervently hoped that the Union wasn't planning to disrupt the celebrations.

To my relief the Director's address went without a hitch. He began with the traditional Neighbourhood greeting. 'Good health and happiness,' he bellowed across the gathered crowd. 'In the Light we trust,' the crowd roared in response.

The Director's speech ended to rapturous applause and the first bars of the Neighbourhood anthem sounded out over the loudspeaker. I could hear the Director's voice ring out clear and strong around the square. After he'd sung the first few bars everyone joined in enthusiastically. I was so busy watching the square trying to catch a glimpse of any possible Unionists in the crowd that I forgot to sing. It wasn't until I noticed the Director staring pointedly at me that I remembered to mouth the familiar words.

We'd barely finished the first verse when the screens around the square flickered and cut away to black. In bold white text the words, 'We are here!' flashed onto the screen. The loudspeakers crackled loudly and the Neighbourhood anthem cut way to be replaced by the first bars of the song that I'd heard the Unionists sing on Christmas Eve. It took a few moments for the people in the square to realise that something was wrong. One by one they stopped singing until the only sound remaining was the music blasting out from the loudspeakers.

The words faded from the screen and were replaced by pictures of unfamiliar places that I didn't recognise. Places I assumed must be outside the Boundary. There were scenes of families sitting around tables eating food, people working on farms; sowing and harvesting crops. There were images of children playing football with parents at the side lines enthusiastically cheering them on; normal everyday family scenes. These were events that could have taken place inside the Boundary if it wasn't for the fields and open countryside.

By now the Director was aware that something was wrong and was screaming at his aides, 'Turn it off, turn it off.' Anxiety filled the ready room behind us as his team of aides scurried around in a state of panic.

The song from the loudspeakers swelled, becoming louder and louder. The countryside scenes faded away and were replaced by the image of a group of people standing tightly together, arms around each other singing the song of the Unionists. They all wore a mask and I noticed that each of the masks bore the face of a leading member of the Light. It was a humorous touch and I suspected that Daryl or Peter had a hand in it.

One of the aides crept onto the balcony and told the Director that they couldn't find the signal to turn off the transmission. The Director's face twisted with rage and my stomach tightened at the sight of it – this was the true face of the Director, the one that was capable of killing and torturing people. His mask had slipped for a moment and what I saw beneath terrified me to the core.

'Long live the Union,' a man wearing the face of the Director shouted loudly. The voice sounded like Uncle Patrick.

'Long live the Echo,' everyone chorused on screen. This chant continued for at least a minute before the screen faded to black and was replaced with an eerie silence.

The Director was incandescent with rage and the people in the square below were confused, waiting for an explanation.

'Director! Sir!' one of his aides exclaimed. 'You have to say something.'

The Director stared at his aide with a complete lack of comprehension. His face was a ghostly shade of white and a thin sheen of sweat covered his brow.

'Sir, they're waiting for you,' the aide gently coaxed. 'They're expecting you to say something.'

The Director gave a sharp intake of breath as he grasped the edge of the balcony and observed the crowd below. His face filled the screens around the square and the murmuring from the crowd faded away to be replaced by an expectant hush.

Slowly coming to his senses the Director addressed the crowd below. His speech was halting at first. 'This year we wanted to bring you something a little different . . . we . . . we . . . wanted to show you . . .' he paused hesitantly for a moment and then seemed to hit his stride. 'We wanted to show you our past, celebrate what life used to be like before the virus. The images you just saw came from old archive footage that we unexpectedly found in our library earlier this year. Now you can see what we are fighting for. The quality of family life that we want to preserve.'

Now that he'd hit his stride he lied effortlessly, never missing a beat. Astonishingly it looked like some of the people even believed him. I could see it in the way they gazed up at him; some of the older people were in tears, obviously remembering life before the virus. I couldn't quite believe they were so trusting. His words sounded hollow and fake to me.

'We wanted to end on a warning for the future. The Feral Echo who threaten our way of life are still Outside. Still coveting what we have worked so hard to build. We must remain vigilant against this threat, against the danger from people who want to tear this life from us.'

There was a roar of approval from the crowd as the speech came to an end. The Director left the balcony to cries of 'Long live the Light.' His mask was firmly back in place and once again he was in control.

When Maud and I followed the Director into the ready room we found that it was in a state of chaos. The Director's aides shouted and gestured wildly while tapping frantically at their PortPads. The Director marched confidently into the middle of the mayhem, barking orders at his staff and demanding to know what had gone wrong.

Maud and I hovered warily at the edge of the room, unsure what to do. I decided that given the Director's mood it was probably a good idea to remain as inconspicuous as possible. It took some time for him to remember about us and when he did he strode over to where we were standing. As he approached I noticed Maud step closer to me. Her face had drained of colour and she was shaking like a leaf.

'You girls shouldn't be here. You need to go back to the house,' he barked at us.

Maud nodded quickly, 'Yes, Director, we'll leave immediately.' She made as if to head to the door, but I didn't move. 'Will you be coming with us?' I asked.

The Director shook his head impatiently. 'No, I have work to do. Take the car and go back to the house and I'll see you later.' He turned back to his aides and seemed to immediately forget about us. As I left the room I heard him demand that the Unionists be rounded up like dogs and brought to justice.

It had been two days since the Boundary Day incident. We'd barely seen the Director and when he was at home he was in such a foul mood that Maud and I kept well out of his way. His rage was so palpable that I could almost see the waves of anger rippling across the surface of his skin. The Union had embarrassed the Director and he craved revenge.

I tried in vain to contact Daryl and Peter, but there was no response on SciFiGeek.com. I expected the Unionists were in hiding waiting for the situation to calm down. They must be well aware of the embarrassment suffered by the Director and the full extent of his rage.

While some of the more gullible citizens of the Neighbourhood seemed to have been taken in by his speech on Boundary Day, there were many others who were not so easily fooled. Questions were being raised on the Portal, people expressed fear that the Union was back and that the campaign of fear that had blighted the early days of the Neighbourhood would start again. People were even questioning the explosion in the Building of Light, expressing their disbelief that it had been caused by a faulty energy convertor – the explanation that had been so readily accepted by the people in the Neighbourhood last year. I'd never heard anyone question the Light before and definitely never seen any negative Contacts on the Portal. There was even concern that the Director had, albeit briefly, lost command of the Neighbourhood. Things were in danger of spiralling out of control.

CHAPTER 14

Rescue

By the end of the second day when I'd still had no response to the Contacts I'd left on the Portal I was in a complete state of panic and almost beside myself with worry. That evening Maud and I ate a very solemn dinner and barely spoke a word to each other. Even though the Director was eating dinner at the Building of Light his mood pervaded the whole house and the meal was a grim affair to say the least. We hadn't even bothered to dress for dinner, completely dispensing with our usual formality.

Maud played with the food on her plate, obviously concerned for her father. As soon as she'd finished eating she excused herself and went straight to bed without even suggesting that we watch Day2Day or play a game of cards like she usually did. I finished my meal alone and then retired to my room too.

I was shocked to find Peter in my bedroom, perched on the edge of my bed. For an instant my heart lifted at the sight of him.

He stared at me without a hint of a smile on his face. His grim faced look told me that he had bad news. News that I was certain I didn't want to hear.

'Are you here to fix another broken toilet?' I kept my voice light, delaying the moment, putting off the inevitable.

'MaryAnn!'

'You'd think someone would get suspicious about all the broken toilets around here,' I continued, refusing to meet his eyes.

'MaryAnn, sit down please.'

'I prefer to stand, thank you.'

'MaryAnn, you should sit down.'

'No, I want to stand,' I said resolutely. I wasn't quite sure why I was arguing with him. It didn't matter whether I was sitting or standing, the news would still be the same. I just felt the need to exert some control over the situation. I couldn't influence the news Peter was about to give me, but I could control what I was doing when I received it.

'It's Daryl, MaryAnn.'

I wanted to clamp my hands tightly over my ears to block out the rest of his sentence.

'He's been captured by the Watch.'

I heard the words, but it took a few moments to fully understand what they meant. 'Is he dead?' I finally asked. My voice was monotone and the lack of emotion surprised me. I could feel a scream building up deep inside, threatening to push its way out. I'd only just found my brother again. I couldn't lose him now.

'No, he's not dead, but the Legislate have taken him to the tunnels so they can interrogate him.'

I clasped my hand across my mouth in horror. Daryl was being taken to the room in the tunnels. My ears started to buzz loudly and Peter's face became blurry.

'MaryAnn, stay with me, we haven't got time for this.' Peter's voice was stern. He grabbed my shoulders and shook them. 'I knew this would happen, that's why I told you to sit down in the first place.'

My vision started to clear. 'They're going to interrogate him, aren't they?'

'Yes, that's why I'm here. We need your help. We need you to show us the way.'

'We?' I looked around the room expectantly.

'Patrick's on his way, he's going to wait for us in the tunnels. We can't risk him coming into the house. If he's discovered the whole place will go into lockdown.'

'You want me to take you down into the tunnels?' My voice came out strangled and unrecognisable.

'Yes, you're the only one who knows how to find the room. Do you think you can help us?' his tone was coaxing, like he was talking to a child.

The bile rose in my throat and I swallowed hard. I had to do this. I had to save Daryl. 'Of course,' I said, trying to sound braver than I felt.

Peter checked his watch. 'We should go.'

Uncle Patrick was waiting for us on the other side of the panel in the library. He looked dishevelled and dirty and his face wore the same grim look as Peter's. 'It's going to be alright,' he said when he saw me.

I wanted to believe him, but I'd seen the room in the tunnels and I had a sick feeling that it wasn't going to be alright at all.

When Uncle Patrick indicated that I should lead the way, I led them directly to the grate in the wall. Peter helped me to remove it and we crawled through to the other side. On the way to the room we passed the metal cages, but they were all empty apart from some ragged blankets on the floor of one of them.

As we approached the room I automatically slowed down keeping a look out for the Watch. Peter and Uncle Patrick were a few steps behind me, guns cocked at the ready. I stopped just short of the room. I couldn't bring myself to open the door. I didn't want to see Daryl strapped to that metal chair.

Uncle Patrick must have sensed my hesitation because he stepped around me and pressed his ear to the closed door. He listened for a few moments and then cautiously pushed it open. I heard him make a gagging noise as the pungent stench hit him. His body went rigid as his eyes surveyed the interior of the room. Peter joined Uncle Patrick at the door and he made a small choking sound. He glanced in my direction and as our eyes locked a look of understanding passed between us. Now he understood the full horror of the room and why I'd acted so hysterically in my bedroom.

'Daryl's not in here,' he said.

The relief that flooded over me was almost instantly replaced by an overwhelming sense of dread. If Daryl wasn't in the room then where was he?

'I don't know where else to look,' I said when I saw that Uncle Patrick and Peter were both staring expectantly at me.

'Those holding cells we passed a moment ago, were they definitely empty?' Peter asked.

'I think so,' I replied.

'Let's go and have another look.'

Uncle Patrick quickly pulled the door closed and we travelled back along the corridor. When we came to a halt outside the cages I heard a soft moan and the pile of blankets on the floor gave a small shudder.

'Daryl,' I breathed. It had to be Daryl! I pulled at the metal gate but it was locked. 'We need a key,' I hissed frantically.

'We don't need a key,' Uncle Patrick responded. 'Not when we have Peter.'

Peter pulled a metal tool out of his pocket and bent over the lock. After a few moments there was a loud click and the door swung open. I didn't waste time asking how Peter had opened the door, instead I flew past him and pulled frantically at the blankets. Daryl was underneath curled into a tight protective ball. I shook him gently and whispered his name. He stirred slowly and as he looked up at me I recoiled in horror. His face was a riot of purple bruises and his left eye had almost swollen shut. He stared at me through his one good eye.

'MaryAnn,' he croaked, 'what the hell are you doing here?'

'We've come to rescue you. Uncle Patrick and Peter are with me.'

He focussed on Uncle Patrick and Peter, standing behind me. 'You shouldn't have brought her here. What if you'd been captured?'

Peter crouched down beside me. 'Honestly mate, go easy on the gratitude, you're going to make me blush.'

'I didn't ask you to rescue me.'

'True, but we have that pesky motto, remember: *never leave the captured dim-wit behind* . . . and today my friend, you're the dim-wit.'

'You still shouldn't have brought MaryAnn with you.'

'We needed her to show us the way.'

'Hey,' I interrupted. 'I'm old enough to make my own decisions.'

Daryl glared at me with his one good eye.

'Apparently not,' Peter said.

'You think you can walk?' Uncle Patrick asked Daryl. When he responded with a mumbled '*Yes*', Uncle Patrick and Peter gently grasped him under each arm and pulled him painfully to his feet. He barely seemed to have the strength to stand and swayed alarmingly.

'Whoa,' said Uncle Patrick. 'Easy, I've got you. It's okay, just lean on me.' Daryl leant heavily against his uncle. Just getting to his feet seemed to have exhausted him and his breathing was coming in short ragged gasps.

My uncle and Peter exchanged worried glances. 'I must say Daryl, you've really got yourself into a right pickle this time,' Peter said.

'I'll be okay,' Daryl said. 'Let's go.'

The journey back down the tunnel was painstakingly slow. Daryl could barely stand and he needed the support of both Uncle Patrick and Peter just to remain on his feet.

When we arrived back at the wall that separated the two tunnels

Uncle Patrick asked Daryl if he could crawl through.

Daryl looked a little dubious, 'Do I have a choice?'

'Not really,' Uncle Patrick responded.

With great effort Daryl crouched down onto all fours and Uncle Patrick and Peter pushed, pulled and dragged him through to the other side. I took up the rear and carefully replaced the grate.

By the time we exited the tunnels Daryl was barely conscious and Uncle Patrick and Peter were sweating with the effort of carrying his dead weight.

Uncle Patrick faced me. 'Thanks for your help MaryAnn, but you must get back to the house before anyone discovers you're missing.'

I looked at him puzzled for a moment and then I understood what he was saying. I shook my head, horrified at the thought of going back to the house. 'No I can't go back. I'm coming with you.'

'MaryAnn!'

I stopped my uncle with a determined shake of my head. 'I have to be with Daryl. He needs me.'

'Don't worry we'll take good care of him. You have to go back to the house.'

'I can't go back. Not after everything that's happened. I want to come with you.' I was ashamed to hear the pleading tone in my voice.

Uncle Patrick's expression was hard. 'This is where you belong, MaryAnn. We can't take you with us.'

'You don't want me to go with you?'

Uncle Patrick sighed loudly. 'This isn't about what I want or what you want for that matter. You have to stay here because this is where you belong and believe it or not this is the safest place for you at the moment. After the incident on Boundary Day the Watch are determined to hunt us down. It's not safe for you Outside. You're much safer here. For the moment the Director doesn't seem to suspect you.'

'For the moment! Great, that's very reassuring.' In my panic I was shouting at him. 'What happens when he does suspect me? Do I become collateral damage?'

'MaryAnn,' Uncle Patrick's voice was sharp. 'Stop behaving like a child.'

'But I am a child. I'm fifteen. How else am I supposed to behave?'

'You stopped being a child when you found out the truth about the Light. Now you're a soldier in this war just like the rest of us.'

I didn't like the sound of that. I'd never agreed to be a soldier and this wasn't my war. I just wanted to be with Daryl.

'Maybe we should take her with us Patrick. It might not be safe for her to stay here.' I gave Peter a grateful smile. It was comforting to know that he was on my side.

But Uncle Patrick was resolute and there was no persuading him. I was to remain in the Director's house on my own. In the end I had no option but to reluctantly agree to stay behind. I was furious with him, but he didn't seem to care.

'We'll take good care of Daryl. I promise you.'

I truly believed that he would but it didn't stop the knot in my stomach tightening as they walked away. I had to resist the urge to race after them and fall to my knees and beg them to take me with them. I was scared to death and didn't want to go back to the Director's house.

Before they disappeared out of sight Peter gave me a brief wave. I think he was telling me not to worry, but it didn't make me feel any better.

I shivered and headed back towards the house. By the time I made it back to my bedroom I was exhausted and fell into bed fully clothed.

CHAPTER 15

Discovery

It seemed like I'd only just closed my eyes when I was woken by a noise in my room. My eyes flew open to find the Director standing by the side of my bed. He smelt of aftershave and soap and I inhaled deeply; a lovely clean smell. He was staring down at me, his hands clasped behind his back.

I was puzzled. The Director had never come into my room unannounced before. He surveyed me silently without saying a word. His eyes narrowed; I'd seen that look before on nature programmes. It reminded me of a hunter stalking its prey.

I pulled myself up into a sitting position. 'Director, you surprised me. Is everything okay?' I tried to keep my voice as light as possible, although I could feel my heart begin to pound loudly in my chest.

'Sorry to disturb you this early in the morning MaryAnn but I have some business to take care of.' His voice was calm, almost devoid of emotion.

'Business?' I queried. I heard my voice come out as a high pitched squeak.

The Director didn't respond but stood perfectly still letting an uncomfortable silence grow between us. I fidgeted uneasily in my bed and had to fight the urge to say something. My instinct was to fill the void with inane babble. Just when I thought I could bear it no longer he spoke.

'I have some questions for you,' he said. 'Do you feel up to answering them?' His voice was measured, giving nothing away. All I could do was shrug in response.

'Good, good. I'm glad you're being reasonable. I was hoping you could help solve a little mystery for me.'

When I didn't make an effort to respond he continued. 'It seems we had some unexpected visitors to the house last night.' Again there was an expectant pause. This time I understood that he was waiting for an answer. My nerves jangled a warning; he was setting a trap.

'Visitors!' I echoed weakly. 'I didn't hear any visitors. I was really tired so I went to bed early.' Even to my own ears my voice sounded pitchy and unconvincing.

His eyebrows shot up in mock surprise. 'You were able to sleep even when the SanTech was fixing your sink?'

Peter! 'Oh, the SanTech,' I blurted out. 'I forgot about him. Yes he fixed the sink and then I went to bed after he left.'

'Ah, I'm glad it's fixed,' the Director said coolly, 'and not causing you any further inconvenience.' There was something about the tone of his voice that warned me that the trap had just sprung closed around me.

'Just one interesting point,' the Director continued. 'I recently installed a camera in the corridor and yesterday it showed a SanTech coming into your room. Then it showed you leaving the room with him fifteen minutes later. Even more interesting was the fact that you returned hours later and this time you were alone and there was no SanTech with you. I checked the security logs and it appears that he never left the premises. According to my records he's still here somewhere . . . maybe he's still in your bathroom fixing your sink?' He raised an eyebrow in enquiry as he examined the room. I detected not a trace of humour in his voice.

The trap had closed and I was well and truly caught in its grasp. We'd made a stupid mistake. Peter had left through the tunnels which meant he was still logged into the security system.

'You've been spying on me?' I said weakly. It was the only response I could think of.

The Director's manner was so calm that for a brief moment I thought that I might be able talk my way out of the situation and convince him that he was mistaken. However as I studied him a little more closely I realised that while his tone was calm his body language betrayed him. The Director was coiled as tightly as a spring; his fists clenched rigidly by his sides so that the half-moon of his knuckles showed bone white against his skin. The sight of those half-moons made my stomach churn anxiously. Every nerve in my body screamed that I should run, but there was nowhere to go. I was trapped in the Director's house.

'Creeping around my house in the dark makes you look like a criminal MaryAnn.' The Director's eyes had narrowed into barely visible slits. He reminded me of a snake poised to attack. 'Do you want to tell me where you really were yesterday evening?'

I stared at him wide eyed, my mouth opening and closing like a goldfish. The one thing I was absolutely sure of was that he knew exactly where I'd been, but I wasn't sure how much else he knew . . . did he know about Daryl? About the rescue?

The Director's voice interrupted my reverie. 'I asked you to tell me where you were yesterday evening MaryAnn.' He spoke slowly and clearly, taking his time to carefully form each word.

I still didn't answer.

'Do you think that playing dumb will save you?'

I shook my head robotically.

'So maybe you can tell me what I want to know?'

'I don't know what you want me to say,' I squeaked.

'I want you to tell me how you went down into the tunnels with your SanTech friend to rescue your Unionist brother.'

At least that answered my question. He knew everything. There was nothing left for me to hide.

There was a nasty smile on the Director's face. 'What you didn't know is that we set up a little trap for you and your friends. We took your brother into custody hoping that the Unionists would come back for him. Fortunately we were able to tag him with a tracer before you were kind enough to rescue him. At this very moment we have a number of our best trackers following him over the Boundary to the Union hideout. Then we'll exterminate them all like dirty sewer rats.' He spat out the last part of the sentence and some of his spittle hit me in the face. I didn't dare wipe it away.

I was terrified for my family and for Peter. They were in serious danger and there was no way I could warn them. More immediate though, was an overwhelming concern for my own safety. Taking a deep breath to steel my nerves I asked the Director what was going to happen to me.

'Interesting question,' the Director responded. 'I thought as you've shown such an interest in the tunnels that you might like to spend some time down there as my guest.'

An image of the gore ridden chair flashed unbidden into my mind. I realised that this was going to be my fate and I was terrified. I had to fight the urge to run to the toilet and throw up.

'I should leave you to get dressed,' the Director said. 'When you're ready the Watch will escort you to your new home.' He waved a hand around the bedroom. 'Unfortunately it won't be as luxurious as your current accommodations.'

He headed to the door. As he passed by my desk he picked up my phone and PortPad. 'I'll take these with me. Wouldn't want you to alert your Unionist friends,' he said as he left the room. He closed the door behind him with a determined click.

I climbed out of bed in a daze. The room in the tunnels had featured so prominently in my nightmares that I couldn't believe this was going to be my future. Without my phone or PortPad I had no way of calling for help. I was on my own.

To quell the rising panic that was starting to claw at my throat I focussed on slowly opening drawers and pulling out some clean clothes to wear. I laid the clothes out carefully on my bed, brushing out any creases. Then I quickly showered and changed.

As I brushed my hair I surveyed myself critically in the mirror. This was probably the last outfit I would ever wear and I wondered why I'd chosen something as drab as a pair of khaki trousers and a blue button down shirt. Maybe I should have chosen one of my nice frocks so I could go out in style.

I imagined the look on the Director's face as I stepped into the room in the tunnels wearing one of my ball gowns and I stifled a manic giggle. I could feel the hysteria swell and threaten to take control so I moved over to the window seat and sat down heavily. It was raining outside and I traced the faltering tracks of the raindrops down the window pane with my index finger. Focussing my mind on the mundane seemed to help keep the hysteria at bay. My greatest fear, apart from the torture, was the secrets that I held inside my head. I wasn't a trained soldier; I was a coward. I'd never stand up to interrogation. I would tell the Director everything and in doing so could cause the deaths of countless people. Knowing that I was going to die terrified me, but what scared me even more was the damage I could do in the hours before I died.

There was a light knock at the door and I froze in anticipation; the Watch had arrived to take me away. I didn't bother to respond. The time for good manners was over.

The door opened, but it wasn't the Watch who entered, to my

surprise it was Maud. Her sallow complexion was even paler than normal and she surveyed me through a pair of red rimmed eyes. Finally she seemed to find her voice.

'How could you?' she hissed through tightly clenched teeth. 'How could you do this to us? After all we've done for you?'

'Maud, please . . .'

'The Director took care of you and this is how you repay him. How could you do this to us?' I was stunned. I'd never seen Maud angry before and now she was standing in front of me visibly shaking with rage.

'The Watch had my brother. They would have tortured him.' I was astonished when the mention of torture didn't illicit any response from her. She didn't even appear to flinch. There was something about the way she held my gaze that made me squirm. I didn't want to believe it, it was too grotesque but I had to ask. 'You knew didn't you? About the torture?'

Her eyes took on a bright, almost zealous, glow. 'The Director has to make difficult decisions for the good of the Neighbourhood and to preserve our way of life. Sometimes that has to involve things that might be considered distasteful.'

'Distasteful!' I stared at her in absolute horror. 'Distasteful! The Director has a room under the house where he takes prisoners and tortures them to death.'

Again she didn't react. There was something nightmarish about this conversation. 'Did you know about the room where they torture people?'

'Of course I know,' she spat at me. 'The Director used to take me down there when I was younger.'

I stared at her, my mouth agape, hardly able to believe what I was hearing. 'You watched him interrogate the prisoners?'

She nodded. 'At first I was scared, but the Director made me watch over and over again until I finally understood.'

'Until you understood what?' I felt sick.

'Until I understood how dangerous these people are. They don't care about our rules. They just want to destroy us so they can take over the Neighbourhood.'

'That's not true. The Light lied to us. The Echo don't want to take over the Neighbourhood. They just want us to leave them alone.'

'You don't know what you're talking about. They've brainwashed you. Turned you against us.'

'It's not me who's been brainwashed,' I responded. 'The Director's a monster.'

'The Director is not a monster,' she shrieked. 'He's just protecting us from people who want to hurt us. People like you.' Her lips curled up into an ugly snarl and her pale face flushed an angry crimson colour. She glared at me, her chest heaving up and down as she gave me an almost deranged look.

'But you're my friend. I would never hurt you.' I grasped at the fragile bond of our friendship. If she could remember the closeness we'd once shared, maybe it would bring her back to herself, even persuade her to help me . . . . I failed miserably.

'Friend!' she shrieked so loudly that I jumped back in alarm. 'You call yourself a friend! You pretended to like me so that you could get close to the Director and then you betrayed him. You aren't my friend. You were never my friend and I hate you, more than I have ever hated anyone in my life.' As she screeched out the last part of her sentence the door opened and two members of the Watch entered.

'Maud, please!' I begged. She was my only hope. Without her help my future looked very bleak indeed.

'Goodbye MaryAnn,' she said. 'You deserve everything that's going to happen to you.' Then she turned on her heel and left the room without even a backward glance. She took her white hot anger with her and once it was gone the room felt strangely empty.

My guards' faces remained inscrutable below the peak of their helmets as they placed handcuffs on my wrists and marched me down the corridor. With each step my insides clenched with fear and my bowels liquefied. I understood what was waiting for me in the tunnels. I also realised that I was a coward and I wouldn't be able to stand up to the torture. People were going to die because of me. Like father like daughter I thought. My father had killed countless people and now I was following in his footsteps.

Unexpectedly we headed towards the Director's study rather than the library. The door was already ajar and the Watch ordered me inside. Once inside the room they led me over to the far wall, where for the first time I noticed a hand scanner. One of my guards placed his hand on the scanner and a wall panel moved effortlessly aside, revealing another entrance into the tunnels. Unlike the entrance from the library this one was clean and well lit.

My legs felt weak and I stumbled clumsily as we climbed down into the tunnels. I grasped at the wall to keep from falling over and a member of the Watch caught me under the armpit. He didn't say a word but his grip was like a vice squeezing my arm and nipping the skin painfully.

'I can walk,' I muttered, yanking my arm away.

As we moved closer to the room I concentrated on putting one foot in front of the other and that helped to quell the panic a little. The world was reduced to the small area under my feet, to taking one step at a time. If I refused to believe that anything else existed then it made the circumstances almost bearable. I couldn't control what was happening around me – but I could control where I placed my feet. My heart rate slowed and a strange calmness descended. This brought with it a feeling of optimism, that maybe I could somehow endure the torture . . . then we arrived at the room and all hope evaporated.

The Director was waiting for me. He'd removed his jacket and tie which was an unusual sight in itself. His white shirt was covered by a rubber apron and upon seeing this my throat constricted into a silent scream. My knees turned to jelly and it was all I could do to remain upright. The Watch unlocked my handcuffs and pushed me roughly towards the chair.

'Please take a seat MaryAnn,' the Director requested with the manners of someone offering me a place at the dinner table.

I climbed into the chair and watched numbly while the Watch fastened the bindings around my wrists and ankles and fitted the strap around my head until I was held fast to the chair.

From the corner of my eye I saw a dark shape appear at the door.

'Just in time,' I heard the Director say. 'Have you met the new Legislator?' He directed the question to me. I couldn't move so I had to wait until the Legislator moved within my field of vision. I instantly recognised the man; he'd been part of my father's team and had been a guest at our house a number of times. I couldn't remember his name but I did remember that he gave me a pair of earrings for my birthday. I must have been ten or eleven at the time.

'You bought me earrings,' I said.

The Legislator laughed at this. His laugh didn't match his appearance. His body was thick set with a wide face bordered by thick eyebrows that almost met in the middle. His laugh was high pitched and had a reedy tonc to it. 'That was a long time ago,' he said. 'I'm flattered you remember.'

'MaryAnn likes her little trinkets,' the Director said. 'She's always had an eye for fashion. Maybe that's what turned her head. Did the Union offer you some nice trinkets to betray the Neighbourhood?'

I didn't bother to respond. He was playing with me like a cat pawing callously at an injured bird.

'Well never mind,' he said. 'We'll find out soon enough.' The

Director addressed the Legislator. 'Let's not waste any more time. Shall we begin?'

The Legislator rubbed his hands together eagerly.

'Splendid.' The Director wheeled a trolley across the room until it came to a rattling halt in front of the chair. My eyes widened in horror as I saw that it was covered with an array of surgical instruments . . . . I assumed there would be no anaesthetic.

Time became a blur, a painful, horrific, blur. The first cut was the worst. It hurt so much that the coward in me screamed until my throat was raw. I was like an anchorless dinghy, caught up in a storm tossed sea, except it was waves of pain that battered me and refused to release me from their merciless grasp.

I heard voices, asking questions, insistent, demanding, often yelling; but the pain roared so loudly in my ears that I couldn't understand what they were saying, make sense of what they were asking. I was ready to confess everything, but my brain was so consumed by the pain that I couldn't understand what they wanted me to say.

My whole body was on fire, as though I was burning from the outside in. I'd never felt pain like it before, even in the hospital after the accident I hadn't hurt this badly. At times when the pain became too much to bear I blacked out. Each time I gratefully embraced the blackness and for the briefest moment I was at peace, but then the blackness was torn from me and I hurtled straight back into hell. It seemed like I'd endured a lifetime of pain before I lost consciousness for the final time and everything mercifully stayed black.

CHAPTER 16

Escape

As I regained consciousness I was overwhelmed by the sharp tang of iron in the air. Everything was blurry and I squinted for a few moments until slowly and painfully the room came into focus.

I was alone; the Director and Legislator had left. My head restraint had been unfastened but my arm and leg restraints were still fastened tight. I stretched my neck and caught sight of the floor below my chair; it was slick with blood. There was so much blood on the floor that I was amazed there was any left in my body.

As consciousness returned so did the pain. My whole body felt like an open wound that stretched from the roots of my hair down to the tips of my toes.

I heard the squeak of the door and a member of the Watch entered my eye line. My body sagged in defeat; I was done. I couldn't take any more pain. If they were going to torture me again then this time I prayed that I would die right here in this chair.

The member of the Watch was beside me and pulling at the straps that bound my wrists. I felt the rough material of his uniform rub against the open wounds on my arm and I let out a moan of pain.

'I'm sorry,' he whispered quietly in my ear. My eyes widened with surprise. 'Please don't hurt me.' My voice came out as a hoarse sob.

The Watch raised a finger to his lips. 'Shush, I'm not here to hurt you.'

That's when I recognised him; it was Mr Murray, the Director's chauffeur. I was confused. Why was the chauffeur in the tunnels dressed up as a member of the Watch?

'I'm here to help you,' he whispered. 'Your uncle sent me. I just need to unfasten these and then we can get you out of here.' He busied himself with the restraints and when I was free he placed his hands under my knees and around my back. He was trying to be as gentle as possible, but even so the pain was almost unbearable and I gave a strangled yell. Mr Murray's eyes darted around nervously.

'Shush. You have to be quiet. Like a mouse, you understand?'

I pressed my face into his neck to muffle any sound as he lifted me out of the chair.

'I know it hurts,' he whispered in my ear, 'but we'll be out of here real soon I promise.'

As he carried me towards the door his foot slipped on the blood smeared across the floor and for a moment I thought he was going to fall over. With a struggle he was able to remain upright, but the movement caused shards of pain to rip through my body and I breathed heavily into his neck.

'Sorry,' he whispered.

Mr Murray was a big man and my weight didn't seem to slow him down as we sped along the tunnel. I must have blacked out, because the next thing I remember was being blasted by freezing cold air as we exited into the clearing beyond the Director's house. I'm not sure how Mr Murray managed to get me through the hole in the grate, but somehow we had made it safely out of the tunnels.

It was dark outside and above us a full moon hung low in the sky. A hunter's moon my father used to call it. Somehow it seemed appropriate.

'There should be someone here to meet us,' Mr Murray said.

'I'm right here.' A figure detached itself from behind a clump of bushes and Mr Murray froze. 'Patrick sent me to help. I encountered a little trouble; it looks like they were planning an ambush.' That's when I noticed the five bodies stretched out across the grass. They lay at funny angles with their necks bent oddly out of shape.

'I had to break their necks,' said the man. 'So they couldn't make any noise. We have to move quickly because someone will come and check on them soon.'

The man led us to the road where there was a car waiting. Mr Murray lay me down across the back seat and I let out a low moan.

'Just try and stay as quiet as possible,' Mr Murray said. 'Once we're out in the countryside you can scream as much as you like.' Leaving me with that comforting thought he climbed into the driver's seat.

The Unionist crouched beside me with a syringe in his hand. 'It's only a very weak painkiller,' he said. 'I'm afraid I can't give you anything stronger until you've been looked at by a doctor, but it should help a little.'

Once the Unionist had finished injecting the liquid into my arm Mr Murray started up the car and we slowly pulled away. The man remained by the side of the road. 'Isn't he coming with us?' I asked.

'No, we can't risk blowing his cover. There's enough damage been done tonight without losing one of our best guys.'

'Damage?' I queried.

'Yes, Daryl being captured and now the Union leadership on the run. It's a complete mess.'

I felt awful. Daryl! How could I have forgotten about him? I'd been so busy worrying about myself that I hadn't even bothered to find out if he was safe. When I asked Mr Murray he said that Daryl had made it safely across the Boundary. That was all he could tell me. He promised to find out more once we were safe.

There was something else I had to tell him, something important but the painkiller was already clouding my brain and I couldn't remember.

'You should rest for a while,' Mr Murray said. 'I'm going to take you to a safe house where you can hide for a couple of days, and then we can try and get you over the Boundary.'

'Aren't we going to be in danger if we stay in the Neighbourhood?' I mumbled.

'We don't have any other option. We need somewhere safe to stay for a few days until you're able to travel.'

I could feel myself drifting off to sleep. Just as I was about to lose consciousness I had a flashback of Daryl and Peter sitting at the table during the Christmas Feast. 'Mr Murray,' I asked sleepily, 'do you like knitting?'

Unexpectedly I heard him give a low chuckle before I fell into a drugged asleep.

I awoke some time later to find that we were on a rough track. When the car came to a standstill Mr Murray climbed out and quickly disappeared. I tried to pull myself into a sitting position to see where he'd gone, but as soon as I moved I felt some of my wounds rip open and start to bleed. I slithered painfully back down onto the seat and waited for Mr Murray.

When he returned he carefully picked me up and carried me towards a large concrete building. It was stark white with windows that glinted in the early morning sun.

'Where are we?'

'We're at an abandoned Delta camp,' Mr Murray answered. 'We should be safe here for a while. At least until you're ready to travel,' he added.

Mr Murray carried me around the back of the building where we entered an annex and climbed a flight of stairs to a room on the first floor. The room was dark, the window was painted over with black paint and the only source of light was a naked bulb hanging from the centre of the ceiling. Next to the window was a rickety old table and two chairs that had definitely seen better days. At the far end of the room was a large double bed. Mr Murray crossed the room and gently laid me down on the bed.

'You should try and get some rest,' he sat down heavily in the chair.

'How long do we have to stay here?' I asked.

Mr Murray shrugged, 'I'm not sure,' he said.

I tried to get comfortable, but every part of my body was aching. To take my mind off the pain I asked Mr Murray how he knew that I was in the room in the tunnels.

He told me what I already suspected, that he was a spy for the Union and had worked for the Director for a number of years. He told me that he was the one that had given Daryl the map of the tunnels. Before the virus the house had been a hotel and his father had worked there as the manager. He'd discovered a map to the tunnels long ago hidden inside the pages of an old book in the hotel library. He'd found out that the network of tunnels had been specially constructed when the house was built to hide the owners in the event of a war or attack. He'd explored the tunnels at length with his sister, and they'd spent many hours playing under the house.

'You didn't think of using the tunnels to bring in an army of Unionists to attack the Director?' I asked.

He shook his head. 'It's too dangerous. The Director has a state of the art security system. If it detected an intruder in the house then the whole place would go into lockdown and the Unionists would be trapped. That's why we had to engineer a reason for Peter to visit.'

'Engineer a reason?' I queried.

'The broken toilets,' he said. 'My handiwork.'

'So Peter lives in the Neighbourhood just like you?' I asked.

'No, not exactly. He comes into the Neighbourhood whenever we need him for a job. We managed to create a false identity for him. One of our Delta allies let us use the papers for her dead son. Peter sneaks over the Boundary, completes his task and then returns to the caves when he's done. Sometimes he stays for a few days or weeks, but never long enough to raise any suspicions.'

'So he's not a SanTech?'

'Not officially no. We have allies and spies in the Neighbourhood who can tap into the Portal network and intercept calls if we need them too. We only do it when there's an emergency or something important is at stake. The Watch are tracking us all the time so we have to be really careful.'

I remembered the time Peter appeared in my room. 'So when Peter came to visit me at Christmas it was because the Union thought I was important?'

Mr Murray couldn't quite meet my eyes. 'Erm, not exactly, it was your uncle who thought you were important.'

'Oh,' I said. Not sure whether to be delighted at finding out how important I was to my uncle or disappointed that the other Unionists didn't seem to feel the same way.

'I should go and check on the doctor, see where he is,' Mr Murray said as he got up from the chair and advanced towards the door. 'I'll be back as soon as I can.'

After he left I closed my eyes and despite all the new information churning around in my brain I must have slept fitfully, because the next thing I remembered was the sound of raised voices outside the room.

'I told you we should have taken her with us.' It was Peter. He sounded angry.

'If I'd known that this was going to happen then of course I would have taken her with us.' Uncle Patrick!

'Instead you left her with the Director, when you knew what he was capable of.'

'As I told you. If I'd known she was in danger I wouldn't have left her there.'

'But now you get what you always wanted don't you?'

'What are you trying to say Peter? Come on, spit it out.'

'After what happened I expect she'll be more than willing to join the Union and that's what you've always wanted isn't it?'

Uncle Patrick's tone was harsh. 'I'm not a monster, Peter. I never wanted this to happen.'

'But it did happen, didn't it.' I detected a bitterness in Peter's voice that I'd never heard before.

The door clicked open and they both entered the room. I kept my eyes closed, pretending to be asleep. I wasn't sure why, but I didn't want them to know that I'd heard their argument.

'MaryAnn,' Uncle Patrick whispered. 'Are you awake?'

I opened my eyes. He was standing over my bed and winced when he saw my face.

Peter was more direct. 'Bloody hell MaryAnn,' he whistled through his teeth. 'You look a right sight.'

'Thanks, that's really kind of you.' I used my best sarcastic tone.

'Has the doctor been to see you yet?' Uncle Patrick asked.

'Not yet.'

'I should take a look at you,' Peter said as he took off his jacket and rolled his sleeves up above his elbows.

'What! Absolutely not,' I protested. 'I'm waiting for the doctor.'

'The doctor might not get here for a while and we probably should check you out for any serious injuries.' Peter's tone was calm and business like.

'Yes and that's why we should wait for the doctor. So a professional can check for any serious injuries.'

Peter's voice lost its calm tone and he sounded indignant, 'I'm a trained field medic. I've got loads of experience dealing with injuries.'

'He's right,' Uncle Patrick said. 'He is a trained field medic and someone should take a look at your wounds. At least clean them up so they don't get infected.'

I wasn't happy with the situation, but I was less keen on getting an infection so I reluctantly agreed. Peter ordered Uncle Patrick out of the room to collect the first aid kit from the car.

As Uncle Patrick was about to leave I suddenly remembered the urgent thing I needed to tell them.

'They put a tracker inside Daryl,' I blurted out quickly. 'When they captured him.'

Uncle Patrick turned around to face me. 'We know,' he said. 'We found it. He's okay.'

'You found it?' I breathed a sigh of relief. 'The Watch didn't capture any more Unionists.'

'No, we found the tracker. All our people are safe. Don't worry.' He gave me a reassuring smile before heading out of the door.

Once Uncle Patrick had left the room Peter approached the bed. 'I'm going to take a look at you,' he said.

'Is it going to hurt?'

'Probably.'

'Great, already loving the bedside manner,' I muttered.

He seemed uncertain for a moment. 'I'm going to have to take off your shirt so I can get a better look.'

'Pervert,' I muttered through gritted teeth.

This diffused some of the tension in the room and caused Peter to laugh loudly. 'At least you haven't lost your famous sense of humour.'

He carefully undid the buttons on my shirt and then pulled it over my shoulders. I knew he was trying to be as gentle as possible, but the movement caused some of the cuts on my arm to rip open and I gasped in pain.

'Sorry,' he mumbled, his mouth close to my ear.

When he'd taken off my shirt I saw him wince.

'That bad?' I asked.

'I've seen worse,' he replied unconvincingly.

Uncle Patrick had returned to the room carrying the first aid kit and a bowl of water. He crossed over to the bed and I noticed him flinch when he saw my arms too. He opened up the first aid kit and rummaged inside pulling out cloths, bandages, plasters and some pots of ointment. Once he'd finished laying everything out on the table he muttered something about going to find Murray and left the room. He seemed keen to get away as quickly as possible.

'I'm going to roll up your vest and take a look at your stomach,' Peter said.

I hissed in pain as he pushed the vest up over my skin.

'I'm sorry,' he said. 'The blood's dried and the vest is stuck to your skin.' He carefully pulled at the vest again and I sucked in painful air as he gently wiped away the congealed blood with a damp cloth.

After Peter had cleaned away the blood he surveyed my stomach thoughtfully. Then he bent over and gently pressed my ribs with the tip of his fingers. I gave a loud strangled yell and nearly leapt off the bed.

'Looks like you might have some cracked ribs.'

'You think!'

'Some of these cuts are pretty deep. I think you're going to need stitches.' He pulled a needle and thread out of the first aid kit. 'This might sting a little.'

I squealed and squirmed away from the needle.

'You have to try and stay still.'

'You try staying still while someone's sticking a needle into you. Don't you have any painkillers?' I moaned.

'I need you to be fully conscious so you can tell me where it hurts.'

'Everywhere,' I muttered. 'It hurts everywhere.'

It took him forever to stich me up. Then just when I thought the ordeal was over he discovered more cuts further up my arm that needed stitching. By the time he'd finished I was in so much pain that I was seeing stars and tears were flowing freely down my cheeks.

Once he was finished he gave me a shot of a painkiller, covered me with a blanket and told me to get some sleep.

With the help of the painkiller I fell asleep almost immediately, but it wasn't the deep comforting sleep that I longed for. It was a sleep filled with monsters that slashed at me with razor sharp claws and teeth. I woke up a number of times screaming with terror. Each time I awoke Peter was sitting patiently by my bedside. The blacked out windows meant that the light never penetrated the room so I couldn't tell if it was day or night. Peter would just tell me everything was alright and talk to me softly until I fell back to sleep.

Finally I awoke to find Peter asleep in the chair next to my bed. Uncle Patrick was slumped on the floor snoring quietly. I lay for a few moments wondering how long I'd been asleep when the peace and quiet was shattered by Mr Murray who raced into the room. 'The Watch are on their way,' he hollered, his voice filled with panic. 'We have to leave now.'

Uncle Patrick and Peter were on their feet immediately.

'Are you sure?' Uncle Patrick asked.

'We just received a message from one of our informants that the Director released a story on the Portal that his adopted daughter is missing. He's offered a massive reward for her safe return. We have to get her over the Boundary. She's not safe in the Neighbourhood anymore. Every low life is going to be looking for her now.'

'We can't move her yet,' Peter protested. 'She's been asleep for two days, she obviously needs rest.'

I was shocked. I'd been asleep for two whole days. It felt like I'd only been in the room for a few hours, definitely not days.

'No time,' said Mr Murray. 'She has to go now.'

'MaryAnn, you have to get out of bed and go with Peter. Do you think you can do that?' my uncle asked.

I nodded uncertainly, my limbs still felt weak and shaky and I wasn't sure that I was going to be able to stand up, never mind walk out of the room.

'I have a truck waiting outside,' Mr Murray said.

'Do you have somewhere safe that you can take her?' Uncle Patrick asked Peter.

Peter thought for a moment and I saw a number of emotions play across his face before he nodded. 'Yes, it's -'

'No, don't tell me,' Uncle Patrick interrupted quickly. 'The fewer people that know the better.'

'Aren't you coming with us?' I asked.

'I can't. The Director knows that I'm your uncle. He'll use you to get to me. I need to be as far away from you as possible.'

'What about Daryl?'

'He's safe. The Director isn't going to find him.'

'We should be going,' Murray sounded impatient.

'You help MaryAnn to the truck,' Uncle Patrick ordered Peter. 'I'll go and get some supplies.'

Uncle Patrick left the room with Murray. Once they were gone Peter crossed the room to the bed and with some effort I pulled myself into a sitting position.

'Here!' Peter pulled his jacket off the back of the chair and helped me put it on over my vest. He zipped it up before wrapping an arm around my shoulder and helping me to my feet. I swayed alarmingly for a moment but managed to stay upright.

'I'll help you to the truck,' he said, 'but we must hurry.' I walked as quickly as I could, holding on tightly to Peter's arm, but we still made very slow progress. Even with Peter's assistance my body was covered in a thick sheen of sweat by the time we made it out of the door. When we arrived at the stairs I stopped uncertainly.

'Not far now,' said Peter in a tone he obviously thought was encouraging.

'Easy for you to say,' I mumbled as I tried to figure out how to tackle the stairs. After a brief pause Peter scooped me up and carried me down the stairs to the waiting truck.

CHAPTER 17

Flight

We found Uncle Patrick pacing up and down impatiently by the truck. When we exited the annexe he opened the truck door and helped Peter carefully deposit me into the front seat.

As I was fastening my seatbelt Murray came tearing around the side of the building.

'Too late,' he yelled frantically. 'They're here already.'

Too Late. Those words struck fear into my heart. The Watch had found us.

Uncle Patrick quickly pushed a backpack into Peter's hand. 'Supplies,' he said. Peter raced around the truck and jumped into the driver's seat.

'Go,' Uncle Patrick yelled. I could hear fear in his voice. 'Get her out of here.'

We could see a cloud of dust appear in the distance and three black cars appeared over the brow of the hill. Peter switched on the engine and the tyres skidded in the dirt as we drove away from the building.

'Keep her safe,' Uncle Patrick bellowed after us.

I craned my neck painfully so I could see out of the rear window. I watched as Mr Murray jumped into a car and hurtled up the road towards the Watch.

'What's he doing?' I shrieked. 'He's driving towards them.'

'He's creating a diversion so we can get away,' Peter said.

Uncle Patrick had disappeared, but Mr Murray continued up the road heading straight for the Watch. It looked like he was playing a game of chicken. The air was filled with the sound of rapid gunfire and Mr Murray's car took off from the road, briefly flying through the air and landing directly on top of one of the Watch patrol cars. The remaining cars ground to a halt and figures climbed out, quickly advancing on the crash scene. Without any warning there was a loud bang and the two cars burst into flames.

'What's happening?' Peter asked. He was crouched over the steering wheel, his brow furrowed in concentration.

'Mr Murray hit a car,' I said. 'It exploded, but I can't see if he escaped.' Despite the pain, I was craning my neck frantically trying to get a better look out of the rear window, hoping to catch a fleeting glance of Mr Murray. All I could see was a dense cloud of smoke.

'Just two patrol cars to worry about then.' Peter pressed his foot down on the accelerator and the truck picked up speed. The remaining Watch give up the rescue attempt and returned to their cars. We bumped along the road with the two cars in hot pursuit.

'They're still behind us,' I squealed, the panic evident in my voice.

'I know, I know,' Peter snapped as we raced down the road. We spun around a corner and I hung onto the door handle as the truck pivoted onto two wheels. For a moment I thought the truck was going to roll over. Then with a crash the wheels slapped back onto the road. The patrol car following us wasn't so fortunate and I watched as it swung around the corner and then flipped over. There was the painful crunch of metal as the roof hit the grass verge. Then the car rolled over twice more until it finally landed in a ditch.

'Two down,' Peter muttered grimly.

The remaining car continued to give chase.

'We need to get off this road,' Peter said as he yanked the steering wheel to the right and we veered into a wooded area. The patrol car turned too and followed us into the wood.

Branches scraped loudly against the side of the truck as we weaved erratically through the trees.

I caught glimpses of the patrol car as it continued to give chase. Peter zigzagged through the trees in an attempt to get away but it remained doggedly on our heels.

'What are we going to do?' I squealed.

We drove out into a clearing and the truck bumped along a small meadow before pitching down into a fast flowing river.

'Peter!'

'Just hold on tight,' he ordered.

I gripped the door handle as water surged over the front of the truck. 'We'll drown,' I squeaked.

'We won't drown,' Peter said as he threw me an optimistic grin. For a moment I felt a sense of relief, until he added, 'What we really have to worry about is water getting into the engine and stalling the truck.'

I held on tightly to the door handle and prayed silently that the truck would make it to the other side. The river wasn't very wide but the water lapped alarmingly at the sides of the truck.

After a few tense moments we reached the other side and the vehicle laboured up the bank onto dry land. Peter brought the truck to a halt for a moment and I breathed a sigh of relief.

'Let's hope the patrol car isn't built like this little beauty,' Peter said as he gave the dashboard a grateful pat.

The patrol car appeared out of the woods and without hesitating it careered down into the river. The patrol car was smaller and less robust than the truck and as soon as it hit the water the bonnet was totally submerged. The engine spluttered loudly and then stalled.

'We should get out of here,' Peter said as he steered towards a clump of trees. As I peered out of the back window I saw that the patrol car was still floundering in the water.

We drove quite a distance through the trees with Peter still maintaining a hectic pace.

'Check if they're still following us,' he finally demanded.

I peered out of the back window but all I could see was trees.

'I don't think so,' I said. 'I can't see any other cars.'

Peter eased off the accelerator and we slowed down a little.

'Are we going to the Boundary?' I asked

'Yeah, but we have to find a new place to cross. We can't risk using the old crossing. The Watch followed us there after we rescued Daryl.'

'They followed the tracker?' I asked.

'Yeah, we realised Daryl must be the reason they were following us. When we examined him we found the tracker and cut it out.'

'Ouch,' I grimaced.

'Not quite the words that Daryl used when we cut it out, but close enough.'

Despite the seriousness of our situation, I laughed. I imagined that Daryl had uttered a few choice words.

'So you have another place where we can cross to the Outside?' I asked.

'Yeah, we haven't used this crossing for a long time so it shouldn't be compromised.'

We continued through the woods but didn't see any further evidence that the Watch were still following us. We arrived at a wide reservoir visible in a clearing between the trees and Peter stopped the truck. He pulled a map out of the glove box and examined it for a few moments before setting off again.

'Do you know where you're going?' I asked.

'Yeah, it's not far now.'

We reached the edge of the woods and Peter stopped the truck. I could see the Boundary in the distance.

'You should probably try and get some sleep,' Peter said. 'We'll cross as soon as it gets dark.'

Peter was shaking my arm and softly whispering my name. The return to consciousness brought with it the pain from my wounds and I groaned loudly in response. Peter rummaged in his backpack, pulled out two small capsules and handed them to me.

'Painkillers,' he said. 'They should help.' He said he couldn't give me anything stronger because I needed to remain conscious so I could walk across the Boundary.

Peter grabbed the backpack and then clambered out of the truck. He moved around to the passenger door and pulled it open, offering me his hand. I grasped his hand tightly and stumbled out of the truck. For a second my knees buckled and the only thing that stopped me dropping to the ground was the arm that Peter wrapped tightly around me.

'You going to be okay?' he asked. I could hear the concern in his voice.

'Yeah, I just need a minute.' My head was throbbing horribly and I felt queasy.

'Okay, whenever you're ready. Take as long as you need.' Peter remained by my side. He was the only thing that kept me upright. I leant my head against his chest until the throbbing receded and I was ready to go.

It wasn't far to the Boundary but I moved so slowly that it took us a long time. Peter kept his arm firmly around my shoulders and did all he could to help me, encouraging me at every step. He kept his manner light, but I could detect the tension in his body and the anxiety in his expression as he carefully scanned the countryside.

When we arrived at the Boundary Peter worked at a hole in the fence until it was large enough for us to crawl through.

Peter said that the safe house was only a couple of miles away but at the speed we were able to travel it took us a long time. Despite the painkillers Peter had given me my side throbbed horribly.

Peter assisted me over the crest of a hill and told me that the safe house was located in the valley below. We'd just cleared the top when I slipped in the soft mud and a searing pain flared up my side. I let out a loud gasp.

'You okay?' he asked.

I grunted an acknowledgement. 'I think I burst my stitches.' The searing pain had been replaced by a dull throbbing ache.

'It's not far now,' he said. 'It's just over there.' I followed the direction of his finger and could just make out a series of farm buildings nestled in the valley below.

'Think you can make it?'

'Easy,' I mumbled. Trying to keep my voice light.

The ground was boggy and even with Peter's help I found it difficult to stay upright. A few times I slipped and felt my side tear painfully.

The air grew thick and heavy and one by one the stars blinked out as they were covered by a thick blanket of cloud. The pressure started to build around us and there was a low growl of thunder. Peter gave the threatening sky an anxious glance.

'I think there's a storm on the way. We should hurry.'

I tried to quicken the pace, but I was wiped out. My strength was gone and there was nothing left in reserve to draw upon.

As we reached the farmyard the heavens opened and the rain poured down. It was only a short distance to the farm house but by the time we arrived at the porch we were both soaked through to the skin.

Peter steered me into the porch which provided some shelter from the rain. He gave the front door an experimental push and found that it was locked. He picked up a bright blue flower pot from the window ledge. Whatever plant the flower pot had contained was long gone, leaving behind parched crumbling soil. I caught the glint of a silver key lying underneath it. Peter unlocked the front door and it opened to reveal a dark hallway beyond.

He held the door open for me and told me that there was a kitchen at the end of the hall. I heard him enter the house behind me but instead of following me into the kitchen he climbed the stairs.

The kitchen smelt musty and damp and there was an air of neglect, as though no-one had lived in this house for a very long time. It was a large room dominated at one end by a wide wooden table and a sofa. It was the sofa that drew my immediate attention and I collapsed onto it with a grateful sigh. A large cloud of dust puffed up around me, but I didn't care. I was too exhausted to worry about how dirty everything was. I wasn't even wearing gloves; I'd left those behind at the Director's house.

I closed my eyes and nestled into the sofa trying to find a comfortable position. The effect of the painkillers had definitely worn off. I was aching all over and the throbbing in my side was almost unbearable. I put a hand under my vest and when I pulled it back out it was sticky with blood.

I could hear Peter's footsteps on the floor above and wondered irritably what he was doing. I needed him downstairs in the kitchen, preferably injecting me with a large syringe filled with painkilling goodness.

At long last I heard him descend the stairs. When he entered the kitchen I saw that he was carrying an armful of clothes and bedding.

'I thought we might need these,' he said throwing them down onto the table.

I looked at him wearily, too tired to respond.

'You doing okay?' he asked. I nodded my head weakly.

Peter strode over to the window and closed the blinds. The storm outside was starting to intensify and the grumbling roar of the thunder had been joined by bright flashes of lightning. Peter pulled some matches from his pocket and lit an oil lamp so that a weak light permeated the kitchen as he joined me on the sofa.

'I should check you out,' he said. He indicated my side. 'You said you'd ripped your stiches.'

My side was still throbbing horribly and I pulled at my wet jacket tentatively.

Peter was rummaging in his backpack and emerged with the first aid kit.

He unzipped my jacket. 'Lift up your vest,' he said.

When I peeled the vest up over my stomach I saw that my side was smeared with red blood. The blood had already started to congeal and harden around the ripped stiches.

Peter took a syringe out of the first aid kit. I smiled at the sight of the painkiller in his hand and waited expectantly. Instead of injecting me straight away he proceeded to fuss around for a few moments, dabbing tentatively at the congealed blood until I couldn't contain myself any longer. 'Just give me the bloody injection, will you,' I snapped loudly. Peter raised his eyebrows in surprise but didn't say anything, instead he carefully cleaned away a little more of the blood before sticking the needle into my side.

I barely felt the prick of the needle, but I welcomed the warm pleasant numbing feeling that spread throughout my body. While I was appreciating my release from pain Peter finished cleaning the blood from my side. In no time at all he'd re-stitched the wounds and was pulling down my vest.

'All done,' he said.

I tried to apologise for shouting at him but he waved the apology away.

'Your clothes are soaking wet,' he said. 'You need to change into something dry.' He rummaged through the pile of clothes and bedding on the table and handed me a pair of trousers, a hooded jumper and a towel.

'There's a utility room at the end of the kitchen. There should be some water because the farm is supplied from a local spring not from the mains.'

Peter was right, there was running water in the utility room and I was able to fill up the large stone sink. I also discovered the remnants of an old bar of soap.

I stripped off my clothes as quickly as possible. Now that the painkiller was working I could move freely without impediment. It had been days since I'd had a shower and I felt absolutely filthy, my skin practically crawling with dirt.

I found that I was able to have quite a good wash in the sink and managed to clean away most of the blood and dirt I'd accumulated over the last few days.

Once I'd finished scrubbing my face clean I studied myself in the mirror and was surprised that a thin gaunt stranger stared back at me. My scar stood out pink and rigid against my white skin and I noticed that it had been joined by a deep gash above my eye and a purple bruise on my cheek.

Despite the injuries to my face it was my body that had taken the brunt of the torture and for that I was grateful. At least I could cover up the burns, cuts and bruises with clothes so that people wouldn't stare at me like some kind of freak.

I quickly towelled myself dry and pulled on the clean clothes. It was amazing how having clean skin and clean clothes could lift the spirits and I returned to the kitchen in a far better mood than I'd left it.

I found Peter settled on the sofa eating a cereal bar. When I took a seat next to him he handed one to me. I grabbed it gratefully and ripped it open with my teeth.

'Hey, steady on,' Peter said. There was an amused tone to his voice.

'I'm starving,' I protested. I couldn't remember the last time I'd eaten. I demolished the cereal bar in three large bites, barely taking the time to taste it. When I'd swallowed the last mouthful Peter handed me another one. I hesitated, not wanting to appear greedy.

'It's okay. Patrick packed a few of these. You haven't eaten in a while and you need to regain your strength.'

I took the second bar and quickly ate that too. After I'd finished eating Peter grabbed the blankets from the table and made a bed on the sofa. He suggested that we both sleep in the kitchen so we could keep a lookout for the Watch. He handed me two white pills. 'To help you sleep,' he said. I was so tired that I didn't think I would need any help sleeping but I took them anyway.

Peter rummaged in the pile of clothing on the table and pulled out a dry T-shirt. He unbuttoned his wet shirt and peeled it off. He turned around anxiously when I let out a gasp.

'What's the matter!'

'Your back,' I said.

He seemed confused for a moment. 'My back . . . oh you mean my tattoo.'

'Can I look?' I asked.

He crouched down beside me and I ran my finger over the delicate artwork. 'A Phoenix,' I said, admiring the mix of vivid colours.

'A Phoenix rising out of the ashes,' he said. 'A new beginning. Daryl and I got matching tattoos after we completed our training for the Union.'

'Daryl has a tattoo?' I was shocked.

'A lot of the Unionists do. It's become an Echo tradition - a way to record and share our stories.'

228

'So the tattoo on your arm, what does that mean?' I traced the outline of the tattoo; ripples of black and grey intersected with flashes of orange, pinks and reds. Eight small stars were etched across its surface.

Peter got to his feet without answering and pulled his T-shirt over his head, covering up the tattoo. 'You should sleep,' he said. 'I'll take the first watch.'

I realised he must be exhausted too as he hadn't slept for a long time, but I was too tired to argue. The pills that Peter gave me really helped and for the first time in what seemed like forever I entered a dreamless sleep.

CHAPTER 18

Family

When I awoke the blinds were still drawn and the lamp burnt dimly. My head was cloudy and my tongue felt thick and dry. I was desperately thirsty.

'I thought you'd never wake up,' Peter said from his seat by the window.

'How long have I been asleep?'

I was shocked to hear that I'd slept for twelve hours and it was already early afternoon. I could hear the rain lashing against the window as the storm continued to rage outside. I asked Peter to get me some water and he poured me a glass from the tap. When he brought it over to me I could see that he was pale and gaunt, his eyes ringed by dark shadows.

Despite the smile he gave as he handed me the glass I could detect a distinct change in his mood. In the hours that I'd been asleep he seemed to have retreated into himself. He looked like he'd gone beyond the point of exhaustion and I resolved to take over the next watch once I'd finished the water.

It took some time to convince Peter that I was fit enough to keep watch and he protested that I needed more rest. Secretly I agreed with him, but Peter hadn't slept since we'd left the Delta camp and I realised that he must be practically dropping with exhaustion.

He agreed to sleep once he'd checked out my wounds and given me another painkiller. When he was satisfied that everything was alright he climbed onto the sofa and fell asleep almost immediately. I pulled the blanket up under his chin and the action caused him to frown slightly in his sleep. His face held a tense, brooding look. I'd seen various incarnations of Peter's personality; his easy, often inappropriate humour with friends, his sarcasm and also his disdain for me, but I'd never seen the brooding intensity that haunted his features now. It seemed to have started once we'd entered this house but Peter wasn't in the habit of confiding in me so I suspected that I would never find out the cause of his melancholy.

After I'd grown tired of watching Peter sleep I crossed over to the window and peeked through the blinds. My watch said it was two o'clock in the afternoon but it was already dark outside. I expected that it was one of those winter days that had never properly gotten light. The storm was still raging outside and seemed to have no end. The thunder and lightning had passed by, but the wind still howled eerily around the house. I watched the trees in the farmyard as they were buffeted by the gale force winds. The slates on the roof above us rattled alarmingly as if at any moment the wind would tear them away, exposing us to the elements.

I pulled another cereal bar out of the backpack and munched on this as I curled up on a chair by the window. I remained by the window for a long time peering out of the blinds. After a while my eyes began to grow heavy and I struggled to keep them open.

I needed to remain alert so I got up to stretch my legs. The kitchen worktops were thick with dirt and I ran my finger lazily across the counter top creating a swirl of pattern. I marvelled at how immune I'd become to the dirt. Only weeks before I'd have hated being in this dusty old place. I'd have been terrified that I'd catch some type of infection. Now I was able to rub my bare finger through the dirt without even the protection of my gloves.

I stopped at the fridge. It was rusting and old and when I pulled it open the dark empty interior smelt like long forgotten food. There were a number of children's drawings still pinned to the front of the fridge. These were old and yellow and curled at the edges. The drawings showed pictures of sheep, cows and pigs; animals that I recognised from drawings I'd seen in books. I thought that in the past this kitchen must have been a cosy place to be. I mentally constructed a picture of what this room must have looked like when a family lived here; a fire cracking in the hearth, candles flickering on the mantelpiece and a family snuggled together on the sofa. It must have been a real family home.

Even though Peter had told me to stay in the kitchen I was curious about the rest of the house and eager to find out about the people who had once lived here. I also needed to keep moving if I was going to stay awake.

Peter was still fast asleep on the sofa, sprawled on his back snoring slightly. I noiselessly padded over to the window and checked outside. Everything appeared to be normal so I picked up Peter's torch from the kitchen counter and let myself out into the hall.

The hall was dark; the only light that could penetrate the gloom came from the glass in the entrance door. By the light of the torch I could make out a door midway along the corridor. When I pushed it open I found that it led to a family lounge. Similar to the kitchen this room was also covered in a layer of dust.

Despite the dirt the room still felt homely. It was dominated by a brick fire which was so large I expected I could almost stand upright in it. Pushed up against one wall was a comfortable looking sofa and two armchairs. At the opposite end of the room was a large piano. There were a number of photographs displayed on top of the piano and, curious, I crossed the room to take a look.

There was an eclectic mix of frames; silver and gold, patterned and flowered. I picked up one of the larger frames and peered curiously at it, keen to see the faces of the people who had lived in this house. As I scanned the photograph I caught my breath. It was a family portrait taken outside the farmhouse; I counted nine people in the photograph - two men, two women and five children. It was one of the children that had caught my attention. I drew the frame closer so I could get a better look. The boy in the photograph was Peter; a younger version of Peter, but the face, the eyes, they were the same. The shoulders were less broad and he had some growing to do, but it was definitely Peter staring out from the photo.

'I told you to stay in the kitchen,' a voice growled from behind me.

I jumped in surprise and let go of the photograph. I fumbled to catch it but it was too late and I watched in horror as it hit the floor and the glass frame smashed into tiny pieces. I stared at the shattered photograph in dismay; the family returned my gaze, their faces distorted and disfigured by the broken glass.

'I'm sorry,' I said bending down to pick up the pieces.

'Leave it.'

'No, I'll clean it up,' I protested.

'I said leave it.' Peter's tone was harsh. As I straightened up I caught a glimpse of his face. He was furious. I could tell he was barely holding onto his temper.

'What were you doing in here?'

'I . . . you were sleeping, and I was bored and I thought I would take a look around.'

'You were bored so you thought you would take a look around,' he mimicked, his voice a tight furious whisper. 'You thought you would take a look around even though I told you to stay in the kitchen and keep a look out for the Watch.'

'I was just curious,' I said. 'I wanted to find out about the people who lived in this house.'

'What if the Watch had surrounded us while you were in here?'

'I don't know. I wasn't thinking.'

'And that's your problem MaryAnn.' His eyes blazed dangerously in the darkness. 'You just don't think. I can't keep on protecting you if you won't listen to me. If you don't care about your own safety then why should I?' He turned on his heel and stormed out of the room. I heard him thunder down the hall and then the slam of the kitchen door closing.

I bent down and plucked the photograph from out of the frame, brushing off the broken glass. I carefully folded it up and placed it into my back pocket before hurrying out of the room after Peter.

When I entered the kitchen he was standing by the window looking through the blinds. Outside the storm may have blown itself out, but I could feel that there was an equally violent storm gathering inside the house. I was desperate to diffuse the tension.

'I'm sorry,' I said. It didn't seem enough. It wasn't enough, there needed to be something more that I could say.

'I know,' he said. The words came out in a short sharp gasp as if he was clenching his jaw. I could see his hands balled up into fists held rigidly by his side.

The silence hung heavily in the air. 'Was that your family?' I asked. 'Was it you in the picture?'

'I don't want to talk about it.'

'Was this your home?' I persisted, 'before the . . . .' I couldn't think of a way to finish the sentence, to ask him whether this was the house where his family had been so horribly murdered.

'I SAID I DON'T WANT TO TALK ABOUT IT. SO SHUT UP WILL YOU.'

He shouted so loudly that I jumped in surprise. Then he punched the wall with a balled up fist. He must have punctured the skin

234

because when he pulled his fist back I noticed a smear of blood across the wallpaper.

I wasn't sure what to do. I thought that I should at least offer to clean up his hand, but I was scared about how he might react. He resolved my indecision by storming past me and out into the utility room. He didn't say a word, but I got the impression that I probably shouldn't follow him.

I lowered myself onto the sofa and waited uncertainly. I desperately wanted to go and check that he was alright. I wanted to take care of him in the same way he'd looked after me, but he'd been so angry I didn't dare. Like the true coward I was, I remained seated on the sofa picking anxiously at my fingernails until they started to bleed.

I must have fallen asleep, because when I awoke Peter was back in the kitchen and was quietly rummaging through his backpack.

I jumped up from the sofa, my heart racing. 'Are you leaving?' I asked.

He looked up from his bag. His eyes were puffy and red rimmed and he gave me a strange look. 'No,' he said. 'I was getting something to eat.' He extracted a cereal bar from his bag and held it up for inspection.

I breathed a visible sigh of relief.

He continued to stare at me with that strange look on his face. 'You thought I was going to leave you?'

I found I couldn't quite meet his eyes. 'You were so annoyed with me. I just thought that maybe you were . . . .' My voice dropped to a barely audible whisper. 'I thought you were going to leave me here on my own.'

Peter responded with a humourless laugh. 'If I walked away every time you annoyed me MaryAnn, then we would barely spend any time in each other's company.'

'Then it's true,' I said. 'You do hate me . . . Daryl said you didn't, but I thought that you did. That's why you're always so nice to other people, but never to me.'

Peter exhaled loudly. 'Of course you want to make this about you.'

I frowned. 'What's that supposed to mean?'

Peter didn't answer me directly. 'MaryAnn, hate is a very strong word and I reserve that emotion for people who really deserve it and that certainly doesn't include you.'

'Well you dislike me then,' I persisted. 'Even if you don't hate me.'

He shrugged. 'I might have taken a bit of a dislike to you when we first met, but you were incredibly rude. So I feel I was justified.'

'I was rude?' I bristled defensively. 'How can you say that. You were the one that was rude to me after I'd spent hours hiking though the dark to meet Daryl.'

'I'm not talking about the night you crossed the Boundary. We met before then.'

'Did we?' I tried hard to remember, searching my memory but I drew a complete blank.

'It was at school,' he responded.

'You went to my school?' Now he really wasn't making any sense. A Delta would never be admitted to my school.

'No stupid, I never said that I went to your school. I said it was at your school. I was working as a SanTech. Daryl and Patrick had asked me to keep an eye on you. You wanted to use the toilets and I told you they were broken. You were incredibly rude and then stalked off with your nose in the air.'

I couldn't remember the incident at all, but as much as I hated to admit it, it did sound like me . . . the old me.

'You don't remember?' he asked, his eyes searching my face.

I shook my head. 'Sorry, I don't.'

'Ah it seems the event wasn't as memorable for you as it was for me.'

His face took on a downcast expression and I found myself about to apologise when he gave me a sarcastic smile. 'I must have been bowled over by your fine manners.' His comment got the desired response and I laughed. Which helped to dissolve some of the tension that still filled the room.

I expected that Peter's attempt at humour was his way of changing the subject, signalling that he didn't want to talk about the events earlier in the evening, but I wasn't ready to let it go so easily.

'Peter.'

He paused in the middle of opening the cereal bar. 'Don't MaryAnn,' he warned.

'Why did you come back here?' I persisted, determined to get to the truth.

He refused to look at me, slowly chewing the cereal bar. When he spoke his tone was matter of fact. 'Because I couldn't think of anywhere else to go. We needed somewhere safe to hide out and this was the only place I could think of that was close by.'

'Is this the first time you've been back . . . since . . . .' I trailed off uncertainly.

'When I found them I just ran away. I left everything behind. The Union must have cleaned up when they came back for the bodies.'

I shuddered at the mention of the bodies. He was talking about his family. This was the house where his whole family had been massacred in cold blood. I couldn't imagine how horrible it must have been for him to return to this place.

There was an uneasy silence and it was only broken when Peter said the strangest thing. 'You think that it's all going to end in some meaningful way,' he said.

The change of topic was unexpected. 'What's going to end in a meaningful way?'

'You think that life is going to end in some profound way,' he said softly. 'Death is so final that you think it has to mean something. But I realised after my family died that dead is just dead, nothing more. One minute you're alive and then the next minute you're gone, and apart from your family and friends no-one even realises that you don't exist anymore.'

'That's horrible,' I said. 'Life has to mean more than that.'

'I'm not talking about life,' he said. 'I'm talking about death. If anything it makes life more meaningful. If death is so meaningless, then you have to make sure that you live well. I'm not just talking about having a good time. What I mean is living properly. Making the right choices. If your death doesn't mean anything then you have to make sure that in the end your life counts for something.'

I pondered this for a moment. 'It just seems like such a morose way to think about things. Death has to mean something more.'

'But does it really? Look at your parents. One minute they were sipping champagne and eating canapés and the next, *'poof'* they were gone.'

I grimaced at the thought of my parents literally exploding out of existence. 'So you feel the same way about your family?' I asked.

'Exactly,' Peter responded. He'd moved over to the sofa to sit beside me and was hunched forward, his hands clasped tightly together. 'One minute they were waving goodbye as I left to deliver the Wilsons' Christmas present, the next I was in the kitchen staring at their bodies sprawled across the floor. If Mrs Wilson hadn't persuaded me to stay for a hot chocolate then I would probably have been at the farm when the Watch arrived and I would have either have been taken away for re-education or killed trying to escape. Then we would never have met and we wouldn't even be having this conversation. My death wouldn't have meant anything to you. You'd be with someone else in some other safe house.'

I shuddered, 'I just think it's a morbid way to look at things.'

Peter started to say something, and then he visibly seemed to shake himself. 'Let's not talk about this anymore. I don't want to think about the past. Not while we're in this house,' he said. 'What's done is done. None of this will bring my family back.'

From the resolute look on his face I could tell that the conversation was over. When I tried to engage him further, he simply refused to answer. Instead he firmly suggested I get some more sleep while he took the next watch.

Reluctantly I lay down on the sofa. My head was buzzing with the conversation I'd just had with Peter and despite feeling absolutely exhausted I found that sleep evaded me. I observed Peter over by the window and noticed that his face looked pinched and grim in the dim light of the lamp. I realised that we had to get away from this house as soon as possible. Staying here was just torturing him. Now that I understood its history the house no longer felt homely. It definitely wasn't the safe haven I'd imagined it to be.

I felt the ghosts of Peter's family press in around me; one minute smiling with welcome, the next screeching in terror. Blood-smeared faces stared out at me from the broken frame of the family photograph. A child's hand; so tiny and white in death, an accusing finger sticky with blood pointing towards me. A shudder raced down my spine . . . I woke with a scream in my throat and realised I was calling out for my father. Peter was beside me in an instant.

'It was a dream,' he shushed, 'just a dream. That's all.' I grasped at the front of his T-shirt with a shaky hand, the dream still vivid in my memory.

'I'm so sorry,' I said.

'What are you sorry about?'

I wanted desperately to make him understand, but it came out all mixed up. 'I can't stop thinking about him. About my father. Sometimes I hate him, but then other times I miss him so much.

Even after everything he did I still miss him and want him back. How could I want him back after everything he did? I must be some type of monster.'

I expected him to push me away in disgust, but he didn't. 'Of course you're not a monster,' he said. 'He was your father. You can't just switch off your feelings for him.'

'But that's what everyone expects. They think that I should hate him.'

Peter responded in a way I didn't expect. He told me that for a long time he hated my father, hated the Light, hated everyone in fact, but then he realised that it was turning him into someone he didn't recognise. *Someone who was no better than the people who had murdered his family.* He told me he'd seen the same thing happen to other people in the Union. How the hate eventually tore them apart. He realised he didn't want to end up like that.

His words surprised me. I didn't understand how he could forgive so easily. His face darkened when I told him this.

'MaryAnn you misunderstand. I haven't forgiven anyone. One day the Light will pay for what they did. But I understand that this fight is bigger than just my need for vengeance. The only real way for me to get revenge is to bring down the whole corrupt system and I can't do that on my own.'

He held my gaze unblinking for a moment. 'I remember that night at the farmhouse. When you said you couldn't join the Union because innocent people were killed when the Building of Light was bombed.'

I nodded, remembering how angry Daryl and Uncle Patrick had been.

'And you were right,' he said. 'The people in the Neighbourhood aren't guilty of the crimes committed by the Light. Maybe they can be accused of being ignorant and burying their heads in the sand, but the Light controls them as much as it does the people Outside. Imagine how scared they must have been during the virus outbreak. Moving to the Neighbourhood must have seemed like their only hope of survival. Fear made it easier to accept that some people had to be sacrificed for the greater good. I expect a lot of the people in the Union would have made the same choice if they'd had the money to pay to keep their families safe. Most people are like sheep and just want to feel safe along with the rest of the herd.'

'But not you,' I ventured.

I saw a fleeting look of surprise cross his face then he chewed thoughtfully on his bottom lip. 'I'm just like that,' he said. 'I do exactly what the Union wants, what Patrick orders me to do, exactly in the same way as the people in the Boundary follow the Light. I'm no different to any of them.'

'You didn't want to plant the bomb though did you?'

'No. I voted against it.'

'Yet you still went along with it even though you knew the damage it would cause?'

'Yeah like the good Unionist sheep that I am.'

'Don't say that. You're not a sheep . . . at least I don't think of you like that.'

This comment made Peter smile. 'The problem with a lot of the Unionists is that they see the people within the Boundary as a faceless enemy. You have to understand we've lived separately for so many years that they barely seem human anymore.'

'In the same way that the people in the Neighbourhood think the Echo are feral animals,' I said.

'Exactly, there are some of us, myself and Murray for example, who've spent time working in the Neighbourhood. We're there to spy for the Union, but you can't help getting to know people, building up friendships and the like. You start to realise that we aren't that different. If the Union kill the people living in the Neighbourhood because we don't like the choices they've made then we're no different from the Light. We should be looking at ways to bring people together, not alienate them even more.'

'Do you really think that things could change though? That we could live together?' I couldn't imagine it ever happening.

'I don't know. It's tricky. Often power just moves from one group to another. There are new people in charge but nothing truly changes.'

'It's true what you said earlier about the people in the Neighbourhood. Now I'm Outside I can't believe that I didn't see what was really going on, what my father was doing. I wonder how I could ever have been so stupid.'

'But you can't spend the rest of your life apologising for your father. At some point you have to let it go. Accept the past and just move on.'

'I wish I could just let it go, but sometimes it's all I can think about. I just don't know how I can ever make up for all the things he did.'

'Listen to yourself,' Peter said. 'After everything that's happened to you in the last few days. You're a fugitive, you've given up everything; your home, hot running water,' at this comment he flashed a smile at me. 'What else do you think you need to sacrifice?'

'I didn't do it for the Union,' I said. 'I don't think I even did it because it was the right thing to do. There was nothing noble about it. I did it for my family, to keep Daryl and Uncle Patrick safe. I'm definitely not the hero in this story. I've been scared every single second since I met you and Uncle Patrick and the Union -' The end of my sentence was cut off by a loud yawn.

'I think that's enough talking for now,' Peter said. 'You need to sleep. If we're going to leave tomorrow we need to make sure you're fully rested, it could be a long trip.'

When I awoke, Peter was sorting through the contents of his backpack.

'You slept well,' he said. It was a statement rather than a question.

I felt more rested than I had in a long time. My wounds still hurt but they'd receded to a dull throb that was almost manageable.

'Do you think you're able to leave today?' he asked. 'The storm's over.'

'I think so. I feel a lot better.'

Peter made me sit on a chair while he checked my injuries. He was keen to make sure that my stitches hadn't burst open again. Once he'd declared me fit to travel he sent me off to the utility room to wash up.

I took the time to have a proper wash in the sink, not sure when I'd have the opportunity again. I was trying to tease the tangled knots out of my hair with my fingers when there was a knock at the door.

'You decent?'

'Yes, come in,' I responded.

Peter pushed the door open and smiled as I finished combing through my hair.

'Well don't you look gorgeous this morning,' he said in a teasing voice.

I winced and immediately stopped playing with my hair. I quickly pulled on my hooded top and busied myself with the zip.

'Did I say something wrong?' he asked.

I shook my head, not trusting myself to speak.

'I did, I said something to upset you didn't I? I was only teasing.'

I could feel him watching me.

'It's not you, it's me.'

'What's you?'

'Isn't it obvious?'

He shook his head and seemed totally lost.

I jabbed at my face, 'I'm not gorgeous, am I. Not anymore. Not after the bomb.'

His face took on a stricken look. 'I'm so sorry,' he said. 'I wasn't making fun of your -'

I cut him off, 'It doesn't matter. I told you it was my problem. Come on, we have to go.'

Before he had chance to respond I pushed past him into the kitchen.

Peter quickly picked up his bag from off the kitchen counter and then led the way out into the hall. I followed close behind. We arrived at the porch and he paused for a moment, carefully surveying the yard. When he was satisfied that it was empty he led us towards a large barn. As we entered the barn he gave a low whoop of joy. 'Great, the truck's still here,' he said. 'Fingers crossed that it still works.'

He opened the passenger door, climbed inside and extracted a key from behind the sun visor. He inserted the key into the ignition and turned it expectantly. This was followed by a hollow click. 'Damn,' I heard him mutter under his breath.

He tried the key a few more times but each time this was followed by an empty click. With a curse he climbed out of the cab and threw open the bonnet; this was followed by a series of loud banging noises. I went over to find out what he was doing.

'Is it going to work?'

'I don't know,' he muttered. 'The truck hasn't been used in a long time. I'm just going to clean off the sparks to see if that helps.'

I didn't have a clue what he was talking about. The only real experience I'd had of driving a car had been the time that I'd taken Reese home from the park. I rose up on my tiptoes and peered under the bonnet, watching Peter as he fumbled around inside.

'What if it doesn't work?'

'I don't know,' he said somewhat irritably. 'Can you move out of the way because you're blocking my light.'

I stepped away from the truck and waited patiently for him to finish. He fiddled with the engine for a little while longer and then told me to climb into the driver's seat and turn on the engine. I did as I was told and again there was an empty click.

I heard Peter curse in frustration followed by more banging noises. 'Again,' he called.

This time when I turned the key there was a loud but determined splutter before the engine faltered and died.

'Now we're getting somewhere,' Peter muttered hopefully. The next time he instructed me to turn the key the engine spluttered loudly to life before settling into a steady hum.

'You beauty!' Peter exclaimed loudly and slammed the bonnet shut. He put his head through the driver's window and checked the dashboard. 'We need some more fuel,' he said.

The vehicles in the Neighbourhood used solar energy or electricity so I watched with interest as he filled a series of cans from a large metal drum and then poured them into the truck. When the gauge indicated that the tank was full Peter stowed the remaining cans in the back of the truck. He refused to let me help, telling me that he didn't want me to exert myself and burst my stitches again.

Once he'd finished he climbed into the truck and then we backed out of the barn and down a narrow track. When the track ran out Peter steered the truck into open countryside. I asked if he knew where we were going and he told me that he knew these hills *'like the back of his hand'*.

CHAPTER 19

Return

We'd been driving for over an hour when Peter suddenly slammed on the brakes and I lurched forward with a grunt. Peter made a hissing noise beside me and fumbled in the glove box. He pulled out a package and then jumped out of the car.

I observed him through the windscreen as he crouched low and crawled up an embankment. The package he'd taken from the glove box was a pair of binoculars. He rubbed the lens with the sleeve of his jumper and then held them to his eyes, concentrating on something in the distance. I squinted, but couldn't see anything. After five or ten minutes Peter packed the binoculars away and crawled back to the truck.

'What is it?' I asked when he was back inside.

'The Watch,' he said. 'It looks like there might be a patrol up ahead. They could be looking for us.'

'How could you tell? I didn't see anything.'

'It's all part of my secret ninja training,' he tried to make his voice sound mysterious. I raised an eyebrow in response.

'Okay,' he admitted. 'I thought I saw something glinting in the distance. It must have been the sun off their windscreen.'

'Do you think they know we're here?'

'Doesn't look like it; otherwise they'd be heading this way. I saw some bushes a little ways back, we'll drive there and hide the truck and wait until they leave.'

Peter drove the truck deep inside the clump of bushes. It was a tight space and the branches scratched painfully down the side of the vehicle.

'What now?' I asked.

'We wait.'

'Maybe we should climb into to the back seat,' I said. 'There's more room and we should probably try and get some sleep.'

Peter agreed and we climbed through to the back seats. He handed me a blanket which I took from him and gratefully wrapped around me as it was starting to get cold.

As we waited I remembered a question that I'd been meaning to ask him. 'Remember when I first met you and you told me that your family were Echo, but you'd been re-assigned Delta. What does that mean?'

'You know how the Light uses Delta to work for them in the Neighbourhood?' he asked.

'Of course.'

'Well in addition to the skilled workers like the nurses and teachers the Light also need unskilled labour for all the menial jobs. Most Alpha families have their own staff of cleaners, drivers and housekeepers.'

Again I nodded. We'd had a staff of five at home. The Director even more.

'There are never enough unskilled workers to satisfy demand and the Light can't risk bringing in Echo because they're scared of catching a disease. So they find the Echo who test immune -'

'But there's no immunity to the Sandman Virus . . . is there?' I trailed off uncertainly as I saw the expression on Peter's face.

'I sometimes forget how naïve you are,' he said. 'You know nothing about the Outside.'

I didn't like being called naïve and wanted to protest, but I realised that he was probably right so I let him continue.

'There's a gene that gives immunity to the virus. The Light discovered it a long time ago. It's how they were able to develop the vaccination. All children designated as Echo are required to undergo a test for immunity every year between the ages of thirteen to sixteen. That's when the natural immunity usually appears. If they're found to be immune then they're re-assigned Delta and taken away to the LightHouse. It's a community college where they're re-educated before being sent to work in the Neighbourhood.'

'You make it sound like a bad thing,' I said. 'Surely it's a good opportunity for the Echo because they get the chance to live in safety behind the Boundary.'

Peter's eyes flashed with anger. 'Yeah right! Being taken away from your family, re-educated, then sent to live in the Neighbourhood as a virtual slave. Absolutely . . . it's a great opportunity. Can't understand why I didn't jump at the chance.'

I flushed red with embarrassment, 'I'm sorry, I didn't realise.'

'That's because you still think like an Alpha. You believe that life begins and ends at the Boundary. But there's a big world outside of the Boundary and most of us are happy to live in it. Why would anyone want to live as a slave in the Neighbourhood, when they could live free on the Outside?'

I felt ashamed of myself. Even though I'd crossed the Boundary, he was right: I was still thinking like an Alpha.

'Sorry. I didn't mean to sound so arrogant. How old were you when you tested immune?'

'I was fifteen.'

'So what happened then?'

'I was told that I would be taken for re-education at the beginning of January. My mam and dad agreed that they wouldn't let it happen

248

and secretly planned to leave the farm and join the Union. We knew they'd protect us.'

'But the Watch found out?' I queried.

'Yeah, someone must have informed on us. The Watch came early, and my family refused to hand me over, and, well . . . you know the rest of the story.'

'But why would another Echo inform on you if they knew what the consequences would be?'

'Echo are people just like everyone else. Some are good, some are bad. Not everyone is loyal to the Union or interested in fighting the Light. Plus there's a lot of money to be made from informing on immunes.'

I thought about this for a moment and realised I was disappointed. Maybe I'd expected something more from the Outside. Some type of solidarity between the Echo, but it was obvious that this wasn't the case. Life outside the Neighbourhood was proving to be as complicated as it was inside.

I was curious about the LightHouse and asked Peter what he knew about it.

'There are stories about the place, nothing good. I'm not sure what they do to people in there, but when they're finished most of them go to work in the Neighbourhood willingly.'

'Most of them!'

'There are a few Delta who seem to be able to resist the re-education process. We try to recruit them to work for us as spies. The problem is that the Light are always refining their techniques so nowadays it's rare to find a Delta who comes out on the LightHouse still intact.'

'Don't they try to escape?'

'No. The LightHouse is so heavily guarded that it's supposed to be impossible to escape from.'

'It sounds horrible,' I said.

Peter nodded and then yawned widely and wiped a hand across

his eyes. 'I'm tired,' he said, settling back into his seat, 'I think that's enough for now. We might as well try and get some sleep. It doesn't look like we're going anywhere for a while and we could both do with the rest.'

Despite being sleepy I couldn't stop thinking about Delta and the LightHouse. I realised that Anita, my parents' maid, had been a Delta. I wondered whether she had tested immune and been sent to a re-education centre too? The thought sent a shiver down my spine.

'Stop thinking about it,' I heard Peter mumble. 'I can hear your brain working from over here and it's interrupting my sleep.'

I gave him a gentle poke in the ribs before pulling the blanket tightly around me for extra warmth. I snuggled down into the seat and closed my eyes and tried to banish all thoughts of the LightHouse. I'd experienced enough horror in the last few days that I didn't need to introduce any more into my life. If I ever wanted to sleep again there were some things that I was just going to have to leave well alone.

When I awoke it took me a few moments to realise where I was, then I remembered that we were parked in a truck waiting for the Watch to leave. It was growing dark outside and I stiffened; I thought I heard a noise. I strained to listen and heard the distinct sound of an engine. Peter was fast asleep, his head lolling against the window. I shook him gently and he woke with a start.

'What!'

I shushed him. 'Quiet. I thought I heard something,' I whispered.

Peter was instantly alert and climbed into the front seat so he could get a better view out of the windscreen. He pulled back instantly, crouching low.

'What is it?' I hissed.

'A car,' he whispered. 'Stay down.'

I squashed myself flat into the back seat and stayed as still as possible. The hum of the engine grew louder and louder until it was right on top of us. I held my breath and waited. Then I let it out with a sigh of relief as the car rolled by and the sound of the engine receded into the distance.

Peter gave a low whistle from the front seat, 'That was close.'

He said that we should probably wait half an hour to make sure the Watch had gone. What followed was one of the longest thirty minutes of my life. The dusk transformed into night and brought with it a blanket of darkness. The air grew steadily colder and even the blanket failed to keep out the chill.

Finally, Peter started the engine. It sounded incredibly loud and we both cringed at the noise. Peter didn't turn on the lights, so we crawled out of the bushes into a dense impenetrable darkness.

'We should probably keep the lights off in case we meet another patrol,' Peter said. 'It's going to be tricky getting over the hills, so you should prepare for a very bumpy ride.'

Peter wasn't lying, even though we crawled along at an incredibly slow pace the ground was uneven and we pitched and dived over the hills. After we'd been driving for a long time Peter stopped and flicked on his torch, glancing briefly at a map. 'Nearly there,' he grunted. From the light of the torch I could see that his face was drained of colour and he was bleary eyed with exhaustion.

We continued our journey until a large rock face emerged out of the darkness. We'd reached our destination and the caves stretched out before us. Without a word Peter brought the truck to a standstill and wearily rested his head against the steering wheel.

'You okay?' I asked.

'I just need a minute,' he mumbled thickly.

'You did good,' I said, patting him reassuringly on the back. 'We made it.'

He grunted his assent, seemingly too tired to speak.

We both jumped at the sound of a knock on the driver window. Three faces peered into the truck.

'Where have you been? Patrick's going off his head with worry. Thought you'd be back days ago,' Will said as he opened the door.

'Yeah, we hit a bit of trouble and had to lay low for a while,' Peter mumbled.

Will pulled a hand held radio from his pocket and spoke in a low urgent voice. When he'd finished he helped Peter out of his seat. He was so exhausted that he didn't even try to resist.

Jake and Max moved around to the passenger door and helped me out onto the grass.

'Let's get you both inside,' Max said.

Peter resisted for a moment. 'The truck,' he mumbled. His words came out slurred like he'd been drinking too much elderflower wine.

'Don't worry, we'll put it away,' Jake said to him reassuringly.

Happy that the truck was going to be taken care of he allowed Will to assist him towards the cave entrance. I followed behind leaning gratefully on Max and Jake; my legs felt like they didn't belong to me anymore.

As we approached the cave two specks of light appeared at the entrance. The lights moved towards us and as they approached I saw that the first speck of light was Uncle Patrick, he was carrying a torch in his hand. The second was Daryl. He trailed behind my uncle, slowed down by a limp.

'Where have you been?' Uncle Patrick demanded as he approached. 'We expected you back ages ago.' He gave Peter a reproachful look. For some reason this annoyed me and I jumped to his defence.

'Don't blame him,' I said. 'I couldn't travel. So we had to wait.'

'We also hit some trouble on the road so had to hole up for most of the day,' Peter explained.

'What type of trouble?' Uncle Patrick asked sharply. He looked at

Peter, waiting impatiently for an answer.

'Watch trouble,' Peter responded. His voice with thick and slow. He looked about ready to drop.

'Patrick, we have to get them inside,' Will said. 'They're both exhausted.'

Uncle Patrick considered us both for a moment, then in one fluid movement he bent down and picked me up. He headed towards the cave entrance. 'You three help Peter,' he called back over his shoulder.

My uncle and I entered the cave and he carried me carefully down the steps into a waiting boat. Things were a little hazy after that. I must have dozed off because in what seemed like only a few minutes Uncle Patrick was hauling me out into the cave. The next thing I remember was lying on a bed while someone injected something into my arm. Peter was in the bed next to mine, his eyes were closed and his face was ashen. Before I slipped into oblivion I heard the loud excited barking of a dog. 'Flash,' I mumbled weakly.

I awoke feeling absolutely filthy; my body was practically crawling with germs and disease. I put my hand to my hair and felt a tangled bird's nest of curls. I desperately needed a shower.

I rolled over to find Peter in the bed next to mine. He was lying on his side, his eyes wide open, staring straight at me. At his feet I could see Flash Gordon stretched out, fast asleep.

I sat up with a groan. 'How long have we been asleep?' I asked.

'You were both asleep for a really long time,' came a voice from the door. It was Daryl. His face was a jigsaw of purple and yellow bruises. 'I've been to check on you a couple of times and you've both been sleeping like babies for the last twenty four hours.'

Twenty four hours! No wonder I felt so nasty and grimy.

'I'll go and get the doctor. He made me promise to tell him as soon as you were both awake.'

He limped out of the room and returned about ten minutes later with a tiny Chinese man in tow.

'This is Dr Lee,' he said by way of introduction. 'He was the one who took care of you when you arrived yesterday.'

'And a right state you were in,' the doctor directed this comment towards me. 'I don't know who stitched you up, but whoever it was should get a job working in the Market as a butcher.'

'Hey!' Peter protested. 'We were out in the field. I did the best I could.'

Dr Lee ignored him. 'How are you feeling?' he asked me.

'Sore,' I responded.

'The soreness will last for a few weeks,' he said, 'but you should heal fine as long as you don't rip those stitches again.'

'Am I okay to get up?' I asked.

'I need to give you a once-over and if everything looks okay then there's no reason why you shouldn't be able to get out of bed.'

'What about me?' Peter asked.

'There's nothing wrong with you that a good night's sleep hasn't fixed,' Dr Lee said. 'You can get up whenever you're ready.'

Peter clambered out of bed and gave a groan as he straightened up to his full height. 'I feel so stiff.'

'You don't fancy a run then?' Daryl joked.

'What, you think you can run in your condition?' Peter pointed at Daryl's leg.

'Even in this condition I could still beat you,' he shot back.

Peter chuckled and threw a pillow at him. Daryl ducked and the pillow flew over his head, landing on the floor behind him. 'In your dreams,' Peter said.

'No-one's running anywhere,' Dr Lee intervened. 'I prescribe lots of rest and gentle exercise until you're back to normal. And that's an order.'

'Sounds like a bundle of laughs,' Peter grumbled.

'Yes but you'll do exactly as the doctor tells you Peter.' Uncle Patrick shot him a pointed look as he entered the room. 'Won't you?'

'Yeah alright, alright. Lots of rest and gentle exercise, I get it.'

'If you've both finished I'd like to examine MaryAnn and I'm sure she doesn't want you two gawking at her,' Dr Lee said.

'Too right,' Daryl responded. 'Come on mate, let's go.'

'Okey dokey, catch you later,' Peter winked at me as he left the room with Daryl.

Uncle Patrick remained in the room and the doctor stared at him expectantly. 'You too,' he said.

'I'm sorry?'

'I want you to leave the room too. Once I've examined MaryAnn you can come back in.'

For a moment Uncle Patrick seemed undecided, and then he turned and walked out of the room leaving me alone with Dr Lee. He gave me a kindly smile. 'Let's get this examination over with and then you're free to go.'

CHAPTER 20

Decision

Dr Lee finished his examination. He made me promise to be careful, no strenuous exercise for a couple of weeks, and then released me.

When I left the room my first thought was of a shower. Uncle Patrick was waiting outside the room. He handed me a towel and a change of clothes. 'Thought you might need these,' he said.

I took them from him gratefully and he pointed me in the direction of the showers.

The shower block was a large room divided into cubicles. It reminded me of the showers in the gym at school. The block was deserted and I found the first empty cubicle and stepped inside. I gratefully peeled off all my clothes and threw them onto a chair. The shower was a mixed blessing. It was great to get clean, but my body was covered in so many bruises and cuts that they stung horribly as soon as the stream of water hit them. After I'd grown used to the pain I carefully wiped at the dirt and grime with a sponge. Finally I tackled my bird's nest hair. I had to wash it three times before it felt like it was properly clean.

When I'd eventually washed all the dirt and grime away I switched off the shower and carefully dried myself, wincing as the towel rubbed uncomfortably against some of my cuts. Uncle Patrick had given me a set of clean clothes; a pair of trousers made out of a soft tweed material and a blue cotton top. I dressed slowly, taking the time to luxuriate in the pleasure of a clean body and fresh clothes. I was grateful that the soft material of the clothes didn't rub against any of my wounds.

Once I was dressed I went in search of food. My stomach was grumbling loudly and I realised that it had been a long time since I'd eaten anything. I followed the aroma of cooked food and soon found myself in the Market. Daryl, Peter and Uncle Patrick were sitting together at a table tucking into large platefuls of food. As I sat down I observed that Peter looked cleaner and fresher than he had in days. He was wearing a clean pair of jeans and a grey cotton shirt. He appeared to have lost weight and I noticed that the shirt hung loosely across his shoulders. Flash was sitting beside him, his body pressed so tightly to Peter's leg that he could have been mistaken for a limpet.

'You want some food?' Uncle Patrick asked.

I responded eagerly.

He left the table and returned a few moments later with a large plate of eggs, mushrooms and toast.

'No meat,' he said as he put it down in front of me.

As I expected the food was delicious. I wasn't sure whether it was because it was fresh food rather than the synthetic food we ate in the Neighbourhood or because I was absolutely famished. I shovelled large forkfuls into my mouth and cleared the plate within minutes. When I'd finished, Uncle Patrick picked it up, left the table and returned with a second helping. I managed to mutter a thank you before tucking hungrily into the second helping.

I listened to Peter as he retold our story to Uncle Patrick and Daryl. He told them about our escape from the Delta camp and hiding out at his family's farm. I noticed my uncle and brother both exchange a brief glance at this, but Peter studiously ignored them and kept talking, giving them no chance to comment.

'That's a hell of a story,' Uncle Patrick said when he'd finished. Daryl nodded in agreement.

I'd finished off my second plateful of food and I pushed the empty plate away from me.

'You want any more?' Uncle Patrick asked. I shook my head. 'I'm stuffed.'

'And so you should be,' Daryl responded. 'You ate like a pig.'

'Give her a break,' Peter said coming to my defence.

I beamed in thanks.

'Not a pig,' he corrected. 'More like a small piglet.' Daryl and Peter burst into fits of laughter.

'Hilarious,' I glared at them both.

'Good to see that everything's back to normal,' Uncle Patrick winked at me and then got up from the table. 'Duty calls,' he said. 'I'd better get back to the office. I have work to do.'

As he made to leave both Daryl and Peter jumped up to their feet. 'Murray,' they exclaimed loudly.

My heart lifted as I saw Mr Murray approach the table. He had a bandage wrapped tightly around his head and his arm was in a sling, but he was alive.

Mr Murray took a seat at the table and related the story of his escape. He'd been able to jump out of the car before it burst into flames, but hadn't been able to throw himself completely clear so had suffered some burns, particularly to his face. He'd crawled away into the undergrowth and had hidden until the Watch had left. Then he'd made his way to the Boundary. He told us that he had had to walk the whole way back to the caves, hiding whenever he encountered a Watch patrol. He'd arrived back yesterday while Peter and I were still sleeping.

Uncle Patrick said that it was a miracle he'd made it back at all and that the doctors were amazed that he had been able to walk such a distance with the injuries he'd sustained.

'Murray's as tough as old boots,' Peter exclaimed, the admiration clear in his voice.

'He's like a superhero,' Daryl agreed.

Mr Murray waved them off impatiently and then excused himself claiming that he had an appointment with the doctor. Uncle Patrick walked out with him. As he walked away I noticed that Daryl and Peter were watching him with open admiration.

'He's the man,' Daryl breathed excitedly.

'He really is the man,' Peter agreed.

I settled slowly into my new life in the caves. Uncle Patrick, Daryl and Peter shared one of the canal boats on the river and they made some room for me. It was very cramped and after the luxury of the Director's house I sometimes found it a little difficult. I had no real space to call my own, apart from a bunk at the bottom of the barge. The washing situation was also difficult. Water was rationed in the caves and there was a shower rota. I was appalled to discover this. I couldn't understand how people survived without showering every day. There were also no chem showers in the cave either, or gloves. The potential for infection concerned me.

Peter and Daryl seemed to realise that this situation was extremely challenging and sometimes gave me their shower tokens. I felt guilty accepting them, but the lure of being clean was too strong. Daryl told me that he had had the same issue when he first left the Neighbourhood and he assured me that I'd get used to it. But I wasn't so sure. It didn't seem to get any easier as the weeks passed.

In an attempt to make me feel better Peter told me that he preferred spending time with me now that I didn't constantly smell like antiseptic. I was so accustomed to the smell that I'd never noticed it before. In truth I missed it a little, especially the feeling of cleanliness and hygiene that it evoked.

I'd been living in the caves for about a month when Uncle Patrick took me aside after breakfast one morning. At first I thought he was going to give me my work allocation. Everyone in the caves was expected to work and in return they were given tokens to buy food and essentials. Uncle Patrick had told me that I wouldn't be expected to start work until I was fully healed, but yesterday Dr Lee had given me the all clear. My burns had healed, my cracked ribs were mended and my cuts had been reduced to delicate silver slithers.

Uncle Patrick led me to the cave that served as his office. He sat down at his desk and indicated that I should take the seat opposite him.

When he leant across the desk towards me his face was serious. 'I need to talk to you,' he said, 'because soon you're going to have to make a decision.'

'A decision?' I queried, although I had an uneasy feeling about what was coming next. This was going to be a discussion about my future, but nothing as easy to resolve as my work placement.

'You've made it very clear in the past that you don't want to be part of the Union.'

I nodded warily in response.

Uncle Patrick watched me for a moment, his face impassive. 'Soon you'll have to make a decision,' he said. 'You'll have to decide whether you're with us or not.'

'And if not?' I asked. Although I feared that I already knew the answer to my question.

'There can be no middle ground,' he said. 'Although we've built a family here in the caves, at our heart we're a fighting unit. Not everyone is required to physically fight, but we expect everyone to support our cause . . . and our methods.'

I valued his frankness and honesty, but I knew I wouldn't change my mind. I couldn't support the Union's terrorist activities. Planting bombs was wrong, however they tried to justify it. I told my uncle this and his face took on a hard look.

'After everything that's happened, you still can't support us?'

'Don't you understand?' I shuddered. 'That's exactly why I can't support you. What happened to me was horrible. I don't want other people to have to suffer that.'

Uncle Patrick scared me by slamming his hand hard on the table and I jumped at the sound. 'I don't understand you MaryAnn. They tortured you for hours and yet you still defend them. Isn't it obvious that we have to fight violence with violence - it's the only thing they understand.' His eyes shone fever bright and there was a zealous glow that reminded me uncomfortably of Maud when she was talking about her father torturing the prisoners.

I shook my head. 'No, it's not right. It's not just the Light you're fighting. It's the ordinary people, living inside the Neighbourhood. You can't target the Light without hurting them too and I can't accept that.'

Uncle Patrick was glaring at me now, there was ruthlessness to his gaze that I'd never noticed before and it scared me. I realised we were on two different sides of a fence and it was unlikely we'd ever be able to come to an amicable agreement. Uncle Patrick seemed to come to the same conclusion because he signed and wiped a hand wearily across his face.

'I expect we could discuss this for days . . . weeks even, and never reach an agreement,' he said. 'As much as it pains me to say this, you'll have to make a choice and decide whether you'll fight with us. If not then you can't stay here. People won't trust you and I can't have you disrupting the unity of the group.'

'So I'll have to leave?'

'I'm sorry, but you're putting me in a really difficult position. You're

261

part of my family and I care about you, but I have a far greater responsibility to the Union and that has to be my first priority.'

I tried to understand, I honestly did, but more than anything I wanted him to make me his priority, to put me before the Union. I realised that it would never happen. He would always choose duty over family. In a way I admired him for his total commitment to a cause that he thought was more important than anything else.

'For now I'll allow you to stay. But you will have to make a decision very soon,' he said.

With those words ringing in my ears I left Uncle Patrick's office and made my way back home to our boat. I smiled mechanically at anyone I passed, hoping they wouldn't stop to talk. I was desperate to get back to the seclusion of the boat. I could already feel the blackness starting to descend and with it the all too familiar feeling of loneliness and despair. With each second it was becoming harder for me to breathe. I realised I hadn't felt this way since I'd left the Director's house. I thought the feeling had gone away, but apparently it had been lurking in the background, silently waiting.

I stumbled onto the boat and was grateful that it was empty. My breathing was coming in short shallow gasps and my heart was beating so fast it felt like it would burst out of my chest. My arms were numb with pins and needles and I flopped down onto the bed. I was definitely having a heart attack and was going to die alone on the boat. I put my head between my knees, but it didn't seem to help at all. If anything it made it even harder to breathe.

I heard a noise; my vision was blurry. Someone pushed a brown paper bag into my hand and told me to breathe into it. I grabbed at the bag and did as I was told. Slowly, gradually, I began to feel a little better as my head cleared and my heart beat returned to a normal rate.

As my vision cleared I saw that Daryl was crouched down beside me, a look of concern on his face. I put the paper bag aside, but was too embarrassed to look at him. Instead I picked anxiously at my finger nails.

It was Daryl who spoke first. 'How long have you been having panic attacks?' he asked.

Panic attacks! At last I had a name for what was happening to me.

'I didn't know what they were called,' I said.

'So you've had them before?'

'Some,' I responded non-committally.

'And when did they start?'

There was something in his voice that made me think that he already knew the answer. 'When I went to live with the Director,' I said.

Daryl nodded as if he understood.

'It hasn't happened for a while,' I explained.

'Since you came to live here?'

'Yes.'

'Then why today?'

'Uncle Patrick and I . . . we, we had a chat -'

'He told you that you had to make a decision,' Daryl interrupted.

I realised Uncle Patrick must have spoken to him already and warned him about the ultimatum.

'And what did you say?' Daryl asked.

'I haven't made a decision yet.'

'MaryAnn, what decision do you have to make? You know what the Light is doing. You've seen it.' He grabbed my arm and rolled up the sleeve of my cotton shirt. 'Look, you can see the evidence for yourself.'

I looked down at the thin silver scars still visible across my skin.

'You've experienced their cruelty first-hand. You must understand that the Light has to be stopped.'

'I agree with you. We have to stop the Light but not at the expense of killing innocent people. I can't be part of that.'

'MaryAnn,' Daryl started to protest, but I put up a hand to stop him. 'I know you think that everyone inside the Neighbourhood is guilty because they live under the Light, but I don't agree. We can't just kill them.'

Daryl got to his feet. I could tell he was angry.

Before he had chance to respond I felt the boat lurch to one side and Peter entered the cabin. Flash followed closely at his heels. Peter came to a halt when he saw us and raised a questioning eyebrow.

'Am I interrupting something?' he asked.

Daryl gave me a hard stare. I avoided his eyes and continued to pick at my fingernails.

'No, we're done,' he said and then left the cabin.

Peter remained by the door, he seemed uncertain. I could feel him watching me. He asked if I was okay. Robotically I told him I was fine.

'You want to talk about it?' he enquired.

'Not really,' I responded. I realised my tone was unnecessarily sharp. I knew this wasn't his fault, but I couldn't help myself. Peter was an easy target.

'You want me to go away and leave you alone?'

When I didn't respond he remained at the door quietly appraising me for a moment.

'MaryAnn, you have no control over other people. All you can do is take responsibility for your own actions and behave in a way that's right for you. Whatever choice you make it has to be the right choice for you. It has to be something you can live with.'

When I still didn't respond Peter sighed and turned to leave the cabin. He called out to Flash but instead of following him the dog jumped up onto my bed. Peter shrugged and left the cabin without saying another word.

Wearily I lay down on the bed and faced the wall. Flash shuffled towards me and his head nuzzled into my stomach. I stroked his fur, grateful for the company. I realised that I was going to have to make a decision, but not now, not today. It had to be soon, but for now it could wait. For the moment I just needed to sleep.

END OF BOOK I

www.theuniontrilogy.com

WATCH OUT FOR THE NEXT TITLE IN

THE UNION TRILOGY

Also by Cillian Press the first book in the new and exciting
TREGARTHUR'S SERIES

www.tregarthurseries.com

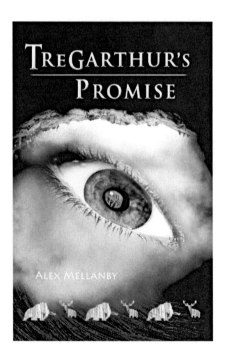

About the Author

JOE KIPLING is a Hull born, west Yorkshire based young adult fiction writer with a lifelong passion for Sci-Fi, particularly the post apocalyptic variety. She currently lives in Holmfirth with her dog Rosie and is a full time consultant and part time writer. A lifetime of travelling and avoiding near catastrophe has provided endless inspiration for her debut novel Blinded by the Light.

www.theuniontrilogy.com

Join in on the discussion
www.facebook.com/theuniontrilogy

Lightning Source UK Ltd.
Milton Keynes UK
UKOW05f1851051113

220514UK00002B/81/P

9 781909 776005